WHAT I LEFT BEHIND

A PREQUEL

THE JAN PEARCE SERIES
BOOK 3

JACQUELINE WARD

www.bloodhoundbooks.com

Print ISBN: 978-1-5040-8600-4

ALSO BY JACQUELINE WARD

The Replacement

————

The Jan Pearce Series

Random Acts of Unkindness

Playlist for a Paper Angel

CHAPTER ONE

MANCHESTER, 2000

I storm into the nursery suite, past the parents of the child who was snatched from her bed. Their grief leaks out and touches me, but there's no time for that. Not right now.

Steve Ralston meets me. He's dressed in casuals. Jeans and a jumper, his greying hair untidy. He's caught by surprise and it shows in his eyes.

'What have we got, Steve?'

He sighs heavily. Steve's the DCI and always first on the scene. I'm usually second.

'One-year-old little girl. Maisie Lewis. Taken from her bedroom about nine o'clock. Parents watching TV. I've called Petra, and she's on her way with forensics.'

Poor kid. And her family. But Petra Jordan's one of the best forensic scientists in the country. 'This must be a big one.'

Steve continues. 'Father. Marc Lewis. Executive Director at Truestat Ltd. Aged forty-four. They're the people who do the security for the nuclear plants. He's the guy right at the top.'

'Mother?'

'Amy Lewis. Thirty-six. Teacher at a local primary school. The girl, Maisie, had her first birthday two weeks ago. She's their only child. The couple moved into the area about five years ago to follow Marc Lewis's job. Previously lived in Farnham, Surrey. I've opened a SMIT enquiry.'

He looks calm, but I know that he'll be panicking inside. From Steve's short description of the child's father, I know that this is a high-level matter. Code red. Steve had fed me some intelligence about local company executives' children receiving threats in recent days, but nothing had happened. Until now. But I'd been ready. I'm always ready. Poor Maisie. Poor Maisie and her parents.

Since I arrived back from London, they have involved me as an Investigative Advisor in the Special Major Incident Team, or SMIT as we call it. They don't know what to call me, really. I'm an expert in surveillance, but more like a criminal profiler. These days, people like me are more integrated into the investigation. More streamlined, fewer Crackers.

I'm in my case, I'm hiding. I'm a marked woman, hiding from my past. I'm only rolled out in cases like this where my expertise is needed. Even then, I'm working in the background with the SMIT team. Away from the media. Away from prying eyes. Away from the people hunting me down.

On the way in I saw Petra's low-slung sports car already parked in the driveway, another sign that the elite team of investigators are gathering in a hurry. It's dark, but from the light of an almost full moon I can see the grey outline of the moorland behind the house. The rocks and the shapes where the sky hits the hills in the distance. I know this place. It's familiar territory. I listen through the silence for the quiet boding of the not so far away bog land, and I can almost smell the water of the reservoir I know is beyond.

Coming into the house, I spotted a camera on the front gates pointing downwards to capture the faces of anyone entering or leaving. Away from the road. They fitted the house with cameras, static units facing toward the outer walls. I commit all this to memory, as I'll need to get inside the head of whoever entered this sprawling property to take a small child away from her parents.

I look into the crime scene. I can see that the immediate area comprises a playroom, a bathroom and a bedroom, all pastel colour themes. Steve's behind me and I turn to the door.

'Alarmed?'

'Yes. But not switched on. They've got a cat.'

He gives me one of his exasperated, eyebrow-raised looks. I continue into the bedroom where Petra is already at work, along with two scene-of-crime forensics guys in white suits, gloves and masks. Steve and I pull on the protective shoe covers that they hand to us. To the naked eye this just looks like an empty child's bedroom, but by the tight-lipped look of concentration on Petra's face, she's found something. We walk towards her as she snaps off her protective gloves.

'We've got fingerprints. All over the cot and the window frame. We've got what could be a hair and some fibres.'

Steve explains what he already knows from speaking with Maisie's parents.

'They spent the day here, in the house, watching TV. Marc Lewis was working for part of the day, and Amy Lewis was playing with Maisie in the garden. No visitors. Not today or anytime last week. Neither of them noticed anything strange until this happened. Got in through the window.'

We all turn to look at the window. It's a standard size and lockable.

'Wasn't it locked?'

'No. I've had a walk around before anyone arrived. Seven windows left open, mostly on the second floor, but two on the ground floor. Mrs Lewis says she shuts them before they go to bed. Their room is adjoining.'

He pulls on a pair of gloves and pushes a maple door. It opens onto a luxurious double suite with floor-to-ceiling glass panels overlooking the Saddleworth countryside. It smells faintly of lilies, and the low yellow lights give it a calming aura. Petra touches me on the shoulder.

'Also, we found this.'

Her almond eyes are solemn, and she tilts her head to one side. She's tiny, and this accentuates her sense of sorrow somehow. She pulls her gloves back on and picks up a pair of oversized tweezers. Going over to the evidence tray, she picks up what appears to be a ripped piece of paper. Steve and I move closer. It was once part of a chain of paper dolls, but ripped so that only one of the dolls has pulled away from her friends. Petra takes a photo of it for evidence. Steve's shaking his head, making a connection.

'Similar to the others, except they were cut-outs from the same sheet. If you look at the last three, they didn't have the tear mark at the end. The first two did. And the difference here is that all the others had messages.'

He'd briefed me a couple of days ago about this. The cut-outs were posted through the letter boxes of senior executives in the same high-profile jobs as Marc Lewis, addressed to their children. Mistaken for party invitations, some of the children had read them and given them to their parents. The messages all said the same thing. *Hold Mummy's hand tight. Don't run off with strangers. Because you never know what those strangers will do to you.* It was handwritten on one side with the child's name and address on the other side.

The sinister messages, the spidery handwriting, and the anxiety these notes had caused their children had made their parents report them to the police, just to be on the safe side. When they reported three of the notes and made a connection between them and the business celebrity of their parents, they alerted Steve. Just to keep an eye on it. There had been several more reported since then. Petra hands me photocopies from her case notes. I study the previous notes carefully.

'Petra, can you get your team onto these? Looks like they're all written by the same person.'

Steve points to the cut-out found in Maisie's bedroom. 'Except this one.'

I pull on a pair of protective gloves from my pocket. I take the tweezers and hold the shape up in front of me. It's a doll. The kind of cut-out dolly you see in paper chains decorating children's classrooms. But this one's a little different. It's a peculiar shape, not cutesy or doll-like. And its feet are blood red. It's an outline of something. Almost misshapen, it looks chubby and slightly angry. I hold it up to the light to see if I can place it. It looks familiar, something I can't quite place about it. Then I see something else.

'Petra, there's an impression on the back of the paper.'

She fetches a magnifying glass and places the paper doll on the evidence tray.

'Yes. We need to get it to the lab. It looks like it's part of a writing pad that they've written over several times. Each time more faintly. We can get impressions from this fairly quickly.'

She puts it in an evidence bag and we turn back to the empty cot. Despite the open window, the room smells of baby products and lavender. I watch as a revolving lampshade casts pale-pink elephant shadows on the wall and over a picture of the little girl with her mum and dad.

I feel a chill as I suddenly snap into a recap of what happened in the room. How someone climbed easily through an open window, holding on to the frame and leaving prints. No gloves. Creeping over to the cot, picking up the sleeping child. But what about the prints on the cot? Did Maisie wake and struggle? Maybe that's how the paper doll came to be in the room, grabbed by a frightened one-year-old without the abductor noticing.

Then out through the window again, snagging clothing on the catch, and back, backwards toward the thick hedge. Climbing through an evergreen hedge with a child wouldn't be easy, then into a waiting vehicle. The vehicle had to be waiting on the dirt track in front of the house. So the perpetrator would have had to carry Maisie all the way around the perimeter wall. It had to be a nearby vehicle. And there would have to be two of them, or at least a child seat.

I try to picture who this person could be, but I can only see a shape. Someone who could fit through a window, through a hedge, even holding a child. Someone fairly light – no footprints in the tightly cut grass. Someone determined. Quiet. Desperate. Someone careless, unprepared.

I look at the picture again and hope that she was asleep when they took her. That whoever has her is kind to her, with the intention of giving her back once they get what they want from her parents. She's adorable, and I commit her face to memory. After all, I must recognise her if I'm going to find her. And I am.

All the cases I have worked on with Steve have involved organised crime. That's the nature of it at this level. SMIT isn't widely publicised, as we don't want to scare the public into thinking that national risks to their safety are happening on a daily basis. But there are enough people out there to constitute a threat.

If SMIT is manned by the top experts in the criminal investigation field, then the people they are after are equally experts. The only difference is the side they're on. Just as we have Petra, they have scientists working on their projects, waiting to wreak chaos on the world. Just as we have Keith Johnson, an IT communications expert, they have their comms people listening in on private corporate conversations and spinning their own evil words.

They're highly organised, just like us. It's a constant battle. We've had kidnappings before. We've had drug rackets, counterfeiting, even murders, all of them increasingly difficult to solve. This is because of the high level of care taken by the operatives to leave no trace. By the time we get to crime scenes, they are practically sanitised.

But not this one. Hair, fingerprints and bits of paper. It doesn't make sense. Granted, the pattern of threats to a common network is in the profile range, but this? Steve is busy looking out of the window where two more forensics people have arrived.

'Anything?'

The tallest figure in a white suit lifts his mask.

'Not here, but farther, just by the edge of the planted area, there's flattened grass. The border's slightly damaged. Probably where the perpetrator stepped on it. We're just assessing that area now. And this.'

He holds up a baby soother in his thickly gloved hand. Petra hurries over with an evidence bag. I move closer to the window and see what the abductor would see as they climbed back through the window. Darkness. A lawn of tightly cut grass. In the distance, a high stone wall. The owner of this house has made a huge effort to make it an oasis of lush calm in the middle of the bleak moors.

The green lawns couldn't be more different from the land which I know stretches out beyond the house. Someone crossing that would be easy to track amongst the broken bracken and dust disturbed by hurried footsteps. Here, though, the springy grass would hide footprints.

'How far does that wall go all the way around the house, Steve?'

'Runs around to the back garden, then it joins a dense evergreen hedge. About six feet high, same height as the wall. There's a gate in the hedge, but it's locked. That hedge looks pretty thick. It wouldn't be easy to get a sleeping child through.'

'That's what I thought. And I'm right in thinking that there are cameras on the house?'

He shrugs. His mannerisms and his general demeanour make him look unconcerned, but I've worked with Steve for a long time. I know that his laid-back dress code is born out of exhaustion and from pulling on whatever comes to hand in the morning. Usually a mac with jeans and a sweatshirt. I know he is right on the ball.

'Not on the house. Facing outwards. Onto the gardens. Static cameras. Sequence photographs rather than video footage. And the camera at the gate. Same again. Placed to capture specifics, like faces. Good for close-ups at the gate, people in cars, that sort of thing. Not much else.'

'What about the outside?'

I already know, but I want Steve to understand it too. This place is right in the middle of nowhere. About fifteen miles from central Manchester and in the middle of the Pennines. A similar distance from Huddersfield. Highest point in Greater Manchester around here is about 500 metres above sea level. No CCTV unless there's a road junction to a major highway, or a roundabout. Steve thinks for a while, then gives me his opinion.

'As good as disconnected from the grid. Whoever did this chose their target carefully.'

It seemed that way at the outset. Remote location, easy escape once out of the grounds. I have my doubts. But, at this point, it can go either way and I need to know more. I can see the front gate from this window, just the edge of it. Several more cars arrive and I recognise one of the drivers as Lorraine Pasco, our Family Liaison Officer. Almost time to go to see Maisie's parents.

I feel my body jolt as I try to imagine how they must have felt to find their daughter's bed empty. How they must have panicked and wondered how they could have left the window open. How they must have run out into the grounds, frantic, to search for her, hoping she'd merely climbed out. How they realised with the ultimate horror for a parent that someone must have taken her from her own bed. I remind myself to tell them that it didn't matter about the open window. If the abductor wanted Maisie, they would get her any way they could. If the window was shut, they would have tried another window. Got in forcibly. I feel a shiver up my spine, my body telling me that every fibre of my being is engaging with this case. That I won't rest until this is over. That I'll use everything I've got to find the evil people who have taken Maisie. Everything.

I cross the room and approach Steve, who's filling in the late arrivals. I can see the scene-of-crime team preparing to seal the suite, unravelling sheets of polythene and yellow crime scene tape.

'Steve, sorry to interrupt. The other notes? When were they delivered?'

'No exact times. We're going to get CCTV from the areas. Luckily, they're not as remote as this is. It would be around mid-afternoon. When the kids came home from school, they found them behind the door.'

'Sounds like rehearsals to me. Rehearsals for this.'

They carry on talking and I zone out into the place where I know I can find something common with the person who has done this. That's why I'm here, because I can look deep, very deep, into the background of life. Into the soul of the world. That's where the less visible clues lie. Ironically, they're usually the things all around us we are so used to seeing that we hardly notice.

Not many people look around, outside their own personal space; they focus straight ahead. The thing is, when you're looking around more widely, outside your own bubble, you see a whole new world. One where words aren't necessary, a world of signals, barriers and boundaries that ordinary people cross without thinking. Same with people's inner worlds. Things from childhood flowing through today and into the future. And, in some people, all the goodness churning into bad and bursting out in unexpected ways. Unless you know what to look for, this will all mean nothing. And I know. I can see them. I can do this, because I've been there, to that dark place where your only focus is revenge.

Luckily for me, I dragged myself free, but the imprint remains. It allows me to recognise the feeling in my gut that tells me the personal reasons someone would take a child, take someone's mother, sister, brother, father. Take a life. Why they would make another human being suffer. I know that reason well, and it simmers just beneath the surface, allowing me to channel into my work. I've been there. That's why I'm always ready. Because it's always personal.

CHAPTER TWO

S teve Ralston doesn't agree with me. He doesn't think it's
personal at all. He believes that there is a certain kind of
criminal for whom the suffering of others is irrelevant. It's not
that I disagree with him entirely. They're usually the people
giving the orders rather than carrying them out. Those who
commit the crime, the hands-on criminals need a reason, a
motivation. Anger, greed, revenge, hate or just pure badness, all
these emotions directed against someone as an outlet. Against a
person.

It's twenty minutes past midnight now, and technically
we're officially into the second day of the investigation. More
importantly, Maisie's been missing for almost four hours. When
we reach the lounge, Steve stops and pulls me to one side.

'So, what do you think?'

I shake my head. It's hard to say at the moment, but I'm
conflicted.

'From the outside it looks like something organised, but
when you look more closely...'

Steve always looks worried. He's got one of those faces.
Etched with lines and always concerned.

'Yeah. Agreed. If it wasn't for the previous reports, I'd be looking at a one-off event. Someone with a personal vendetta.' I can tell by the way his lip curls that he hates to admit this. Steve likes organisation. It feels simpler to him, more of a match for our skills. Personal is unpredictable. 'But as it is, it's got all the hallmarks of a campaign. Probably best to keep an open mind at the moment. Keep it basic with the parents until we know they won't disclose.'

We enter the room and Lorraine Pascoe stands up and shakes my hand firmly.

'Jan, good to see you. Amy, Marc. This is Jan Pearce. She's one of the best investigators in the country. You're in expert hands. And you've already met Steve.'

They look drained. Amy slumps against Marc as he leans against the arm of the huge burgundy sofa. They look tiny in the spacious lounge and are clearly traumatised. I perch on the edge of a recliner and Steve stands beside me. He starts his explanation of the investigation.

'Okay. Marc. Amy. Is that okay?'

They both nod, hypnotised by Steve and their expectations for their daughter's return immediately. I look a little closer at Marc Lewis. It never ceases to amaze me how incorrectly TV drama portrays powerful people. He looks like a gentle man and his voice, a soft Scottish accent in contrast to Steve's low Manchester vowels as he asks Steve the standard first question in their scenario, confirms this.

'So, what happens now?'

He has demanded nothing. He's a professional. He knows the way things work. Complex and difficult situations take time. Steve bows his head a little, pauses, and then answers.

'So, Jan and I have had a look around and spoken to the forensics team. We're going to have to seal off the nursery area for a while until we're sure we've collected all the evidence. It seems that the perpetrator entered the property through the nursery bedroom window and escaped the same way. We haven't established how they arrived and left as yet. We're just in the process of collecting and analysing CCTV footage as soon as possible.'

Marc frowns and puts his arm around Amy. I see him pull her closer to him, protecting her as much as he can.

'So how will you find her? How will you find Maisie?'

'We'll be deploying search teams at first light. We will bring in all our resources to search the surrounding area. Jan will profile the perpetrator and we'll do some background research. I've got people out there right now interviewing potential witnesses and checking all available CCTV. Forensics will fast-track everything they can, and we'll keep you fully updated. There are three things you can do for me in the meantime.'

Amy's crying. She's a small woman with a wiry frame and her shoulders rise and fall with each painful word. Deep sobs punctuate her voice as she answers him.

'What? What do we have to do? We'll do anything to get our daughter back. Anything.'

Steve struggles in situations like this. With emotions. He's trying to be as casual as he can, but he's itching to get out there and review the evidence.

'First, let us know if anyone tries to contact you about this. What I'm saying is there may be a demand for money or action of some kind, and it's tempting to keep it to yourself and try to pay it secretly. Don't do that. It'll make things worse. Tell us if they contact you and we'll negotiate on your behalf. Second, don't talk to the media.' He glances at me. I know his reason for this is dual, to keep the case contained and to protect my identity. It has to happen sometime. I know I can't run forever. But the coppers protect their own, so for now, Steve's keeping me out of the limelight. 'Third, make a list of anyone who you think might do this. Enemies. No matter how small the motive, include everyone.'

Marc lets out a small cry.

'Enemies? You do know what I do for a job? I rip up the countryside and upset people. Those people hate me.'

Steve pauses. I know he's assessing the situation. He needs to get a full picture.

'This might be a good time to tell us exactly what you do. I know it's a traumatic time, but the sooner you explain, the better.'

Marc swallows hard.

'I'm a director at Truestat Ltd. Executive Director. There are four of us in similar roles. It's an international operation, but my interests are in the UK.'

Steve looks at me. We already know who the other three are from the previous threats. Marc continues.

'I started off as a surveyor, looking at potential sites for nuclear power plants. As time went on and people retired, I became a director. But I still do the same kind of work. Except now I work in security. That means protecting the sites from anyone who wants to do harm. Terrorism, activists, lone gunmen. That sort of thing.'

Steve interrupts, echoing what we're all thinking.

'So, this could be blackmail.'

He nods sadly and I feel my hardened heart breaking.

'Yes. Yes, it could.'

I've worked on cases involving the energy business before. People so passionate about their cause, whichever side they are on. Motivated not only by money, but by more deeply rooted, primal issues over land and sea, warmth and food. Then there are terrorists who know the damage they could wreak for destroying a power plant.

Marc wipes his eyes.

'People feel strongly about it. But I never thought anyone would go this far. Sure, I've had death threats before now. I do business deals to the tune of billions of pounds, and where there's a contract, there's a loser. That list would be miles long.'

I pick out the obvious big issue.

'Death threats?'

'Yes. The office receives regular threats from members of the public demanding all sorts of stuff. Some of it quite nasty.'

'And have you reported these threats?'

He's desperate now. He's wringing his hands and sweating.

'No. I guess we got used to them. Desensitised. Nothing ever happens. There might be a demo outside our offices or some protesters gluing themselves to our trucks and drills, but never anything personal like this. Anything criminal. I didn't think people would stoop so low.'

I want to tell him that there is no low point. The lowest point for criminals is hell. Steve nods and continues.

'Even so, try to think of the obvious first, then move on to the less obvious. Petty stuff. Lorraine will help you. It's very important that we have names to look at. And could you let your office know that we'll need copies of all the threats to compare with the ones we already have? And, again, don't talk to the press. Not until we tell you to. Whoever has taken your daughter may be looking to raise the profile of their organisation. Don't play into their hands or you might prolong this process.'

Marc suddenly looks alert. 'The ones you already have? Is there more than one?'

Steve looks at me and I nod. Might as well be up front, as Marc and Amy will find out eventually. I explain.

'Several members of your company have received threats in the forms of notes posted to their homes in the last twenty-four hours. There was a blank template left in Maisie's bedroom.

We're not sure if this is accidental at the moment, along with other forensic evidence. They acted on none of the other notes. We think the perpetrator rehearsed the crime before they acted.'

There's silence for a moment. Marc Lewis stands up, angrier now.

'People from my office? Who? And who else? That points to blackmail, doesn't it? Definitely something to do with work? So, you think it's blackmail? Oh my God. What if we don't pay? What will they do?'

Steve shrugs. It's a habit he has when he's under stress.

'We don't know anything just yet. There could be several reasons.'

Marc's face clouds over with grief as he goes over the reasons in his mind, but he doesn't say what he's obviously thinking. He doesn't say it, because perhaps his wife hasn't thought about it yet. He doesn't speak the unspeakable. Instead, he errs on the side of hope.

But we know. Me, Lorraine and Steve. We all know exactly what the different scenarios are here. In a way it's lying by omission, but we have to keep believing in the best outcome. We have to. Suddenly Marc falls to his knees.

'Look, we're in bits here. I know it doesn't mean anything to you, but Maisie's our world. I'd give my job up tomorrow if it meant we got her back. Please. Please help us. Please.'

He's in front of us and Amy runs to him. He stands again and faces me.

'Do you have children?'

I don't answer. I go over to them and put my arms around them. It's not police practice and I know Steve doesn't like this sort of thing, but I do it all the same. I speak quietly to them.

'It does mean something to us. All I can tell you at this point is that I will do everything in my power to find your daughter. We've got a specialist team looking at the evidence right now, and I won't rest until I find her. I won't waste a moment of this investigation. I promise that I'll do everything I can to find Maisie.'

Amy collapses against Marc again. Lorraine signals to us that this is enough, and that they can't take any more. She guides them back to the sofa and speaks gently to them.

'Is there anyone I can call? Relatives? Any friends who could come?'

Amy Lewis shakes her head. 'No, Marc's parents are... no longer with us. And mine live in Canada. We're both only children. We only have each other. And Maisie.'

They're devastated and I'm drinking in their grief, the power of their feelings motivating me, but it's time to go. Looking through the initial evidence will take time, and I'll brief the entire team in the morning with Steve. We leave them to grieve for their daughter. Once out of the room, I hurry up the hallway. Steve's behind me and Lorraine catches up.

'I want all the forensics on those notes as soon as possible, Steve. We need to get back to the station straight away to look at the CCTV. I don't like the sound of this. It's not what it looks like.'

I turn to face him. Steve stops in his tracks and speaks..

'No. There's a certain way to go about these things. You know the procedure. Do what we can with forensics until the ransom demand comes. It looks pretty straightforward. Perpetrator takes rich influential person's baby. Demands money or action. Victim returned. Or not. But either way, we need to make sure all bases are covered. Not go off the beaten track. Not until we have something else to go on.'

But I can't let it go. The empty cot and Maisie's face are imprinted on my psyche and I need to make my point.

'No. Something's not right. It's too sloppy. Too much visible forensics. The notes. Amateurish. And there's something connected to this place. Not sure what yet.'

Lorraine intervenes. 'Look, I'll stay here. Marc said there's a spare room I can kip in and I'll keep you both informed if he hears anything.'

Steve heads for the front door. I watch his long strides and hear one of his leather brogues squeak against the parquet floor. I'd put Steve at about forty-five, but he could be nearer fifty. Rather than argue and have an unpleasant confrontation with a member of his team, he'll wait in his car. His philosophy is by the book, and we both know that he needs me to ask the difficult questions, the ones that his procedural ethics won't let him. Despite me being a good twenty years younger than him, we make an excellent team. I'm there to avenge the dead and the missing, and he's there to avenge our police principles and make sure the case stands up in court at the end of it all. It works for us.

'Yeah. Stay here, Lorraine. Jan and I will be back at the station looking at the CCTV. Because it doesn't matter if it seems a bit strange at this point, Jan, we need to get a detailed picture of what went on tonight. Then we'll decide which direction to take it in.'

Right on cue, he heads for his car rather than face it out. It's a good thing, because it always gives me space to calm down and think before I approach him again. He disappears out of the front door. Lorraine puts a hand on my shoulder.

'Keep going, Jan. You and Steve make a wonderful team. And Petra. If anyone can do this, you can.'

She's right, of course. Steve and I bounce off each other. He starts at one end of the investigation, the logical end, and I start at the other end and we meet in the middle. When I get outside, he's waiting for me.

'Bloody big wall, that.'

I look over to the perimeter wall.

'Yep. And no cameras looking over it.'

We walk towards his car.

'Not much to go on at all, is there? Not outside those four walls?' He auto clicks his car doors open and I get in the passenger side. 'Still not driving, then?'

I momentarily zone out of this investigation and into a previous lifetime when I drove a very fast car around the streets of London. It was a convertible. And in that moment, I feel the wind through my hair and hear Dusty singing 'Son of a Preacher Man', as I tap my fingernails against the leather-bound steering wheel. In my mind's eye, I glimpse graffiti and a luminous tag pointing to the invisible pathway where danger waited.

'No.'

He sits there for a while, waiting for the engine to warm up. My dad used to do the same thing, even though most cars usually drive perfectly well without this. Then he speaks.

'Know this area well, don't you?'

'Yes. Yes, I do. In fact, I don't live far from here. Just over that hill. But you have to drive round it to get there. That's what this place is like. All nooks and crannies. So many places to hide. I spent the early part of my childhood about five miles north.'

'Right. So you'll know where most of the cameras are because this isn't like an inner-city enquiry. Someone's gone to a lot of trouble to find this place to take poor Maisie Lewis.'

I know where every camera is. And every phone mast. And the distance between them. I need to know the terrain in case I need to escape. I've already got a full map of the area in my mind, with the Lewises' house in the middle. There's no way they could do this without a vehicle. So now all we have to do is find out which vehicle that is. He revs the engine.

'Busy round here is it, then?'

'No. Not busy at all. Just down the road, in Greenfield, it gets busy, traffic taking the scenic route over the tops, but further up here it's quiet.' I don't mention that it's the reason I bought my home, an old farm cottage, because of the relative solitude. 'Several villages all on the road through, Uppermill, Denshaw, Diggle, but that's on the other side of Greenfield. This side is mainly remote sheep farms and isolated houses like the Lewises'. Owned by rich people craving privacy. So busy around Greenfield, then busy around the Dovestones reservoir. Lots of local people out walking dogs. Pretty sure they'd report anything suspicious. It's a funny place, Saddleworth. You can be on a busy transit road one minute, then in the middle of a deserted moor the next.'

Steve looks at me. He's obviously tired.

'Fond of it, are you?'

I smile a little. Fond. Understatement of the year.

'Like I said, I grew up round here. What's not to like? Plenty of history and acres of moorland. That's why I moved back.'

He knows it's a lie. He knows I moved back here to slip into the background. To be anonymous.

'I'll drop you off then, if you tell me where to go. Better get some rest before this kicks off big time tomorrow.'

I snort. He's clearly underestimated my commitment to this case.

'No chance. I'm coming back to the station. I need to have a look at that CCTV and get a feel for this bastard. Whoever it is could be bloody long gone by now, but one thing's for sure, there aren't that many ways out of Greenfield and I'm going to have a look at them all.'

CHAPTER THREE

W e arrive at the station and make our way through the Major Investigation Unit. A corner suite at the very back of the Greater Manchester Headquarters houses SMIT, abandoned until a major case arises. Steve's phoned ahead, and the team is already gathering.

As we walk through the MIU, the detectives and staff fall silent. It's something I'll never get used to, the reverence with which I am treated by my peers. In my mind, I'm just a girl from the backwoods of Oldham who got into a difficult situation but managed to get out of it. To them, I solved Operation Lando and almost died in the process. Still in danger, but still on the job. Not because I'm a hero but because I'm compelled. I feel their eyes follow me. The first time after I returned from London there had been an embarrassing handclap. Now just silence.

We reach our newly resurrected office and find Lauren Dixon and Keith Johnson already at work. Our area is at the far end of the suite, cordoned off, and at the other end is a call centre, staffed with operators seconded from the main force who will take any calls from the public and, in the event of a televised appeal, calls routed from the Crimestoppers line. All case meetings will be held in here, as well as all briefings to the press and any television and radio appeals.

The office is on the fifth floor of the building and skirts a corner. It's normally used as a networking area, with the tables and chairs hurriedly removed and replaced by SMIT equipment in a situation like this. Security-wise it wouldn't have been my first choice, as the outer walls are reinforced glass columns which allow a panoramic view of central Manchester. It also allows the press who frequently gather outside, news vans with huge satellite dishes waiting to broadcast our every action to the outside world, a perfect view of us working. I could tell from news reports which journalists had been spending the time between statements peering through binoculars, and sometimes night vision glasses from the pictures they publish, into the inner recess of SMIT.

Tonight I'm not looking towards the city. The advantage of being so high up is that I can see the hills, the dark Pennines that have spawned this crime. The more I think about it, the more I think the perpetrator knows the area. The timescale for the distribution of the previous notes was fast, indicating that whoever it is knows Manchester and Alderley Edge. A map would be no good for the Lewis's house on Link Lane. I haven't checked, but I'm fairly sure that it wouldn't show on the Ordnance Survey as much more than a dirt track.

Lauren is going through the records for the reports of the other notes, and Keith is looking at the CCTV. They look up as I wipe a wall-sized whiteboard clean.

'Lauren. Keith. We've spoken to Amy and Marc Lewis and looked in on the crime scene. Petra's there now and she's going to fill us in on forensics at the briefing tomorrow morning at eight o'clock.'

I see Lauren's eyes dart to the clock on the wall. One forty-five. I continue.

'It's late, I know, but we need to make a head start.'

I pull over a large screen that's attached to a computer and type in the postcode for the Lewises' location. I select Google Maps and focus in on the area around the Lewises' house. As I suspect, neither the house nor the lane that leads to it is labelled or marked. It's new technology and it grips the team.

'So, this is Saddleworth. Link House is two miles outside the village of Greenfield, with one narrow road leading to it. Dirt track, really. No other vehicle access. As you can see, the track goes around the house and ends just past it where the moorland starts. There's no turning point at the end. Whoever goes up the track would have to reverse down it again, unless they turned in the Lewises' grounds. To the back of the property there's a peat bog, then a reservoir about half a mile on. To each side moorland. The road opens onto a narrow country lane, Link Lane, which is circular, serving local farm traffic. Link Lane opens onto a junction. Right turns into the village and through to the Oldham Road, left turns towards Huddersfield and the M62, over the Pennines to Yorkshire. Taking the village route, the Oldham Road runs between Oldham and again toward Huddersfield and the M62. Keith, can you get the CCTV from those two junctions and any along the route for Saturday evening? They're busy routes.'

I pause and look at Lauren. She's doodling on a piece of paper but stops when I fall silent. I've worked with Lauren before. Her background is in surveillance, whereas mine's in psychology. She's worked her way up through the force, hands-on policing. My route to this point was to study psychology, then to specialise in surveillance. Then serve a short apprenticeship in the halcyon days of criminal profiling when anything remotely relevant was admissible from the hard-partying profiling community.

Nothing was out of bounds and the people I worked with

often went to great lengths to secure a conviction for which they had little evidence, just a gut feeling and a hangover idea usually. I'm not being unkind, that's the truth. They worked on hunches and used honey traps. One of my mentors, the former Holy Grail of profilers, would regularly bring in a psychic to back up his vague claims. I learned a lot from them. I learned to work on gut feeling, on instinct, but then to make sure you back it up with action and facts. Intuition and intelligence. And to always turn up on time.

Things have changed, but Lauren's opinion hasn't. She still remembers my predecessors: late for meetings, stinking of whiskey, operating separately from the rest of the team. She's wary of me and at the same time resentful. She wants my job and sees me as the only barrier to her goal. But this is no time for personality differences. I give her a break.

'Lauren. Now's the time to put all that training to good use. Can you plot out the reception points of the notes in relation to the crime scene?'

Lauren moves only to press a single button and her map appears on the screen. She folds her arms and smiles.

'Done. Already done.'

I look at her. Always ahead and that's why she's sitting in this room.

'Thank you. Of course you have. So, we can see that the locations of the other threats are situated between Manchester and Cheshire. No particular geographic pattern. We already know that they selected the recipients in the context of the parent's job, and this is the connection. So, I would expect the perpetrator to have taken the road through the village in order to return to the area they have been operating in.'

Lauren interrupts. She likes to have the last word. 'Unless they're taking Maisie to somewhere more remote.'

Steve takes over. He's not a great fan of theories and he shuts this down.

'We're treating this as a campaign. All the signposts so far are pointing to someone with the motive of causing disruption to the oil and gas drilling industry. Putting the evidence together, we know that one parent of all the children who received the threats and of the abducted girl works in the same job description, some in the same company as Marc Lewis, some of them in competitor companies. That's the connection. And it's a dangerous one. They all work in nuclear security.'

A murmur moves in waves around the room as people begin to understand what this case is all about.

'Because of the location of the threats, we're working on the initial assumption that the perpetrator is or has been travelling around Manchester, Oldham and parts of Cheshire for the past day or so. The chances are, they are still around and most likely scenario is that there will be a ransom demand. So initially we're focusing on getting her back within seventy-two hours.'

Steve looks at me and I explain further.

'To make sure that we have all the evidence and that we haven't missed Maisie being kept in a location near to her home, we'll be deploying a large search team around the house tomorrow morning at first light, extending to the neighbouring areas later in the day.'

Keith looks worried. It's his job to manage the press and media, and I know he's assessing the full magnitude of Marc's status and how soon his home will be crawling with journalists.

'That's very visible. Will we issue a statement to the press?'

Steve peers out of the window, prioritising.

'No statement as yet. But these days we don't always need to. As soon as anyone sees a police car, it's all over the papers. We need to keep a tight rein on it, Keith. If this is led by activists as I strongly suspect, there'll be a website and a forum page and someone will eventually spill the beans. The internet's a nuisance sometimes, but its strength is that it puts people with a lot to say in a forum right where we can easily watch them. But the focus for the moment is tracking the vehicle that took Maisie away and increasing security on the nuclear plants.'

Keith thinks for a moment, and then he asks another question.

'How will we field them, then, when they ask? As you say, it'll probably break at first light. And depending on how key Marc Lewis is, and how much they know about the previous activity, it could make national headlines. Do we need a cover story for when people spot the search teams?'

I think about the yellow tunics moving through the purple heather, and the haze of pollen in their wake. Disturbing the dusty moorland, birds flapping in their faces as they flee. Moorland creatures running from heavy boots. Leading away towards the boggy ground with the outcrops of rocks. Easy terrain to hide a child. And the Dovestone reservoir beyond, four miles in circumference and lined with dense forest. Plenty of hiding places out of the city, near to the crime scene. We have a huge job on our hands to even search the surrounding area for places they could hide a young child. Dead or alive.

Steve reassesses. The ideal position would be to never tell the press anything unless it helps us, but he knows that it never ends up that way.

'We'll have to tell them something. The official line is that there's a child missing from Greenfield village and the search focuses on that. Unfortunately, the minute they abduct a person from their property, it becomes a public event. I think that whoever has done this has carefully calculated the impact it will have. Always the same in these sorts of cases. The fewer details the better at that point so that we don't exhaust the coverage. Because that's when it becomes dangerous, when the captive is of no more use to them. But I don't see any way we can search that area and avoid the press. We'll just have to keep it low profile. Hopefully, we'll find Maisie soon and we won't need a Plan B.'

Maisie. We know the name, but this needs to be more personal. They need to see her face. I'm already fully engaged with the case, and Steve and Petra have seen pictures of little Maisie at her home. But the rest of the SMIT haven't. It's all been hypothetical until this point. I turn to Keith now.

'Keith, I believe they have uploaded a photograph of Maisie Lewis to the system. Could you distribute it throughout the SMIT intranet, please?'

We all need to know what the little girl looks like. This way, her face will immediately arrive on the computers of all members of the team and embed itself into their consciousness. It flashes up on the vast screen in front of us in a second. Even Lauren's features soften as the young child smiles out at us. I can see a strong resemblance to Amy Lewis. Brown curly hair and hazel eyes, she's hugging a teddy bear, and wearing a badge that says, 'I am 1'. So pretty. Obviously taken on her birthday just two weeks ago. We're all dumbstruck for a second, then Lauren speaks.

'Adorable. My God. How could they?'

Keith lowers himself over his laptop, shaking his head, red in the face. It affects us all differently, but the minute it registers that we are looking for a person, a child, everything changes. Maisie is adorable. She could be anyone's niece or cousin. Or their own child. I know Lauren has five-year-old twins and I know how this must be affecting her, even if she doesn't show it on her hard exterior. But we all have a job to do and this relationship to Maisie, a face to a name, spurs us on. They return to work and Steve comes over.

'I'm going to head off now. I'll be back for the team meeting at eight o'clock. If anything happens, ring me straight away. You should get your head down, too.'

I pick up my oversized handbag, and he heads for the door.

'I intend to. I'll call you if anything happens. Oh, before you go, Steve, you were first up at the Lewises' home, weren't you?'

He stops in his tracks.

'Yep. Me, then Petra, then you.'

'So how did you find it?'

He thinks for a while. So much has happened today and we're all so tired.

'Oh. It wasn't on my AA map. I drove around the lane twice, then drove back into the village to ask. Didn't spot the track up to the house that easily.'

'That's what I thought.' I shout back over my shoulder. 'Lauren, can you go out there first thing and ask at the nearby farms for anyone asking directions in the past twenty-four hours? You should get a description of Steve and Petra, but anyone else, take a statement.'

I'm still not sure why, but I have a growing feeling that the perpetrator is local. Rehearsal abductors usually make their ultimate target in a location where they feel most secure. Know the area. I suddenly think that whoever has taken Maisie may come from the area, but they also knew the best way to take her away, as quickly as possible, without being seen.

I want to call after Steve and tell him what I suspect, but he looks beat. And he'll be back in less than six hours. I watch him leave and then I call down to the warrant office.

'Hi. Jan Pearce. Is there an empty cell I can use?'

The warrant officer gives me a number, warns me it's early Sunday morning and that the remnants of Saturday night are in most of the other cells. I grab my bag and go downstairs where a young officer meets me. I'm always ready. Not just in an investigative sense, but also in a practical way. I always carry a change of underwear, a clean top – you can usually get away with wearing the same trousers two days running. No one even notices if you wear the same jacket for a month. Comb, deodorant, mascara and a selection of hair clips. Always look professional. That's the only way people will take you seriously. The officer takes me to an empty cell and unlocks the door.

'There's a Holiday Inn across the road, you know.'

I smile at him. He could never understand. I have to be nearby. So near to the case that I can almost feel it.

'This isn't the first time I've slept in a cell, believe me. I'm used to it.'

I *am* used to it. I carry a change of clothes, because I know I need to be on site during an investigation. There's a point where I have to go home to change and check in with my neighbours, the ones at the end of my garden who look after my Kirby. I have a red setter, still a puppy, all gangly and bouncy at one-year-old. I'd told them earlier that I was out for the night at a hen party. The celebrations included a nightclub and a stay in a central Manchester hotel, which I had paid for up front. But I'm staying in a different kind of hotel tonight. The young officer jumps as one of the other occupants lets out a piercing scream, but I don't flinch. I pull out a pair of silicone ear plugs and hold them up. He laughs loudly.

'Be prepared!'

'I'm prepared for anything. There's a cup of tea with my name on it at the other end of tonight.'

What I don't say is that also waiting there is a chain of paper dolls and a missing one-year-old.

CHAPTER FOUR

I 'd slept fitfully and when I wake for my seven o'clock alarm call from the warrant officer, the first thing I think of is Maisie. The second is the doll. The one from Maisie's bedroom. Its shape had punctured my dreams, still familiar, but just outside the reach of my consciousness. And the red feet. I desperately wanted to search the internet and the depths of my memory for that shape, scanning the outline for a match.

No time, though. I have to find Maisie. I jump up and push my dirty clothes into my bag, then hurry to the staff showers and have a quick wash and clean my teeth. All eyes are on me as I walk through headquarters to the team meeting. I nod and smile at familiar faces and take a coffee offered by one of the operations staff who has just been to the café.

At exactly eight o'clock I enter the SMIT meeting and step up to the front with Steve. I spot Lauren and Keith, and Pete Nelson, the detective who I know from CID back in the days when I worked on more junior cases. He smiles widely and gives me a thumbs-up sign. Several other members of the SMIT operations team arrive along with computer analysts and plainclothes officers who are coordinating the search and the door-to-door interviews. We're ready to start. Steve pulls me to one side.

'Where's Petra? Not like her to be late.'

I scan the room and then go to the window. Her car is missing. Steve thinks for a moment. I know that he'll want to get this briefing over as soon as possible so everyone can get out there.

'Okay, let's make a start. Although I was kind of relying on her to give a forensics report.'

He stalls a little by grabbing a coffee from the machine, and while I'm still looking for Petra, I spot the first news van. Keith notices it too.

'Bloody hell. They took their time.'

The van parks on a grass verge directly opposite the corner where we are standing. I see the reporter step out and I automatically back away from the window. It's the last thing I need right now. To be spotted. I look at Keith.

'Local or national?'

He stands up and stares out at the tall man in the dark suit. He's leaning against a white transit van with an enormous dish on the top. There are sound technicians and a cameraman with a handheld TV camera.

'National. ITV News.'

As he speaks, another news van arrives and parks farther up the road at the roundabout. Steve spots them on his way back and swears under his breath. Then he begins. The first slide flashes onto the screen. It's the same picture of Maisie that we distributed last night.

'Okay. This is Maisie Lewis. A one-year-old abducted from her home in Greenfield. Case notes and assignments are on the intranet. Jan Pearce is going to give you an overview.'

I step forward.

'I'll keep this brief, because we need to get out to find

Maisie. You'll all know by now that there have been threats received previously from who we believe is the perpetrator or perpetrators. They are linked to this abduction by a series of paper shapes. Dolls. The rehearsal events communicated a message. They timed the abduction to coincide with nightfall. Abductor got in through a window and escaped through the same ground-floor window with Maisie. Escape from the property, most likely through a hedge. Petra can tell us more about the forensics when she arrives, but I must stress that there were visible forensics at the crime scene which usually means that this has been carried out by someone who is not a professional. Someone has made mistakes, left a calling card.'

I glance behind me. Still no sign of Petra. I fill in.

'So, operations wise, we've already got a forensics team up there sweeping the property and the surrounding area. Backed up with a search team, scanning the moorland farther afield. There'll be a break at noon for reports. Usual comms rules apply. Don't take comments to the press, especially important in this case, as DCI Ralston strongly suspects that this is industrial espionage. Kidnapping an influential man's daughter. So, we're expecting a demand of some form anytime soon. But that doesn't mean that we should hold off on the search. Any questions?'

There's silence for a moment, then Lauren holds up her hand.

'That's what DCI Ralston thinks. But what do you think, Jan?'

I always think the best of people. I want to believe that Lauren is asking this for the best of reasons, but I suspect she wants to put me on the spot. To unsettle me, to make the team see that I'm floundering a little. It's not normal practice for a young DC with no portfolio to work directly on an operation with the Senior Investigating Officer, but Steve and I always work this way, for balance. She's complained about this before and usually makes a point of raising it. But like Steve says, if it ain't broke, don't fix it. I sip my coffee and think.

'Well, I agree with DCI Ralston. It does seem like Maisie's abduction is linked to the industry her father works in. It just seems like whoever has given the command hasn't hired someone very professional. This can work in our favour. It means they leave a lot of clues. But it can also work against us. As we all know, finding a perpetrator without a criminal record is never easy.'

She nods, but she isn't satisfied.

'So, is that what you think? The person who took Maisie is a first-timer?'

Steve shoots me a look. Because we've worked together on so many cases, sometimes we need no words.

'I couldn't possible comment until I've heard what Dr Jordan has to say about the forensics.'

I glance behind me and Petra's car is there. I see her in the doorway, looking unusually flustered, which makes me slightly anxious. She picks her way through the gathering to the front.

'Sorry, sorry, everyone. I was waiting for the result. You know how it is. Wait one more minute and they might be ready. As it is, they were not. But hopefully I will receive a call during the meeting.'

She pulls her notes from her bag and pushes her reading glasses up her nose.

'Okay. Bedroom. Twenty-six complete fingerprints on the bed and window frame. We've run a check on the national database and the prints are not registered. Fibres from denim material found on a window catch and on the hedge on the perimeter of the property. No footprints. No hairs. Turns out the one we found was from the nanny who's employed Monday to Friday. She's being interviewed today. We've gone over the property with a fine-tooth comb and the only other prints we found were on a picture in the bedroom.'

I think back to the room. The elephant light throwing shadows over a framed photograph of Marc, Amy and Maisie. Petra continues.

'I get the impression that Maisie wasn't snatched away quickly. The prints on the picture seem to indicate that the abductor had a look around the bedroom first.'

I step forward. Even though I have my own feelings about this case, I'll tow Steve's line. For now.

'I would think that the perpetrator looked at the photograph to get a positive ID on Marc Lewis. To make sure that they had the right property and the right child. Was there anything to indicate the type of vehicle used, Petra?'

'No. No tyre marks. No footprints at all. We're still running tests on a soother found on the escape pathway.' She pauses and swallows. It's unusual for Petra. She's usually as cool as a cucumber. It makes my heart rate increase and my alarm bells ring.

'Also, the dolls. Jan noticed some imprints on the doll in Maisie's bedroom. When we looked closer, there were two sets of distinct writing. They will take a little longer to analyse, I'm afraid, but we did pick out some words. There were two words that matched with the addresses that they sent the other dolls to. The less imprinted hand was more difficult. Nothing solid from that at the moment.'

Steve intervenes. He's agitated, raring to go on the case.

'Okay. We need to wrap it up soon. Thanks, Petra. Keith, Lauren, could you let us have what you found on the CCTV, please?'

Keith starts to get up, but Lauren beats him to it. She's got a PowerPoint slideshow prepared and a laser pointer. I want to shake her and tell her that it's not business cards and

PowerPoint that get you the big job, it's results. Results she's skimping on while she's making pretty slides. She sees Steve looking at his watch and begins.

'DCI Ralston asked us to look at the CCTV within the property boundaries and at two junctions nearby the property.' She clicks the first slide. 'So, the camera system inside the property is static, so we viewed the still pictures from 8am until midnight. This allowed us to audit the efficiency of the system by monitoring DCI Ralston and Dr Jordan arriving at the property. Basically, there were no arrivals or departures in the allotted time period. No vehicles passed the gates during this time.'

She hasn't mentioned the light. The CCTV is poor quality and grainy. It was nine o'clock when Maisie was taken. Dusk. The light would have been fading fast.

'Is the lane outside the property lit, Lauren? Would it be easy to see a car without headlights?'

Her expression doesn't change. Lauren's cool and collected.

'No. The lane isn't lit, save for an ornamental lamp post just outside the gate which has a fairly dim electric lamp on a timer. So, on to the junctions.' She clicks another slide over. 'In the four-hour period, two hundred and seventy-two vehicles passed over the junction nearest the lane. They positioned the CCTV in a manner so as we cannot see the turn off, or cars turning into the junction from Link Lane. The other junction was much busier. Seven hundred and twenty-six vehicles passed over the junction in the four-hour period.'

Steve snorts. He's pacing now. For a quiet man, his tone is loud.

'Bloody hell, Jan, I thought you said it was quiet up there.'

I did say it was quiet. But Saddleworth can change from moment to moment. It's an ancient thoroughfare between Lancashire and Yorkshire and is still used as the scenic route.

'It is. But this was Saturday night. There could have been a big wedding at one of the halls, or something on in town. That's something we need to add to the enquiry list. What we need to remember here is that Maisie was in one of those cars. Lauren, can you go back and see if any of the cars had child seats? Or someone in the front or back seat holding a child? I've got a feeling that there was more than one perp. One to drive and one to hold Maisie.'

Lauren presses on. 'Other possibilities we can consider are the CCTV options in Greenfield. If the road through the village is the preferred route, then there are shops and a supermarket that might have cameras. Also, there's a railway station at the top of the Oldham Road junction. There will be cameras in place there.'

Steve's patience has ended. He's had enough now. He's gesturing towards the door, trying to get everyone out.

'Thanks, Lauren. Excellent work. Right, everyone. Back to it. You'll find your tasks on your worksheets. If you're in any doubt whatsoever, or have any bright ideas, let me or Jan know.'

It seems Lauren has a bright idea.

'Will there be a press conference? An appeal? I'd be happy to conduct it.'

Steve considers this for a moment. Out of the corner of my eye, I see Petra back out through the swing doors and answer her phone. I can see her through the clear glass, nodding and speaking animatedly. As she ends the call, she waits for a moment. I see her face cloud with what looks like fear and it makes my heart pound. She hurries back through the doors and makes her way to the front again. Steve's answering Lauren.

'Not just yet. I need to know for sure what this is first. Problem is, although Maisie is our priority and our first concern, we have to take into account the underlying reason for the abduction. If we draw attention to this, we're automatically drawing attention to whatever twisted reason the people who did this are giving for it and putting the sites in more danger. Once they have the right amount of publicity, they have no reason to keep the child. That leaves them with two options. Before this gets to that point, I want Maisie found and back with her parents.'

I return to the front. 'Any questions? We need to get onto this now, folks, and not stop until we've found Maisie Lewis.'

But Petra steps forwards. She hesitates and looks at Steve. 'Apologies, but I've just had some recent information. Jan has told you about the paper dolls posted through the doors of the threat victims. Can we get some pictures of them on the screen, Keith?'

Steve interrupts. He's blazing now, ready for the road. 'With all respect, Petra, we have to move on this. Everyone's got the pictures on the intranet.'

She shakes her head. Normally she would defer. When she doesn't, my heart is in my mouth and fear levels creep up.

'Please, Steve. Give me a moment.'

Keith pulls up pictures of all the paper dolls and they appear on the vast screen in a montage, labelled in delivery order and ending with the one from Maisie's bedroom. Steve's pacing now, and Petra continues.

'There's so much to look at here. We started with a shape and material comparison to make sure that they were from the same source. I'm content that they are from the same batch of paper. Then the handwriting imprints. We did a general surface analysis and came up with fingerprints. The same fingerprints found in Maisie's nursery. On some of the dolls we found nicotine.'

She pauses now and I'm close enough to her to see her pupils dilate and her breathing alter. I silently urge her to get to the crux of the matter.

'The other trace we found was ammonium nitrate.'

I feel my soul lurch and there is a collective murmur around the room. Petra takes a laser pen and turns to the pictures.

'The ammonium nitrate traces are stronger on the first three dolls. Then, as the day wears on, they reduce to a scant trace. But on Maisie's doll, it's strong again. Whoever has done this, the person who has taken Maisie has been in close contact with ammonium nitrate in the past twenty-four hours.'

I look at Steve for a cue as to which one of us will explain this. He's stopped pacing now, and he's standing, arms loosely at his side, staring out at the glassy-eyed gathering of police officers. It's as if a wave of terror has just washed over us and we're waiting for it to subside. I'm stunned. Steve collects himself a little.

'Explosives? How much? Enough to detonate?'

Petra shakes her head. 'It's perfectly safe for fertiliser use, this stuff, but this isn't diluted over an area. It's concentrated.'

The room is silent and I can hear my own pulse in my ears. Steve rallies and joins me again.

'Thank you, Petra. Jan. Right. So, we've got a new angle now. Not only has this criminal abducted a child but also potentially has the materials to make an explosive device. One thought, though. Petra, there are farms around the scene of crime. Could the fertiliser be from a farm?'

I know this area well. I know that a person's natural instinct is to disbelieve that someone will intentionally set out to hurt others, and Steve's looking for a reasonable explanation. There's an air of panic around the officers and Steve's trying to dumb it down.

'Sheep farms. There are only sheep farms in Saddleworth now. No industrial crop farming.'

He's struggling now, and I know a personal battle to keep it together is going on inside him, as it is with all of us. I take a long drink from a bottle of water to relieve my fear-dried mouth. Steve finally speaks.

'In short, the scenario is that we're now looking for an abducted child, possibly being held near explosive materials. Potentially, targeting a high security site. We need to find the vehicle and find Maisie. Extreme caution, folks. If you feel you're getting close, call for backup. Understood? Let's get to it. More information as soon as we have it.'

The police officers disperse and Steve turns to us.

'So how much, Petra? How many explosives?'

Petra looks at us, her expression full of sadness.

'I don't know. But if it's being repeatedly transferred onto someone's hands, it must be accessible. Not in a sealed container or suchlike. It's in raw form. Maybe not made up yet. Maybe that's their next move.'

Steve takes out his mobile. Before he uses it, he speaks in a low voice.

'I'm going to alert national security. Just as a precaution. I'm going to close the roads and air space around all the nuclear plants. Because of Marc Lewis's job, they could be targets. This has got all the markings of someone with a little bit of knowledge and a potential bomb. Whoever took Maisie isn't some hardened criminal. No fingerprint match. If they were a professional, there would have been no trace. No. This is some nutter with a grudge which makes them more volatile and more dangerous.'

I think about Maisie. My hopes for her being treated kindly were fading into genuine fears. Who has her? It was certainly clear from what Marc Lewis said that he had enemies, and we know what their motives are to disrupt nuclear power plants. I can see where Steve's thinking is leading. If they'll take a child, they'll go further. The problem is if they haven't thought this through, or are inexperienced, what could be a professionally planned attack could turn into an amateur fiasco with the potential for even more casualties and chaos.

I quickly check my lazy stereotyping of some hippie protest and tell myself that I've been watching too much TV. In the back of my consciousness, I see the perpetrator as seething, and I conjure up the emotion from my wide repertoire of suffering. Seething and committed to their cause. So angry and desperate they're out on a limb, reaching into an area that they've probably only ever dreamt of before. There are people out there who will do anything to get what they believe is the right outcome. I believe they are called extremists.

Steve dials a number and waits. I see his eyes flicker as he hears a voice.

'Sir. DCI Stephen Ralston. 3246. I'm sorry, Sir, but I believe we have a Code Black.'

CHAPTER FIVE

Steve finishes his call and we hurry over to the forensics lab on the other side of headquarters, on the instruction of the Chief Constable of Police. Petra drives. She always drives into the police compound, even the short distance from the lab, as she can't be bothered with the press. I join her this time so that I can avoid being recognised. She's cool and collected as she crosses the car park. She has to be ice cold, because her job demands clinical detachment. If she gets too close to the investigation with its heated emotions and human pain, she can't be objective. It would colour the evidence, make it lean towards the good. And she is completely detached.

The Chief Constable wants a full forensic report from Petra, signed off by Steve, so that he can make the necessary security arrangements. Both of us know that from now on, until we find the perpetrator, Steve will be answerable to John Miller. That reduces the time he'll have on the investigation. Until now I've been in my comfort zone, working with Steve as my wingman, and although he still will be, I suddenly feel a little jolt of fear.

At the end of my time in London, I had a lot of space to sit and think about what was important to me. I came to the conclusion that it was passion. Passion for my job, passion for my friends, the ones I grew up with, and passion for the place I love. The job and the people were easy, and it didn't take long to work out what that place was. I was in love with Manchester.

I had grown up in Uppermill, a village in Saddleworth, and each week my mother had taken me to the city on an old rickety bus. She'd pointed out the gargoyles on the cathedral and taught me how to notice everything around me. She'd been a dressmaker, and she called it the fabric of life, the little things other people miss. Her Galway Irish voice echoes through me now, just as it always does at critical moments.

'Sure, Janet, there's more to life. More than people. More than talking. Life's made up of colours and pictures too. They're the real pointers. Problem with people, Janet, is that they put themselves ahead of what's right in front of them. Can't see the wood for the trees.'

Even as a child I was as mesmerised by the city, so rich in its hidden stories, as I am now crossing the police car park and seeing it in the distance. Is it possible to be in love with a place? I'd asked myself this question, because in my fractured state of mind I had to get it right. I had to find somewhere I felt was the safest place on earth, because now my life depends on it.

Petra and I have discussed this over cocktails between cases. She originates from Iran, from a picturesque valley between two mountain ranges. The daughter of a medical doctor, she was sent to London to train to be a pathologist. From there, she studied forensic science and excelled. But she left London for different reasons. The pollution, the hustle and bustle, the flatness. Like me, she had the passion for the job, but she hated the surroundings. She longed for the hills, and after travelling north she chose Manchester. Like me, she lives outside, on the outskirts; nestled in the Pennine hills and valleys.

For me, I just followed my heart. This area is deeply imprinted into my psyche; coming back was like a key in a lock, filling the gap where pain and heartache constantly lived. Once away from the Met, the Greater Manchester Force welcomed me with open arms. I had to work – it was my lifeline, my passion – but I had to be safe from the people who wanted me dead. The team was my safety net and the high-level cases fed my adrenaline. Now this was a step higher. Back to national security and I wonder if the net will stay intact.

But I'm DC Janet Pearce. Like Petra, cool and collected, but in my case I'm both determined and broken. On the mend, but still broken. I think about Maisie. And Marc and Amy. How they will take it when they get the news that this has gone national. I know this is my coping strategy, to focus on the victims, to put everything I have into a case. So I don't have to think about my own pain.

We reach the forensics building. Steve doesn't speak to me until we're in the lift.

'Right. This is going to be tricky from now on. We need to give this everything. We've got to find that vehicle. We've got to find that kid. Straight after this you need to go up to the scene of crime and do what you do. We need extra on this, Jan. Extra.'

I nod. I know what he means by extra. He's giving me permission to work on instinct, to look in the places his detectives might not think of. To ask the awkward questions. To point his officers in the right direction.

'Roger that. What I said before, about things not being right.'

He waves his hand at me.

'Yeah, yeah. That's all part of it. This is a random crime, but acting in an organised way. I'd think it was just management on the part of the criminal organisation, getting the wrong person and all that. If it wasn't for the chemical trace. No one's that stupid. It doesn't add up and I need you to make it add up and more.'

I know what he means. But it's hard to see what else there is to look at. All the teams up at the Lewises' have gone over the house and the area with a fine-tooth comb and come up with what we have.

'But forensics have scanned now. What more is there?'

He wipes his forehead. The lift stops, but he holds the doors closed. His pale skin looks grey with worry.

'There's something else. Something we've missed. We've found fingerprints and bits of paper with a connecting chemical signature. But we can't find the vehicle. Think around it, Jan. Go back up there and think about it.'

The doors try to open, but he holds them firmly closed.

'You can do it, Jan. If anyone can do it, you can.'

When the doors part, we walk into the lab. Petra's already there and she shows us to a room where two technicians are waiting. We join them and she puts out the lights.

'I wanted to show you the effects of ammonium nitrate so that you know what we are dealing with.'

My heart sinks. This is going to be difficult for all of us. Especially Steve. But he steps up.

'Wasn't it used in the Trade Centre bomb? And... others?'

I see him wince at not-so-distant memories. In response, she presses play on the remote control and the screen flickers into life. A film showing a sizeable amount of ammonium nitrate being detonated runs and then changes to a different perspective. The resulting explosion is so large it makes us turn our faces away. I see the flames reflected on Steve's pale face and in Petra's glasses. Fear rushes through my body. She turns the lights back on.

'Of course, it has to be detonated. It's unlikely to explode without a detonator or the presence of other chemicals.'

Steve's calm, but obviously shaken. His hands are trembling and he's blinking fast. 'Do you think the chemical is in the vehicle, Petra, or stored somewhere?'

She thinks for a moment.

'Impossible to say. All we know is that the person who abducted Maisie, and handled the notes, has been near it. Until we find the vehicle and Maisie, we're in the dark.'

Petra gives Steve the paperwork and they both sign it. Steve leaves us and goes off to arrange for the necessary security, and I wait to speak to Petra while I push my own terror down to the depths and struggle to keep calm. She's busy finding out if the handwriting analysis is back, which it isn't. Eventually, she sits with me and speaks.

'What is it? Is there something else?'

There is something else. Something that's been playing on my mind and I need to share. 'Yes. This case has escalated big time. To frightening proportions. But I can't get past the crime scene. So careless.'

It's difficult for Petra to give an opinion and I feel bad asking her. But she does anyway.

'My job is to analyse whatever's there. I've seen worse. But agreed, it seemed like the work of an amateur.'

So, I'm not imagining it.

'Mmm. Not just that. What's really bugging me, what doesn't fit with any of this, are those paper dolls. Who would go to all that trouble? It's the MO of a single operator, unbalanced, with their own signature. This is much bigger. Abducted child and ammonium nitrate. Steve's right, this is more like the work of a group or organisation, someone with a plan. The dolls? Well, I could understand it if it was some kind of symbolism known only to the perpetrator. But that seems unlikely if it's a group. What organised criminal gang is likely to sit cutting out paper dollies?'

She's more animated when I mention the dolls.

'That's been bothering me, too. Dolls mean a lot of things to a lot of people. Childhood. Collectables. Babies. Then there are the messages. They hardly seem like threats. Against children. More a statement of fact. Out of keeping with hardened criminals. More stalker or... oh, I don't know. We need more, Jan. We need more.'

I stand and she hugs me.

'You go back and do what you can.'

I leave and as I look back, she's watching me. I can see her sadness, and I know she shares my fear for Maisie and what could happen with the potent chemicals. And the unspoken fear that we all share. Whoever had Maisie was going to take out a nuclear power plant.

———

This is one of the times I wish I was driving. As it is, I have to get a police van to take me up to Saddleworth. I hop up into the front and watch the concrete turn to rolling hills as I consider what Steve said. I should do what I do. I can't accurately describe how I do what I do, but it involves being in the right state of mind and taking action. It's a bit like the lines out of Shakespeare's Henry V. 'But when the blast of war blows in our ears, then imitate the action of the tiger: Stiffen the sinews, summon up the blood, Disguise fair nature with hard-favoured rage...'

Summon up the blood. It's like becoming a more acute version of me, where all the little details stand out from the background. But it isn't some magical process. It comes after years of reflexive training and excluding the outside world for the duration of enquiries. I've never taken drugs, but some of my close friends have told me that LSD produces a distorted world of altered sensory perception. I guess my experience of being in the zone is close to this, but without the bizarre ideas that go with tripping.

I can dip in and out of it once the blood, as it were, is summoned. Right now, as we arrive at Marc Lewis's home, I can confirm that the blood is truly here. The vista that meets me is a blanket of yellow making its way up the sloping moor behind the Lewises' house. As we turn onto the dirt track, I see two cars parked at the end of Link Lane, behind a cordon. One occupant jumps out and presses a camera against the van window, and it momentarily blinds me. Oh my God. It's happened. For the first time since I've left London, they have snapped me.

The flash hits my retinas and I'm back in the middle of the Met investigation, the paparazzi hounding me on bikes and me driving through the busy London streets, winding in and out of lanes and pressing the blue light onto the roof of my car. My heart beating fast in my chest. Pulse racing. That's how you learn to control it, by doing it and facing the fear.

I'm shocked, but I have to carry on. I have to put Maisie first. As we draw to a halt just before the gate, I realise that this is probably the start of the abductor's journey. I turn to the driver, a young officer who was at the morning briefing and knows what is going on, hence his driving just a little bit faster than normal.

'Thanks. Can I just ask, what made you park here? Just here. Before the gate?'

He thinks for a minute.

'Instinct, I expect. Not wanting to block the gate. Not wanting to park farther on and have to walk back. I dunno. Seems the natural place.'

I get out of the van and walk around the outside of the wall. None of the duty officers stop me; they recognise me and nod. At first the grass is short, but further on it gets longer. Even in daylight the path is hard and all I can see is the moor to one side, backed by black hills, and the wall to the other side. I can't see the house.

I walk on until I reach the hedge. It takes about forty seconds and I manage to squeeze through the end of the hedge fairly easily, although I'm scratched by the sharp edges of branches. I'm facing the outside of the Lewises' bedroom with its enormous windows. The perpetrator would have taken a gigantic risk; there was no way to check that no one was in the bedroom, and nowhere to hide if there was. I step onto the lawn and continue to Maisie's room, which is sealed off now.

I call inside for someone to remove the polythene from the window. The tall forensics officer I met yesterday pulls it away and I climb through. It's no struggle for me at five feet five inches and one hundred and sixty pounds. Once inside, I get a feel for exactly what the abductor saw. The picture, the cot, Maisie asleep. I turn back to the window; climb out again, then back in, taking care to note the points where the window fastener catches my clothes around the shoulder and the waist as I step into the room.

I know they found the doll on the floor, folded as if someone had stepped on it. I look back out of the window. What was the doll? What's its significance? It's still bugging me when Lauren Dixon comes up behind me.

'Jan. Anything?'

I snap out of the zone and face her.

'No. I only just got here. What about you?'

'Not yet.' I see her glance at the picture. 'I hope you don't mind me asking, but how do you do it in cases like this?'

I look at the floor. I know where this is going.

'Do what?'

'Well, wouldn't you have to empathise with the parents? And how would you do that? You don't have any children.'

I stiffen up, but only imperceptibly. No one would be able to detect the tightening of the sinews in my jaw, and the crushing of my heart. It sounds like a genuine question, but from Lauren it has undertones of 'wouldn't I be better based on the premise that I've given birth?'

I suddenly flash back to a cold office. Three plastic chairs and only me sitting there. The one next to me is empty, and a chill runs through my soul as a door opens and someone different to who I was expecting enters and smiles tightly. I push it down, down into my soul. It's not time for this. Not now.

'Lauren, I've studied. I've got several years in the field. I know what I'm doing. I'm not coming at this from a purely subjective level at all. You should know that. It's a mixture of that, objectivity and powerful instinct. And knowing how to use them.'

She looks at me but says nothing. It's one of those 'you're not getting significant results with that though, are you?' looks. I ignore her and press on.

'Did you get the camera footage from the shops and the station?'

She pulls down her peplum jacket.

'All underway. Keith should have a complete set of CCTV for the whole proposed route in about half an hour.'

I look at my phone. No messages, but I realise that it's ten o'clock. Thirteen hours since they took Maisie. Lauren is staring at me.

'So, what's next, Lauren? Have you been up to the farms to see if anyone asked for directions?'

Her eyes go to her thin-heeled shoes and natural tights under a tight short skirt.

'No, not yet. I thought one of the interview team could go.'

I walk round the room and Maisie's eyes follow me. I wonder what she's seeing now and what she's feeling. Missing her mum. Missing her dad. I hope beyond hope that she's safe. A sick feeling makes me unnecessarily sharp with Lauren.

'Look, just go up there, will you? Borrow some wellies or something. This is important, Lauren. More important than your suit.'

She hurries off and I'm immediately sorry. She's a city girl, not used to mud and bogs. Not used to endless dusty tracks and heather. Even so, it's better that I'm alone again to get a feel for this place. The geographic profiling is pretty clear. The other locations were very public. The perpetrator took a chance by walking through the garden, lit by the bedroom lamps. It was easier pickings than the city. But why hang about in the bedroom? Picking up pictures? Touching everything without gloves?

I turn to go. Before I leave the room, I have a last look at the picture of Maisie and the flame of my rage rises higher, and I promise her again that I'll find her soon.

I walk down the hallway and turn off into the lounge. Lorraine gets up quickly. Amy Lewis looks like she has taken a sedative. Her eyes are docile and hooded from crying, and she barely registers my presence. Marc is at his computer and I can see, even from this distance, he's scanning news sites for any snippet of information. He's so involved in his task that he doesn't see me in the doorway.

I look past him, out of the lounge window and into the garden. I can see the front gate clearly from here and I wonder if, with the curtains drawn as they were yesterday evening, they could hear traffic from the road. I get my answer before I test the theory. Lorraine greets me.

'Hi, Jan. I didn't see you come in.'

'Didn't you hear the van? It's parked just outside the gate.'

I move over to the window. I can't see the van from here. Lorraine shakes her head.

'No. And I wouldn't have heard it either. The entire building is triple glazed. Industrial level. Amy said it's so cold they have to keep the heating on, even in summer. Come round the back, did you?'

I nod. 'Yes. I came around the back. And no one saw me arrive. Not Lauren, not the forensics team and not Lorraine. And not the Lewis family.'

CHAPTER SIX

M arc turns around when he hears me. I immediately
sense a change in his demeanour from last night. His
eyes are red-rimmed and his skin the pale grey of someone
worried for their child's safety, but he's more alert and
businesslike. He shakes my hand.

'DC Pearce.'

I meet his eyes. Fear mixed with sadness. No sign of anger.
Not yet.

'Jan, please.'

He signals for me to sit down on the sofa, in the place he
was sitting last night. He stands beside me.

'Right. The thing is, I've been thinking. I can be part of your
investigation. I can help you look for Maisie. It's an impossible
situation, me sitting here and doing nothing.'

I glance at Lorraine. She's out of his line of vision and makes
a confused face and shakes her head. I think fast. I need to keep
him on side. Stop him from speaking to the press. From
meddling and making matters worse.

'Well, I wouldn't say that you've done nothing, Marc. I

wouldn't say that at all. You've been very helpful. All the information about your daughter and the house.'

He paces around. All the energy he needs to use to look for his daughter is trying to escape any way it can. Anyone could see that he's like a caged animal.

'Look, I need to be out there searching. I need to be looking for her. I need to be visible, so that she knows I'm there for her.'

Amy cries again and Lorraine comforts her. I think quickly. What's the best way Marc Lewis can help us?

'Actually, Marc, I'm here to ask you a few questions. About the threats you mentioned yesterday. I need to talk to you about any organisations that might target you and your business. I need as much information as you can give me.'

He thinks for a minute.

'But I sent all the threats from my work server to someone called Keith Johnson.'

'And he'll index them. But I need your impression, Marc. That's just a list. I need to know who you think this is. Your best guess.'

He's mulling it over. I know how tough it is to dredge your memory banks when you are under immense pressure. How all thoughts lead back to your current problem and away from logic. He's trying. Finally, he sits down and looks at me, his eyes filling with tears.

'There are so many. It's hard to say. On one hand, there are the financial aspects. My business is worth millions of dollars. There's a lot of competition, but there are unspoken rules, even amongst third world countries. Once we win a contract, once the land is claimed, we leave each other alone. We don't piss in our own backyard, so to speak. I'd be surprised if that had triggered someone breaking into my house and taking my daughter. They'd take me. Sad to say, but to them, I'm worth more than Maisie.'

I take my phone from under my bra strap and text Keith with some notes. Marc watches me and frowns as I remove my phone from my clothing.

'So I can hear it. I need to be available at all times.'

He's satisfied with this and continues.

'So, if it's not the business end, it's got to be the activists. I'd have thought their best bet would be to get the media to cover whatever protest they have thought up and beat us down that way. They've already got massive PR this way and again, I'm fucking astonished that they would use my little girl to get attention. Although some of them have been getting closer to us more recently.'

I look up from my notes. He's angry now. Going through the natural stages of trauma.

'Oh. Who?'

'Names? They don't go by names. Sometimes they use code names, but we don't take much notice of them. Usually poster campaigns, and sometimes they pay for adverts in the press. Sometimes personal stuff, like throwing eggs and paint, or damage to our vehicles. They're different to the financial organisations, which are running a tight ship where money is no object and they bribe people to achieve their objective. But don't get me wrong. The activists are just as organised, but in a different way. They might appear to be haphazard and a bit bumbly with their camps, but they go for the long haul. The organised gangs have the quick hit; the activists have the sit-in. Both are as damaging in their different ways.'

Both effective, but neither fit the profile of this crime. I look at my phone. Two messages. One from Steve. *Integrity secured.* He's done it. He's shut down access to the national infrastructure. Lorraine has just read the same message and again she looks confused. That's good. It means the communications blanket strategy has worked and word hasn't reached her yet. The second message is from Keith. *First sweep complete. No further evidence found.*

Fuck. The sweep of the evidence area up here will be much easier than somewhere urban, where they collect all nature of items, most of them of no consequence. Up here, in an almost barren wasteland outside the property walls, save for some heather and scrub, there's not much to find at all.

I carry on with Marc, ever mindful of the time ticking on. I repeat my question.

'Who's been getting closer, Marc?'

'A couple of specific activists. You could probably find their photos in the newspapers. Their faces come up again and again, not just with us, but on the banking protests and suchlike. We think they're professional protesters. They've been round at our offices in London, trying to get in. We have a key fob security system, all the latest technology, but they somehow got hold of someone's fob and gained access. We found them in one stairwell. One of the security guys noticed them acting strangely.'

'Doing what?'

'Just looking around. When we looked at the cameras, they'd been at someone's desktop computer earlier, but they couldn't get at any of our data. Not the important stuff. It's all encrypted.'

I sigh. I expect he has the tightest security around his sites, but IT systems are often the easiest to get into.

'Not even HR stuff. Names and addresses?'

His eyes widen.

'You think...?'

'I don't know, Marc. I have to look at all the possibilities. You said you've got access to the server. Would you mind if I tried to get in? Just as a test?'

We move over to his computer and he taps away until a welcome screen appears.

'Okay. We're at the start of the system. Exactly what they would have seen.'

I move the mouse around and enter the system. I'm no IT whiz kid, but I can get around a system. I get as far as the security console and I hit the open access area. There's nothing obvious listed. No HR tabs or address lists. I play around with it for a while, and then I see a way in. I return to the home screen and press F3 – return to start-up.

The computer reboots and I'm faced with an option screen. I choose 'root' and I can choose from a list of directories. I choose Human Resources.

'Hardly encrypted.'

Marc fumes behind me. I feel bad because he's suffering, but I need to get to the bottom of this. To find out how whoever delivered the messages to the addresses.

'That may not be, but the valuable stuff is.'

I swing around in the chair.

'What's more valuable than personal information?'

He returns service.

'There's little more on there than they could find out from Companies House. All the people from Truestat are directors. I'd put money on all the other people who received threats being directors, too.'

I concede, but make a note of it. He's right. That information may be available to anyone anywhere, but if someone's been sneaking around his computer system, alarm bells are ringing for me.

'Maybe they didn't get into your system. Maybe they got their information from elsewhere. Maybe they're unconnected. But I need every single instance like this. And access to all your CCTV files for each incident. You said they go by code names?'

'Yeah. Too many to mention. They've all got them. But there is one that sticks out. Like those two guys and I've no idea if they're connected to this, but the name that comes up again and again is Magellan.'

'Magellan?'

'It's scrawled on the back of photocopied protest flyers they stick up all over our windows and car windscreens. Our information analysts watch the internet forums for news of any activism near our workplaces, and they've seen it there too.'

'Thanks, Marc. We'll look into this. It's all helping.'

He nods and begins to write an email. I text the word Magellan to Keith. He'll know exactly what to do with it. My phone rings.

'Hi, Steve. How did it go?' I walk into the hallway for privacy.

'It went well. Heightened security at all vulnerable targets. All-ports warning too, a bit late, but better late than never. You?'

'Just interviewing Marc Lewis about possible inciting incidents. He thinks it's protesters. Two guys broke into his London office recently and they were what he describes as activists, as opposed to financial dealings. Seems quite convinced but can't name any of them. I've requested all records.'

I look at the clock. Quarter to eleven. Time ticks on. Steve continues.

'Look. I've been thinking. You can tell Marc and Amy Lewis about the ammonium nitrate. If you look outside the gates now, you'll see plenty of press gathering. The second sweep is underway and once that's over we're empty. We've got nothing. We need to warn them we're stepping up the investigation.'

I pause to think. It's a gamble. It would be better if we could get a confirmed lead first. But Steve's right. We've got nothing new.

'What have you got in mind?'

'Petra's just called me to tell me the paper analysis is almost complete. She's going to call you as soon as it is. If that doesn't give you anything new, you need to tell him. Then, someone needs to go outside and give a brief statement to the press. Obviously not you. Something like "We're following all lines of enquiry". But we'll have to give them something or they'll start digging and everyone's tetchy. I don't want any information blurted out. I want a tight control on it. Public interest. I'm on my way there now. Let me know if anything happens.'

The line goes dead. Just as I turn to go back to the lounge, Lauren appears wearing Wellington boots and oversized waterproof trousers.

'No one's asked for directions other than Petra and Steve. A foreign-looking lady and a middle-aged Mancunian in a black car, apparently. No one else. I don't see how the perp found it then. It's a bastard. I missed the turning twice.'

I smile at her and she smiles back. Maybe I've been too hard on her.

'Sorry. It's all a bit on top at the moment.'

She shrugs her shoulders. 'I asked for it. Sorry if I pissed you off.'

My phone rings. 'Anything new, Petra?'

The ensuing pause tells me it's not good news. When Petra has discovered something, she doesn't waste any time.

'Yes and no. The impressions on the paper dolls are from two different hands. One is part of a list of names pertaining to the threats perceived. Including part of the Lewises' postcode. This was the oldest imprint. Over that was a different hand. This isn't so clear. I'm going to come over with the details, but I'm not sure they're relevant.'

I feel my stomach turn over. I was hoping the handwriting would lead us somewhere.

'Okay, Petra. I'll see you in a while.'

It would take her about half an hour to get here. Enough time to explain the rest of the case to the Lewis family.

'Lauren, do you want to take those off and come through to the lounge? I need to brief Marc and Amy and you need to be there.'

She's quick. In less than three minutes, she's beside me in the lounge. Marc's still on his computer and Amy's sleeping. Lorraine's looking out of the far window, watching the line of yellow tunics descend the moors. I would have known by now if they had found anything. Now I've got to break this to Marc.

'Marc, this is DS Lauren Dixon. She's part of the team. We have news.'

He jumps up and rushes towards us. I see his pupils dilate and he breaks into a slight sweat.

'You've found her? Is she okay? Where is she?'

'No. No, we haven't found her. I'm sorry. There's something else. The operation has escalated.'

He sits down and holds his head in his hands, the excitement subsiding.

'Escalated? My God? Have they taken another baby? Someone else's child?'

I look at Lauren. She's poker-faced.

'No. That's not it either. The thing is, Marc, our forensics people have been analysing the previous threats. The notes. And the one found on your property. They found fingerprints, but unfortunately they are not on our database, suggesting that the person who did this hasn't got a criminal record.'

He snorts his derision. I see him flush more red. His usual calm exterior is close to breaking point and no wonder.

'Or you just haven't ever caught the fucking scum. Like you're not catching them now.'

Still angry. It's perfectly understandable. I nod. Lauren bows her head.

'No, we haven't caught them. Yet. But we will. As I said, there's been another development. But you must understand that it doesn't necessarily mean that your daughter is in any more danger. This thing is, our forensics team has found traces of ammonium nitrate on the paper dolls. The messages.'

His face contorts and he makes a silent scream. I know it comes from deep inside him, somewhere primal, and I know to wait until it exhausts itself. When it finally does, he collapses onto a chair. He is, of course, imagining his daughter in a room with a large amount of explosives. No amount of warning could have prevented this image. I continue.

'We've put out an all-ports warning. And, as a precaution, we've secured the infrastructure.'

He rallies a little. Marc Lewis is a fighter. He would do anything to get Maisie back.

'I want to make an appeal. Directly to them. Me and Amy. I want to go on the TV and appeal directly to them. Look at me. Look at Amy. They're destroying us. If this is about money, they can have everything. They can have it all, just give me Maisie back. If it's about anything else, I can fix it. Just let me go on TV.'

I hear Steve's voice behind me.

'I don't think that's a good idea at the moment, Marc. As I said before, we need to find out what they want first. If we broadcast an appeal, it might spook them. We don't know who we're dealing with, but I can assure you that within the next few hours we will have developments. I've brought in extra resources and half the UK police force is out looking for your daughter. We're keeping a news blackout as far as we can for the same reasons I mentioned.'

I jump in with a suggestion that I hope will dissuade him from taking things into his own hands.

'I'm going to ask Lauren here to give a statement to the press in a few minutes. It will just be a basic statement, no details. They know that something high level is going on.'

He sniffs, more confused than ever. 'How? How do they know that?'

'They'll have seen the members of our team. We only come together when something... critical happens. They know this is big.'

Marc shakes his head. 'My God. My God. I can't believe this is happening. Why isn't the press in here right now? Surely they can help find her?'

Steve looks at me and I raise my eyebrows. It has to come out sometime.

'That's not a good idea. First, like I explained before, if they give the exposure the perpetrator requires then... and then we have other reasons.'

He looks at me. 'In complete confidence, we're keeping Jan as our best kept secret. She's one of the best coppers in the UK. Well, I can tell you she worked on the Lando case. In London. The one where they held two young girls for months. Jan was on that case and almost didn't survive it. She put her personal safety on the line for that case, and she would do the same for Maisie. Wherever Jan goes, her reputation follows. So, we must try everything else before we involve the press.'

Marc stares at me. I can see his expression, the one that says that I look so young – which incredibly I do, much younger than my twenty-five years – so how can I be so experienced? But he's got offices in London and spends time there.

'Lando? Were you the woman who faced off the gunman and escaped?'

I nod. I faced off a gunman all right, and I escaped. But what they don't know is how I paid for it later. *I feel the wind on my face again, the hood of my convertible down, and London rushing by. Aretha now. 'Respect'. The colourful shop fronts and the piles of fruit and vegetables stacked outside, as I wait in a traffic queue. The semi-suburban streets lined with trees, stretching away into the distance at the end of every block. The smell of a laundry, crisp pillows and sheets, as I follow the traffic flow. I breathe it in, glad to be alive. I've picked up Chinese food and a bottle of single malt whiskey and I'm heading home to my beautiful apartment.*

Marc Lewis is shaking his head and his next words shake me out of my nightmare.

'But wasn't that a grudge? Gang related? Between two brothers in rival gangs? This is different. This is about my business. This isn't personal.'

It's unbelievable how many people think that crime is apart from them. Detached.

'No. That's where you're wrong.' I don't want to point out to him that somewhere Maisie is with another person. Captive. Someone is feeding her, washing her, tending to her. Hopefully. Someone is intentionally keeping her from being with her parents. How much more personal can you get? 'When it comes down to people, Marc, everything's personal.'

CHAPTER SEVEN

A moment later my phone rings. It's Keith. There's no time for greetings and he launches straight in.

'Magellan? Code name? Tag? Operation?'

'Marc Lewis gave it to us. Magellan. It's a name that comes up on forums and on activist literature. I need you to find everything on it. Everything. And quickly. Any more on the CCTV?'

I hear him tapping frantically on his keyboard. The internet hasn't been around long, but it's made policing different, not necessarily better, but different.

'No. Not yet. The stills from the cameras around the house are poor quality, so I've sent them to some guys who can enhance them. At the moment, it's difficult to see anything. Doesn't help that it was dark.'

'Thanks, Keith. Let me know about that and the Magellan thing. It's all Marc Lewis came up with.'

The call ends. He'll know that we're running out of leads and time. I hurry back to Steve and Lauren. Steve looks tired. Or worried. Probably both. He looks at us and shakes his head.

'Bloody hell. We're getting nowhere fast. We need

something. Anything. I don't like the thought of letting them out there what's going on. You know what they're like. As soon as you go out there, they'll be like vultures. They'll be all over this place, asking questions. It's bad enough they know about Maisie, but if they find out about the rest...'

'They won't.' I can see he's being pushed to his limits. Steve's an outstanding leader, but he likes to do things his way. He doesn't like making statements or going after people too soon. I understand his reasons; too much, too soon means not enough evidence. Not enough evidence means no prosecution. 'Lauren's going to give them the statement. She's going to read it.' I nod at Lauren and she smiles. 'She'll read the statement and come back without answering questions. That way they have something to print, and they'll focus on finding Maisie. And we're controlling what the perpetrator knows we know.'

I can see Steve's still worried about the whole story getting out. He's right to be worried. There'd be mass panic, not to mention the abductor reaching saturation point and being forced into making decisions. But knowing the tabloid media, they'll take the abduction story and run with it. In the process, we might even get a witness. The downside is that they'll harass the family, but if we leave officers on the gates and Lorraine stays here with Marc and Amy, they should remain untouchable. In the end, he agrees.

'Okay. Let's go with that.'

I watch as Petra drives up the gravel causeway and round the side of the house. She appears in a few seconds with a gigantic bag of paper.

'Is there anywhere we can look at these?'

We go through to the kitchen and Petra shuts the door.

'Okay. We've analysed the rest of the paper and the handwriting impressions. The problem is that they folded the paper in a zigzag in order to cut it and make a chain of doll shapes. So, to read the fragments of writing in the right order, it was like a jigsaw.'

She gets the individual dolls out of the bag. They're oversized copies and the impressions of writing on them overlays them with grey. She lays them out, side by side, and although we can pick out individual words, they are faint and make little sense. Then she lifts out a large sheet and unfolds it.

'This is the top sheet of writing. If we number this, with the addresses on it and ripped off the pad as one, they made this piece of paper dolls from number three. As you can see, we've rebuilt the doll pattern in the sequence of the writing. You can see the partial addresses. Including the postcode for this property, marked in red.'

The dolls are laid out on the sheet, holding hands. The dolls lay landscape format, and the writing is portrait format. Some of the addresses are almost complete, some fragmented, and I scan the words, hoping for some clue to jump out at me. The extra. But they're just addresses. Worse, they're addresses that we already know. Petra continues.

'The second sheet, the one that would have been just above the sheet they cut the dolls from, has a list written on it. The writing is in large letters and block capitals, and it's not clear at all. There are lots of doodles that obscure most of the words. Even our high-tech analysis couldn't separate them. The doodles appear to be more dolls. This sheet is almost certainly in the same handwriting as the handwritten messages on the dolls that they posted through the doors. The top sheet, the one with the addresses, someone different has written it.'

Steve looks puzzled.

'At least two people then? At least we know that now. Anything else, Petra?'

She pulls out another sheet.

'Even fainter, thinking of this sheet as the one above the

addresses is what could be another list. We're still working on that one. The pressure on the paper was very light, and dissecting it from the other clearer text is difficult. But we think there may be a telephone number. So, these are the sheets above the messages, first the phone number, then the addresses, then the doodles. Then the dolls.'

No one says it, but we all silently acknowledge that we've learnt nothing new at all from this. I clutch at straws.

'So, the second sheet, Petra, is there any indication what the writing means? The parts that are readable?'

She pushes the enlarged sheet forward. It's a blur of scribbles with some words visible. *Don't. Woman. Say. Dance. On.* It reminds me of the notes I used to take as a student, neat at first then, as I lost interest, I'd draw outlines of stained-glass windows all over the notes until you couldn't read them at all. Well, no one else could. But I'd be able to decipher most of it from memory, because I was there and it mattered to me. I'd read the material, and I remembered it. That's why I could scribble on it, because I already knew what it was. By heart. Whatever was on that sheet is important to the person who wrote it. To the person who posted the notes. To the person who took Maisie.

It's the nearest I've got to them. It's the first real sign of what they are like, what they know. Who they are.Putting this layer of scribbles over a list of things etched into their being. Together with the message text on the paper dolls, I'm pulling together a picture of someone brooding, someone preoccupied by something. Something on the periphery of their consciousness, something that distracts them while they're list writing. Something that makes them warn people. Warn? Is that the right word? Wasn't it a threat?

I pick up another sheet where Petra has collated the doll messages. They're clearly individually written, each one slightly different. *Hold Mummy's hand tight. Don't run off with strangers. Because you never know what those strangers might do to you.* All perfectly punctuated. Someone has sat and written each one out individually. I breathe a sigh of relief. Maybe we're dealing with someone who has patience, will wait for us to react once they state their demands. But are the messages a warning or a threat? I'm not so sure now. Steve's getting impatient.

'Okay. So, are we agreed that this doesn't move us any further forward?'

I can't agree with him. They may not give us physical evidence, but they hold meaning. They hold information about the MO.

'I think it tells us something about the perpetrator. They're in no hurry. They've taken time to prepare, and that usually means they're in no rush to wind it up. They've made arrangements for the long haul. I also think they're preoccupied with something.'

He hasn't really grasped my meaning. He continues along his previous route.

'Yeah. I think it's pretty clear now that these people are activists who object to, are maybe even obsessed with, Marc's work. Their preoccupation and their probable motivation is to get Marc, or his company, to change their direction or to stop them from doing something. The presence of explosives means they will go to any lengths, in addition to abducting Maisie, to reach their goal. Putting it all together, I feel we should still expect a demand for money or action sometime soon.'

Petra gathers the paper together and I call Keith.

'Anything?'

He makes a sound of desperation.

'No. Not much at all. I've found some references to Magellan on Green forums, mainly cryptic references. For example, stuff like "Magellan will sort it" and "Leave it to

Magellan". It's as if this Magellan is the Holy Grail of anyone who's ever been an activist. The ultimate activism. But no real clues as to whom they are. No website. A real urban legend. It's almost as if they're saying, "leave it to the professionals".'

I think for a moment. Professionals or gifted amateurs?

'Thanks, Keith. Keep going. Any news on the CCTV?'

'Not yet. I'll text you the minute it's through.'

I end the call just in time to see a reporter climb up onto the top of the perimeter wall and photograph us. One of the uniformed officers guarding the property shouts at him to get down, then there's a scuffle. Steve finally loses his temper. It doesn't happen often, but when it does, it signals a turning point.

'Get him down. Jan, write out a bloody statement for Lauren to read out. We need to get them off our backs, then think what our next move is. I've got fifty back-ups on standby for when we find the vehicle. It needs securing and we need to find Maisie. We need to do that as soon as possible.'

I know he's reaching his critical mass, but I have to make my point.

'We haven't got anything. Short of tracing every single car that went through that junction last night. Maybe we should do that. It's the only thing we've got. It's midday, Steve. She's been missing fifteen hours and we haven't got further than this house. We've got a lot of information, lots to go on, and we've laid the foundations. But all we know is that someone's out there with Maisie and some fertiliser.'

I know why he doesn't want to go down the car tracing route. It takes time. Lots of time. And it's visible. But we have no choice. I take out my notebook and write a brief statement for Lauren to read out. She reads it twice. Steve's still fuming.

'And don't answer any questions. They're like bloody jackals. They'll try anything to get it out of you.'

But that's Lauren's strength. Her measured way of stating the obvious and no more, and her poker face. Even in extreme situations she appears, on the outside, to be expressionless and emotionless. She reads it a third time and then we walk out of the property and towards the gate. I can see Amy Lewis out of the corner of my eye, standing in the enormous bay window of her luxurious home, looking for Maisie. How many times over the past hours has she looked out for her? Hoping that one of us will bring her back, up the gravel path and into her arms.

Lauren sees her too, and for a moment I catch the sorrow in her eyes, a window opening in her mask and the light escaping. I shoot her a warning look and she nods. We reach the gate. She needs to walk up to the top of the dirt track and stand just behind the police cordon at the turning on to Link Lane. Steve's radioed ahead to warn them to cover her.

'Ready?'

Lauren's more than ready. This is her forte. She looks calm and confident.

'Absolutely.'

She rounds the corner and steps out into the lane. Already camera flashes puncture the dull day and I hear a buzz in the distance. She takes about a minute to walk the track, then she's standing in front of them. I back off. I need to keep out of sight. I don't want to make it worse than it is.

I step backward into the grounds, behind the gates. Steve's talking on the phone in the hallway and Petra's walking back towards her car. I catch sight of the outline of the dark moorland on the grey sky. It's impossible to believe in this day and age that no one has seen anything. There's a phone mast up on the northern hill, and a glint of light in the distance. I scan the horizon for nearby houses, anyone and anything that might have seen someone drive up here on Saturday night.

The area is really quite remote. I know that there's a farm

over the next hill, farther up Link Lane, but they wouldn't be able to see the road, even from a bedroom window. Link House is completely hidden. My phone rings. It's Keith.

'CCTV's back. It's completely enhanced as far as they can. The camera works on a thirty second frame switch. There are three different placements on each camera of thirty seconds each. Here's what I've got, and it isn't much. In fact, I'm not sure that it's anything.'

My heart beats furiously. Anything is something at this point.

'At 8.57 the camera on the right-hand side of the main door, looking outwards, clicks onto the right-hand side of the gate and the wall beside it. Then it clicks over to the next piece of perimeter wall, then the next piece, then back to the gate. There's a slight difference between the first picture of the gate and the second. The second one, at 8.59, has a minute white line on the ground outside the gate. Headlights. So small that it isn't spotted on the unenhanced version, because it merged with the white coping stones on the side of the wall. The camera clicks round again, and it's gone. Then again, then seven more times it's there, then it's gone.'

I turn around and look at the camera and then at the wall.

'Text me the images. Both enhanced and unenhanced. Great work, Keith. There's got to be something in this.'

I switch off my phone and it beeps the text to me. I don't look at it. Instead, I go outside the gates. Lauren is still at the top of the dirt track; I see her turn to walk back. I look at the ground around the police van I arrived in. They have scoured every inch of it for evidence, so I'm probably wasting my time.

Lauren reaches me. She blinks rapidly to rid her retinas of the camera flashes.

'How did it go?'

She smiles widely.

'Really well. I read it slowly and there was complete silence. I think they bought it. I think they were satisfied.'

'Great.'

Just as we turn to go back inside, I see Amy Lewis run towards me. At first, I fear she's going to run straight into me, but she dodges both me and Lauren and runs at the gates. She's screaming, just one high-pitched scream. As she gets nearer, I can make out what it is. She's screaming 'No.' No. It resonates deep within my soul.

I move quickly and grab her just before she reaches the gate. A uniformed officer sees us grappling with each other and rushes forward, but Steve and Lorraine reach us, and he stops just short of grabbing Amy. She's pulling at my hair and my clothes, shouting loudly.

'My baby. Not my baby. No. Don't hurt her. Don't hurt her.'

She begins to hit me and I hold her tightly. The others stand and watch, unsure of whether to intervene. I know that someone must have told her about the ammonium nitrate, and she can't hold her pain in any longer. But I can soak it up for her. I can be the vessel she needs to scream into. The one who understands her desperation. She cries hard and loud, and I know she's run out of emotional energy. I can almost feel it ebb away from her.

I release her and she stands there, a broken woman, her eyes begging me to return her daughter to her.

'She's my only child. You need to find her. You need to. None of you can ever know the lengths we've gone to to have a baby. To have Maisie. She's so beautiful, she's so...'

She's bending into me, then suddenly straightens.

'I left the window open. It was me. I left the window open.'

She whispers, almost hisses the words, flagellating herself with each syllable.

'No, Amy. It isn't your fault. Whoever did this did it for a reason. They would have found another way in. Don't blame yourself. It's their fault, not yours.'

I put my hand on her shoulder and talk gently to her.

'Go back inside, Amy. Lorraine will look after you. I promise we'll let you know as soon as we know any more.'

Lorraine leads her inside. She goes with her, then turns back.

'You said you'd find her.'

I meet her eyes and no words are necessary. I will find her.

Steve's talking on the phone again, making arrangements with the powers that be. I look up at the cameras again and then up at the wall. I go inside the house and up to one of the bedrooms. I can easily see over the wall from here, but the camera just sees the one-dimensional flatness of the wall against the background.

I go outside again, to the police van. A young officer, a newbie, passes me with a tray of sausage barm cakes and I take one. I haven't eaten since last night. I lean against a post and go through all the vehicles it could be. It would narrow it down from the hundreds of vehicles going through the junction. But I need something more conclusive. It's times like these that I wished I still smoked, so I could light up a cigarette and think hard.

I know from experience that moments are mirrored against the world and often leave a trace. That could be a picture or a memory, seared into someone's mind. Otherwise, who's to say it ever happened? The records are in the most unusual places. Sand can hold the records of where the tide has been, and bones can tell us stories of ancient lifestyles. The soil holds secrets we uncover the more we work it and even our own, live bodies, retain the marks of our battles, either mentally or physically. But what, here in the middle of the moorland, has recorded ten minutes when someone took a little girl? Had it, despite cameras and security, escaped?

It couldn't have. Only the most remote places are anonymous these days. Somewhere around here, something must have seen the vehicle and its driver, and little Maisie. I look around at the trees and the high wall, beyond it the house. Upwards, a passing plane assures me that this place can't go unseen. My line of vision falls and I see it.

The curved glass of the ornamental lamp at the top of the post I am leaning on. Curves and prisms. And reflected in that glass, the image of the police van.

CHAPTER EIGHT

I dial Keith's number as I try to swallow the half-chewed sandwich. My mouth suddenly feels dry and my fingers won't find the right keys. This is what it's like for me when I'm on the edge of discovering something. Finally, it rings and he answers.

'Keith. The CCTV. The one that shows that lamp.'

I know it will be at his fingertips. Keith is a top-class IT surveillance officer. The SMIT team specially selected him from the civilian staff. There were big objections when he first came on board from trained IT officers in the force, but rumour had it he was Echelon trained. He had worked on top-secret cases over the years and, with the contacts he has, he could execute a surveillance warrant in seconds.

'Yep. It's on both cameras.'

'Okay. The one on the same picture as the white line. Can you have a look at that lamp? Have that part of the picture enhanced.'

I hear him tapping on the keyboard again, faster and faster.

'I'll get it done right now.'

I pause. It's a gamble to tell the other person what you're

looking for. It can bias the outcome if there's any ambiguity. But I have no choice. I have to find the vehicle.

'I'm looking for a vehicle. Headlights on. I think it might have been reflected in that lamp.'

The line goes dead and I know he's on the phone to the lab, ordering the enhancement, checking everything he's already got. I look over to the front doorway of the Lewis's home. Steve's still talking on his mobile and Lauren's gone back inside. I stare at my phone. Come on, Keith. Come on.

I walk around the back of the house now, ever checking that I've still got a mobile signal. My mother used to send me out across the moorland to buy eggs and milk from a local farm. I could have spent hours sitting amongst the heather, picking at rocks and watching bugs under stones. I bet that's what Amy wants for Maisie, that idyllic countryside childhood. Village life. No one could have ever predicted what has happened today. Marc and Amy, they probably felt safe out here. Safe from the hustle and bustle of the city where too many people push and shove. Where all doors need to be locked.

I gaze at the imposing house. Amy left the windows open, never dreaming that someone could creep in and steal her sleeping daughter. Never once thinking that her husband's job would bring criminals to her door. She was safe. I expect she'll never feel safe again. And that's a horrible feeling. The insecurity seeps under the skin and trickles into every feeling. It isolates happiness and builds a cage around it, until, eventually, carrying out the minutiae of everyday slides over the slippery slope of fear. And all enjoyment of life disappears.

I'm suddenly back in London and walking toward a car park, carrying an old-style brown suitcase. I'm dragging my body across the tarmac, heavy with sadness and uncertain of the future. No happiness there. I'd left that behind in the weeks before.

My phone rings and it makes me pull my breath in.

'Keith?'

'Got it. Not very clear. Not clear enough for a registration number, too small. But it's a silver 4x4. Land Rover Range Rover Classic. 1992. The first model with air suspension, if I'm not mistaken. Parked up just before the gates.'

All the hairs on my arms prickle up.

'Finally. Finally. Right. The vehicles at the road junctions. Did Lauren index them?'

He laughs. Keith's a jovial person, always first with a wisecrack, but this is the first time I've heard him laugh. We must be getting somewhere.

'Duh. Lauren indexes everything.'

'Right. I want all the silver Range Rovers that passed those junctions. Registration and registered owners. Stand by while I run this by Steve.'

I thought we'd never get here. I was beginning to think that we were at the end of the road. I end the call and sprint over to where Steve is drinking tea from a polystyrene cup. He knows before I reach him.

'What? What you got?'

'I've got the vehicle. Silver Range Rover. Keith's searching for all vehicles of that type now.'

He doesn't smile. But he stands a little bit straighter and runs his fingers through his hair.

'How?'

I point at the lamp.

'Reflective glass. Ornamental. I got Keith to have all the CCTV enhanced.'

The corners of his mouth turn up a little, and that's the most I'm going to get out of him. Until Maisie is safe and well.

'Let's get out of here. We need to get back to base and move quickly on this.'

We hurry inside and I signal to Lauren that we're going. Lorraine follows Marc Lewis into the hallway.

'What's going on? Has something happened?'

I blink at him. He looks dishevelled and tired and it's no wonder. They've both held up under the pressure of this. I've attended parents of abducted children who've become violent and hit out at the police. But Marc's coped by doing his own research, keeping himself busy. And Amy's coped with a cocktail of tranquillisers. I don't know which one I would do in their circumstances. No one does until it happens to them, and I'm mindful of this when I reply.

'We've got some recent information. We're just going to make some more enquiries, Marc. We'll keep you informed every step of the way.'

He stands at the door and watches us as we get in our cars and pull out of his driveway. I meet his eyes as I pass him, strapped into a passenger street. He's losing patience. Despite appearances, he's at the end of his coping capacity and I'm momentarily worried that he'll go to the end of the dirt track and talk to the horde of reporters when we leave.

Cameras flash as we pass the reporters and I pull my collar around my face. In twenty minutes, we're back at headquarters. Lauren rushes to help Keith. Steve and I grab a coffee. It's one o'clock. Eighteen hours since someone took Maisie from her bed and put her into a silver Range Rover. Two things are still bugging me about this. I'm convinced that this is someone with local knowledge, someone who knows Saddleworth very well. And the doll. I know it's there somewhere, locked into my synapses. Etched on my neurons. Somewhere, tidied away in my memory banks. I know what that doll is. It feels like it's there somewhere in half sleep, on the edge of my dreams. I've seen it before. I know I have.

Keith comes up with nine silver Range Rovers of different sizes. Steve looks over his shoulder at the CCTV.

'Get them all checked out.'

Keith gets to work with almost immediate results.

'Lauren's earlier work has helped with that. Seven are registered to local businesses. One to someone in Greenfield and one to a London address.'

Steve thinks for a minute. 'Okay. I'll get the team on it. Priority. It might be difficult to the track the business owners with it being Sunday, if they're registered to premises. But we need to find all of these vehicles and their owners.'

Lauren picks up one of the tasks from the list. 'I'll get onto the London one. I can ask someone in the Met to check on the owner.'

The Met. London Metropolitan Police. My temperature rises at the sound of the words. *I'm back there, in my car, roof still down, driving through Camden. The wind in my hair. The sunshine beating down on my bare arms and the sound of my own laughter in between verses of Aerosmith's 'Love in an Elevator'. Staring into the windows of furniture shops at Moroccan-style throws and wondering if I should buy one. Feeling the glow of contentment as I head for home. Longing for feet up and the chink of ice over whiskey. Dim sums and hot and sour soup. Stopping at traffic lights and watching a woman with a tiny dog crossing the road. Her heels making an impression in the hot waxy surface of the zebra crossing.*

Lauren taps me on the shoulder. 'I've made the call. They're going to run a check on the guy who the car is registered to. They'll get back to me. You know London, don't you?'

The sadness hits me. I know London. I know it very well.

'Yes. Yes, I do.'

'Is King's Cross central then?'

'Yes. Why?'

'Well, that's where he lives. 5a Swinton Street. Glen Wright.'

Steve joins us. He and Keith have arranged for the other eight vehicles to be traced. I stare at Lauren in disbelief.

'Swinton Street? King's Cross? That's really central. What would a car registered there be doing in Greenfield on a Saturday night?'

Something inside me shifts. It doesn't seem right. Not right at all. But all we can do is wait. Wait until they have narrowed all the vehicles down to one, then swoop. Steve explains that his backup team will make sure that all the vehicles will be traced quickly, probably within half an hour to an hour for the local ones. He pulls me to one side.

'I've had reports from the power plants. Nothing as yet. No sightings.'

His skin is pale and his eyes tired. It's as if his worry is leaking out of him.

The waiting's the worst. No one knows what to do, how to just wait, so everyone picks up some aspect of the case and goes over it again. I pick up the notes and wonder how long it will be before we find Maisie. Before we discover who has taken her.

The first call comes in fifteen minutes. Keith opens up the communications portal and we hear the information over the speakers.

'Vehicles one and two clear. Owners traced and present with vehicle. Vehicles located and searched.'

Over the next twenty minutes there are five similar calls, leaving just a Range Rover that's parked in a locked yard, and the attending officers are waiting for the boss to arrive with the keys.

Then Lauren's desk phone rings. Keith grabs the call and puts it on speakerphone, and DI Patrick Knowles from London

Metropolitan Police gives us the rundown. His voice suddenly fills the room.

'Okay. We've got a Glen Wright. Aged twenty-five. Address as stated. Registered owner of silver Range Rover registration HT2 4SG. Previous convictions for public disorder and breach of the peace.'

Steve shouts out into the silent room. 'Any further intelligence?'

Knowles clicks at his keyboard.

'I've just sent an email with his mugshot and some intelligence stills from his file that have been taken at rallies. He's been a long-time attendee of various events held by a number of organisations. We have reason to believe that he's part of a core gang that turns up at demonstrations and anywhere someone might want a brick through their window. As far as we can see, he's been in full-time education all his life and he's financed by his parents.'

Keith flashes the email up on his screen, and in a few clicks of his mouse he's cut and pasted a security picture from Marc Lewis's company security CCTV of the two intruders he'd mentioned in his interview. It's him. Steve stares at the screen, his watery blue eyes wide and alert.

'Okay. I think that's who we want. We've got one more vehicle query to receive, but I expect that'll be negative. We'll go with this one. Can you bring him in? You need to find the location of the car quickly. The evidence so far shows traces of ammonium nitrate.'

There's a pause. I know Pat. I know he's frowning hard and saying 'Fuck, fuck, fuck' under his breath and wondering how he can shut off a part of central London.

'Right. Can you confirm that?'

Steve confirms. 'Our lab signed it off. We don't know that

it's in an explosive state. There were traces found on material left at the scene where Maisie Lewis disappeared.'

Pat sighs heavily, and it's clearly audible in the room. 'So, we're not just looking for a missing baby, as if that wasn't enough, but there might be explosives as well?'

Steve nods to himself. 'Affirmative.'

I speak now. I push the words out. It's better he knows. 'Pat. Hi.'

I can hear the shock in his voice when he realises it's me. 'Jan. Jan. That's you, isn't it?'

'Yes. I'm working with Steve on this. I'd really like to see this guy you're bringing in. I need to assess him. But it takes two hours minimum to get down there. Do you think one of the investigating officers could wear a headcam? Those body cams? And that we could watch the interrogation of the suspect?'

We can hear his breath on the line. The team thinks that he's considering my request, but I know he's trying to work out how I got to Manchester, and how I'm working on this case. Finally, he answers.

'We'll try it. It's new technology and I don't know if it'll work. We'll try to livestream it through. It'll be recording in any case. How are you, Jan?'

I bow my head. As good as can be expected. Okay. Not too bad. What can I say? It's been a long time since I last came face to face with Pat Knowles.

'Fine. Okay. Good. So, we're all set then? You'll get a team to pick him up when?'

'As soon as possible. Obviously, we'll have to secure the area, but until we know where that car is...'

'Understood. I'll wait for your call for us to tune in.'

My God. I can imagine what Pat has to do now; evacuate lots of bystanders from a busy London Street. They'll have Glen Wright's telephone number by now and they'll have called him, telling him they're a plumber or a joiner who the landlord has sent round, confirming that he'll be in. Pat can convene a large team in less than fifteen minutes. Now we've told him about potential explosives, less. They'll be scrambling right now, all making their way to Swinton Street from different locations. Like bees to honey. I can see the street map in my mind, and even spot the convergence point at King's Cross Bridge. That's what I'd do. Traffic stopped, maybe a removal van broken down in the middle of the King's Cross Road to obscure the view.

We're all tense. Glen Wright's picture looms large on the screen, and Keith is scanning the intelligence files. Ten minutes in, he's found it. A grainy picture of Glen at a banking demonstration. Dressed in black cargo pants and a white vest, a black fringed scarf partly covering his face, but slipped away. He's just thrown a brick and the shot has caught it mid-air. His arm stretches and Keith has focused in on an intricate tattoo on his shoulder. It's a sunrise with a flock of birds flying away from it. Underneath is a line and, in Broadway font, the word Magellan.

The last vehicle call comes in. The owner had unlocked the gate and the officers had him unlock the car. It was full of counterfeit cigarettes and they had arrested him for customs offences.

We are joined by some of the officers who've returned from the Lewises'. Steve briefs them and brings them right up to date with the case, and everyone waits around for the phone to ring, and for Pat to tell us that the operation is live. I stare at Glen's face on the vast screen, three times larger than normal. He's a wiry, lithe young man with a wide grin. Above average looks, but not classically handsome. The question is, has he driven up to Manchester, kidnapped a one-year-old and driven back, all in three days? It's possible, and anyone with a plan would be able to do it. And the ammonium nitrate? Is it in the car? Is it in his flat?

Pat Knowles would be thinking the same things. The mere mention of explosive chemicals in central London would have sent his already spot-on reactions into overdrive. It's the Met's worst nightmare. Then there's reputation. Pat's a proud man, good at his job. He wouldn't want anything going wrong with the recovery of a child from an abductor. Not on his patch.

But one thing that Pat Knowles wouldn't be wondering is whether Glen would be interested in paper dolls. Would he have driven to Manchester and cut out some dolls to post through the doors of his victims? Or even cut them out in his flat before he went? The criminal mind is a mystery, but this young man, who seemingly loves to disrupt and, by the joyful look on his face, to throw bricks through windows, doesn't strike me as the paper doll type. I call out to Keith.

'Those pictures of the suspect. Any more tattoos?'

It's worth a shot. If he *was* so obsessed with paper dolls that he cut them out and doodled them, then perhaps he would have inked them into his identity. Keith flashes up some images. A tribal band around his wrist. 'Mum' tattooed on the inside of his arm. Lauren sighs and I read her. She's wondering how someone involved in a plan to take a child could love his mother.

There are no doll tattoos. But by looking at the pictures in his intelligence file, I'm seeing someone who likes to incite. In many of them he's standing in the background with another man, the other face on Marc's security camera watching while other people commit various criminal acts. He's ever-smiling, ever-laughing, his wide grin belied only by his cold eyes.

'What's he studying, Keith?'

He taps in another query.

'Environmental science at City University. Been there for

four years. It's his second degree. First one, chemistry. But he didn't finish it.'

Steve hasn't spoken since I ended the call with Pat. His eyes are on the clock. It's five past two. Maisie's been missing for eighteen hours. Part of me wishes I could be in London, banging on Glen's door, backed by two armed officers, calling for him to come outside. My plan would be to get him out then to go in. I know Pat would do it differently, despite what I recommended. He'd push his way in and detain the suspect inside the property. Too confused. Too much room for error. That was part of the reason Lando went on so long. And part of the reason that another part of me, the larger part, never wants to go back to London.

In my mind's eye, I can see Pat's team making their way up to the suspect's residence. The streets will be clear of people and all access nearby sealed off. I catch my breath when I think of the back alleyways and stone walls, so many places for people to access a scenario. But Pat will have it sealed off. He won't take any chances. He'll have called in the explosives team and just about now they'll be moving into position. I check my phone to sync the time with the clock on the wall.

A phone rings out over the speakers and a slightly shaky video image flashes onto the screen.

CHAPTER NINE

P at Knowles appears on the screen.

'As you can see, we've got an officer set up with a body cam. I've been patched into your comms so I can hear any comments you have. We've got a full explosives team on standby and a team ready to go to the vehicle. We know he's in there. We've called the property, and he's waiting for a visit from his landlord.'

I check the background behind him. Swindon Street is all residential buildings with cars parked either side of the street. 5a is the third house from a busy road junction with a large hotel at the end of it. I can just see uniformed police officers outside the hotel doors, preventing anyone from leaving. Traffic cones everywhere. A gas van for credibility. Nice work.

My gaze strays to Pat, now in profile and my heart jumps. I scan his familiar face and feel the emotions flood back.

The road is cordoned off and two police vans are at the junction blocking the view of anyone in nearby buildings. Several officers stand at the end of the street and four of them turn off and go towards the back of the property as I'm watching. Not much movement at all. Pat turns around and the body cam turns toward 5a Swindon Street. Three officers approach the property and one of them bangs on the door. Another signals for someone to cover the back alleyway at both ends. No one answers the door.

'Glen Wright. Open the door, Mr Wright.'

Nothing. I glance around the SMIT suite. There are thirty officers glued to the footage. The room is completely silent. Keith pulls up Sky News on the oversized TV and although there's no sound, I can see the reporter pointing at the front of King's Cross railway station, and St Pancras, and crowds of people being herded up York Way. Away from the cordoned off area. They've shut the underground and the railway station.

'Open the door, Mr Wright. This is a final warning.'

Thirty seconds tick away on the clock and then the body cam swings round to show Pat giving the command. We see two officers ram the door open and a stream of men with body armour flash by and into the flat.

The camera follows Pat into the lounge where Glen Wright is pulling on a pair of jeans. Next to him is an overflowing ashtray and two glasses of what appears to be whiskey or brandy. A woman stands in the doorway in her underwear. Her hair is tousled and she's crying loudly. One of the officers grabs a throw from the sofa and pulls it around her shoulders. Pat approaches Glen Wright. He's suddenly standing nose to nose with him.

'Glen Wright. Are you the owner of a silver Range Rover? Registration number HT2 4SG?'

Glen stops stock-still and looks at the four officers flanking him.

'Yes. Is that what this is about?'

Pat sucks in his lips as though he's going to explode any second. But he doesn't. He speaks quietly.

'Where's the vehicle, Glen?'

Glen's grinning the wide grin we've seen so many times before in the intelligence photos. The cold grin, devoid of humour. My first impression is that he's a narcissist. He's arrogant and very aware of himself.

'Round the back. There's the key on the table. I've been a bit preoccupied lately.' He nods at the girl and straightens to full height. 'The car's parked round the back, out of the way, on the grass verge in the alleyway.'

An officer wearing a stab jacket takes the keys and hurries away. Pat doesn't move. He stares at Glen for a second.

'What's in the car, Glen?'

At that moment one of the officers comes into the lounge. Other officers are pulling apart the sofa, turning out drawers. In the background is the crashing of plates and pans as the kitchen is fully searched. Pat continues to stare at Glen, cool and calm, but speaks to the officer.

'What is it, Pete?'

The officer shows him the cardboard box he's holding. He shows it to the body cam. There are bags of powder and some paperwork. Pat picks up the paperwork and takes what seems like an age to read it. Then he pulls on some white protective gloves, which I know he always keeps in his pocket just as I do, and picks up the bag. He shows the label to the body cam's lens. Ammonium nitrate.

'Seems like it's what we've been looking for, boss. Some delivery notes for chemicals. Ammonium nitrate. Pure sodium. Bicarbonate of soda. There's more out the back.'

Glen looks around the room for an escape route. I see his pupils dilate and all the muscles in his sinewy body tense as he prepares to make a run for it. He makes a tiny move towards the doorway and one of the officers blocks his route.

Pat Knowles matches Glen's grin. I've seen that before. It means trouble. If the body cam wasn't running everything would be different. But as it is, Pat is calm and collected. He moves his lips close to Glen's ear.

'Glen Wright, I'm arresting you on suspicion of terrorism, you do not have to say anything but it may damage your defence if you do not mention anything that you later rely on in court. Anything you do say may be given in evidence.'

Two of the officers struggle to cuff him. The grin has gone, replaced by confusion.

'Terrorism? What the fuck?'

Pat sits on the sofa. The body cam scans the room for the benefit of the record. It's a smart flat, nicely decorated, with a rack of CDs and a large TV. Pat flicks on the TV and selects Sky News. The reporter is standing at the end of Pentonville Road, with a vantage point of both the station and the cordon at the bottom of King's Cross Road. Pat turns up the volume.

'... And a police spokesman says that the area may be cordoned off for some time to come. The official line is that there's a large gas leak at the junction of King's Cross Road and Swindon Street. The stations remain closed until further notice. Anyone travelling...'

He reduces the volume and looks at Glen.

'So, you see, we've got all day. So, two things, Glen, before we take you in. I'm going to give you the opportunity to explain to us, in the comfort of your own home, on camera, where Maisie Lewis is and why you have the components to make a bomb in your flat.'

Glen tries to soften his features, but he's still pumped with stress and instead he looks terrified.

'I can explain about the chemicals. They're for an experiment. I'm a chemistry graduate. But who's Maisie Lewis? I don't know who that is.'

Pat doesn't answer for a moment or two. This gives me enough time to assess Glen's reactions.

'Okay, I'll give you a clue. A one-year-old child was abducted at nine o'clock on Saturday night. Your vehicle was used in the abduction. We're fairly sure of that because we found ammonium nitrate traces at the scene of the crime and now we've found ammonium nitrate in your flat. It all kind of adds up, doesn't it, Glen?'

He flushes. He's starting to put together the severity of the situation and how he might be implicated.

'I've been here all week. I haven't been out of the house for three days. I've got a witness. She's been here all the time. Haven't you, babe?'

The girl in the doorway nods slowly. She's pale and shaky and tearful. Pat picks up a small zip-lock plastic bag from a nearby coffee table. It contains a white powder.

'I'm going to repeat the question, Glen. Where's Maisie Lewis? We'll get to the explosives later on. At the station. But right now we need to find that child.'

I lean forward to see Glen's reaction. I wish I was there to gauge it. To feel his fear and see his pupils dilate and recede, to catch him on the edge of a lie.

'I swear I don't know anything about any kid. I swear.'

The officer who took the key appears. He shakes his head. Pat turns to him.

'No vehicle?'

He nods. Glen loses it. He jumps up and Pat lets him.

'It's definitely there. I left it there myself on Thursday. I checked on it and locked it up. It was there on Thursday and like I said I haven't been out since. I swear.'

Pat's silent for a moment. I feel bile rise in my throat. Where the fuck is the car then? Who has it?

'Okay. Just to be sure, you can show us where the vehicle is. Better make the most of it, Glen, because you won't be back for a while.'

The two officers lead Glen to the door. Pat remains. He looks around the rooms, checking for anything that might have been missed.

'Get SOCOs here. Full forensics. As soon as possible.'

He follows Glen and the officers out of the flat, down the road and up a gap between the townhouses. Body cam follows, more fragmented now, and in seconds they're all around the back in a built-up off-road area. A small courtyard with bays of white lines for residents' parking. Pat looks around for cameras to confirm Glen's story, to see who drove away, because the car has gone. He's standing in the middle of the courtyard, staring at the spot where he says it was parked. He doesn't look as confident now. I can see the doubt in his stance, the looking around desperately for clues to who took his car.

'It was there. I swear. I checked it Thursday morning. I parked it up Wednesday night. I'd been out of town. To pick Jane up.'

He signals towards the flat, vaguely. Pat beckons the body cam closer, close enough to hear what he says next.

'So you're telling me, Glen, that after driving out of town you left a shedload of potentially explosive chemicals on a side street in central London?'

Glen's silent for a while and I wonder if he's going to take the bait. There are several responses to this question. There are no chemicals in the car. There isn't enough in there to explode. I didn't know they were explosives. He could even laugh in Pat's face. Or ask for a lawyer. But he goes on the defensive.

'It's not a full car. About three-quarters full. And they're not collated. That was going to be done later.' He realises just a second too late that he's incriminated himself. 'It wasn't me, though. It wasn't. I've got nothing to do with this. I want a solicitor.'

Pat breaks out his smile again.

'We're already onto it. But let me just clarify. Where's the little girl?'

Glen's shouting. In the unusually silent London streets, it echoes.

'I don't fucking know. I don't know anything about no girl. That wasn't the plan.'

Pat stops in his tracks. He turns to face Glen and raises his eyebrows.

'Oh. The plan. Would that be the Magellan plan?'

Glen's knees buckle. His face contorts in pain and he shakes his head.

'I want a solicitor. I'm not sayin' nothin' else.'

Pat shuts it down. He knows that anything else will be extracted in the privacy of a police van on the way to the station.

'Okay. Have it your way. I gave you a chance. Let's take them in. Him and the girl, both of them. Get that flat sealed off and get the roads and the station open as soon as the chemicals have been removed from the property. I want CCTV from all the roads around here from Thursday morning onwards. Let's see if Glen's telling the truth. I can't see any surveillance on these buildings, not overlooking this area, but it would be worth checking private systems in the properties around here.'

He breaks out his cruel smile again and stares into the body cam lens.

'Okay, Manchester, over and out. We'll resume when we get back to the station and start the questioning. Any questions?'

Steve breaks the silence.

'No questions. Jan will represent us at the interview. She'll let you know what we need from him.'

Pat's expression softens a little.

'Jan. Great. I'll look forward to it.' The smile reappears and I feel a little bit sick. I know what will happen between now and the interview. Pat will do his best to persuade Glen to talk. One way or another. Not my kind of policing, and nothing I can prove, which is partly why I am here and not still there. He looks back into the camera. 'Body cam off.'

The screen goes blank and we sit in silence. It slowly sinks in that the silver Range Rover that someone used to abduct Maisie isn't there. Keith articulates my hope.

'Probably one of his Magellan mates, driven it off. He's covering for him.'

We all nod, but I'm not sure. Lauren taps her fingers nervously on the desk. There's an uncomfortable feeling in me, a sense of foreboding. Like when you think something good's going to happen but it doesn't. Like a burning in my chest that I know is going to force me to take action.

'So, we're no further forward. And I still think that whoever took Maisie is from round here.'

Steve swivels his chair to face me.

'Thanks for that, Jan. Thanks a lot.'

I know my strengths and I know my weaknesses. My weaknesses are mainly to do with my more recent past, the one that forced me out of London and into hiding. But my strengths lie in something that happened when I was very young. I grew up in isolated surroundings, not many friends. Only because we lived in a village and I attended a village school until secondary school. The thing is, I never learned to feel less than.

I never developed a sense of others being better or worse than me, and I never really picked up on gender roles, despite my parents' completely dysfunctional relationship. I spent a lot of time on my own and when I encountered other people, it was on my own terms. I was astonished to find out later on that other people had insecurity issues and this is what made me study psychology. What makes the world that way?

In spite of going through police training, I've never lost it. I've never lost a sense of being able to speak up when needed, to critique and to challenge. I've never really had that sense that other people have told me about of looking foolish or stupid or of others resorting to ad hominem insults. I'm not insensitive. I care deeply about other people. I'm just not too concerned what they think of me.

So, I'm here to ask the difficult questions. I know that whatever reaction I get is down to the person reacting and their life filter, not mine. It doesn't make me popular, but it does make me strong. And now is the time to be strong. I face Steve off.

'That's okay, Steve. I wouldn't want us to meander down a dead end now we're onto something. All I'm saying is that the MO of the perpetrator isn't consistent with a hardened activist like Glen Wright. Too disorganised. And knows the area.'

Steve looks doubtful. 'I don't think so. I reckon Pat Knowles will get the names of the other members out of him and it'll be one of them. Maybe it is someone from round here. Maybe not. But what else have we got?'

Keith has resumed tapping on his keyboard and the rest of the officers have drifted back to the comms stations to avoid the tension. It isolates me and makes me question my own judgement. I know that Steve has to go on what he has, and it's obvious that Glen Wright has something to do with this, but I'm still not sure.

'Nothing. Except some pieces of paper and circumstantial. But there's something in the back of my mind about those dolls. It's a connection with the Lewises' house and that area. I can't quite place it.'

I can see a vein in Steve's forehead throbbing and he breaks a sweat on his forehead. I hate doing this to people, placing doubt when they think they're on the right track. Eventually he blows.

'For God's sake, Jan. I know what you're saying, but we have to follow the trail. The chemicals. All linked to Glen Wright.

That Range Rover. We've just had half of London on a detour and we still don't know where that fucking car is. I've got the whole police force looking for it. Every officer in the UK has the registration number, and all the motorways have it programmed into their auto number plate recognition grids. It must be somewhere.'

I move closer to him.

'Yes, you're right. It has to be somewhere. The car and the chemicals have to be somewhere. But you know, Steve, you didn't mention Maisie. Not once did you mention that little girl. It's almost as if you've separated her abduction and the bomb-making material in your mind, because the evidence doesn't fit.'

He steps backwards, avoiding my accusations. 'I haven't. No. I haven't. We find the car, we find Maisie.'

I lean in because he needs to face the truth.

'But the thing is, Glen Wright knows all about those chemicals. He knows all about Magellan and the collation, as he called it. The plan. He's going to tell Pat who he thinks has that car. I know Pat. He'll have him ready to talk by now. But the problem is, Glen knows nothing about Maisie. Nothing at all.'

He's silent for a moment. I know he's going over the arrest footage in his mind.

'He could be lying. It's not unknown, you know.'

He's right, he could. But all the signs say he's not. I'm sure of it.

'Believe me, he's not lying. He completely panicked when Pat hit him with the abduction. He's desensitised to the chemicals, convinced himself that it's all in a good cause, for the greater good and all that. He's all ready to defend that. But the kid threw him. That's when he lost it.'

Steve's thinking. Trying to work round this revelation.

'So, one of the Magellan members takes the car and takes Maisie. They'd have a motive. You heard what Marc Lewis said

94

about them. They're everywhere he is, all over his business, and the intelligence.'

I look at him. He's pale and tired and it's five past four. I don't expect he slept last night. His greying hair is greasy from him running his fingers through it and his shirt collar is slightly blackened around the crease.

'The only thing is, Steve, if it's a gang thing, this Magellan, and they're so tight, why didn't whoever it is just tell Glen they were taking the car? And where's the ransom demand?'

Steve looks at the clock, too. More than 24 hours since Maisie disappeared from her bed.

CHAPTER TEN

An hour later, I'm taking a call from Sally Rushworth. Sally used to be my Lauren at the Met, my understudy, always willing to go above and beyond, forever waiting for me to leave. So that she can step into my shoes.

'Oh my God, Jan. How've you been?'

I snort under my breath. How've I been? I would have thought that was obvious from my absence.

'Good, Sal, good. You?'

'Yeah, I'm working with Pat now, and sometimes Andy. You know.'

Yes, I do know. I know exactly. When I don't speak, she launches into the reason for her call.

'You sure you're okay, Jan? Only you seem different. Not different but... I don't know. I can't put my finger on it.'

I roll my eyes at the phone. Some people have no tact. She's more like Lauren than I thought.

'I'm fine, Sally. Just fine.'

'Right. So, could I have your number? Only I'd love to keep in touch.'

And there it is. Right there, right at the beginning of my

return to London. Someone asking for my mobile number, after I haven't been in touch for a long time. It's always awkward with phone numbers. You feel almost obliged to give your number out to anyone who asks for it, for fear of snubbing them. But it's not awkward for me. Not awkward at all, and the wave of panic that passes through me when she asks reminds me why.

'I don't have a personal mobile. You can ring me at the station.'

There's a short silence.

'Don't have a mobile? Bloody hell, Jan. You used to have one, though. I have your old number here. I tried it a couple of times.'

I sigh. I really didn't want this scenario. I wanted to disappear, stay anonymous. Away from all those people in London who knew so much about me. Who wanted me dead.

'Yeah. I have a work one, but you know. The rules. No outside conversations and all that.'

'Even at your level? Harsh. Anyway. I'm going to be in on the interview with Glen Wright. Is there anything in particular you want me to observe? I'll be doing the behavioural analysis stuff.'

I know that 'just like you did' is on the tip of her tongue, but she doesn't say it. Just like you did in the job you loved so much. Lived for. And almost died for. Just like you, with your colleagues and in the city that's so vibrant and loved by you, but where you can't go now. But my panic retreats now she's firmly focused on work.

'Yes. Yes, there is. I expect he'll be in the mood to speak about the chemicals, but in the initial interview he said he had no idea about Maisie Lewis, the little girl who's gone missing. I need you to watch him very closely to see if he's lying. There's got to be a connection, and he's got the key to it.'

'Right. Will do. I'm sure that Pat will find that key, and

lovely to speak to you again, Jan, really. If you're ever down here, let me know. We could go for a drink or something?'

'Thanks, Sally. I definitely will if I'm ever in London.'

I won't be. Ever. Not if I have my way. I end the call and go back to the main room where everyone is gathered to watch Glen Wright's interview. Sky News looms large in the background of a nearby monitor, which is good, because it's another resource to find the Range Rover. I watch as the news helicopter swoops over Dovestone Reservoir. I watch for a silver oblong amongst the high rocks and back roads, or parked up in the many picnic sites that I know are dotted around the place that I know like the back of my hand. I wonder how Amy and Marc are coping and get my phone out to call Lorraine. But the large screen flashes blue, then Pat Knowles appears.

'I can see you all the time. But the sound will go off for me during the interview. If you have anything, signal it by raising a hand. Jan, I've missed you, mate. Looking good.'

Looking into the background of the stark interview room, I can see a small screen in front of Pat and Sally, turned away towards the opposite side of the desk. I wave weakly and some of the officers smile at me.

'Hi, Pat. Good to see you too. What's the crack, then?'

He laughs loudly. It was our catchphrase. What's the crack? In another life when none of us knew what was just around the corner. We all had passwords that would let us know that it was really us when we text each other, and they were never disclosed to anyone, but in the team we all knew each other's. If the chips were down, we'd have to repeat where the password was sourced, for extra security. Mine was Rhiannon, as in Fleetwood Mac, as it's the name I would have loved to have been be called and a fabulous song. Pat's was Hollywood. After Bob Segar's 'Hollywood Nights', his theme tune. I've never seen anyone look less Hollywood than Pat. Maybe that was the point.

Pat looks much greyer and has more lines than when I last saw him, when he was thirty. Now he looks nearer fifty. He's aged about twenty years. None of us got away lightly, it occurs to me.

'What's the crack? Bloody hell, Jan, that takes me back. Happy days, eh? Happy days.'

Some of them were, to be sure. And what else can he say now? But I can tell from his eyes, the depth of the sorrow that still remains, that he's fared no better than me in the meantime.

'Yeah. Yeah, they were.'

He relaxes a little, both of us safe in the knowledge that we're on the same page.

'Right. This little fucker, Glen Wright. I've persuaded him that if he tells us what we want to know we'll try to reduce the terrorism charge. I think he'll talk. But just to let you know, he's still saying he knows nothing about the kid and his dad has got him a shit-hot lawyer. Sally's going to assist. You remember Sally, don't you?'

I smile. It's odd to see Pat and Sally in an interview room I know so well, and not be there myself. But there's no time for reminiscing because the back door, the one that leads from the cells, opens, and Glen Wright comes in followed by his solicitor. Glen's deflated and his shoulders droop. I look at Steve and he looks surprised. He leans over and whispers to me.

'Jesus. What's he done to him?'

'Oh, he's got his methods. He's not big on the cognitive interview. But he won't have laid a finger on him.'

They all sit and Pat begins.

'For the purpose of the recording are you Glen Phillip Wright of 5a Swindon Road, London? Owner of a silver Range Rover registration number HT2 4SG?'

Glen looks up. His eyes are red-rimmed and I expect Pat's made him cry. A lot.

'Yes.'

'Okay, Glen. I'm going to ask you a series of questions and I would like you to tell me as much as you can. There's a young child missing and the information you give me may help us locate her. So, you'll be doing a public service in a way.'

Glen looks subdued, too. Not as cocky as he was before.

'I don't know nothing about the kid. Nothing at all.'

I see Sally lean slightly forwards, watching him closely. Pat shifts in his seat.

'Okay. We'll start with Magellan. What's Magellan, Glen?'

He glances at his solicitor but doesn't heed his slight headshake.

'It's an environmental collective. About ten of us, all fighting for the same cause. We oppose the rape of the environment.'

Pat nods slowly. I can sense him revving up, moving in for the kill.

'And the vehicle you own, which you say was stolen after 10am on Thursday morning and which we believe has been used in criminal activity. Is there any chance that some of these Magellan chaps could have taken it? For any reason? Maybe some kind of, I don't know, plan?'

Glen starts to cry. He's sobbing.

'I didn't make the fucking plan. I had no part of that.'

Pat pushes a piece of paper over the table to Glen and rolls a ballpoint pen at him.

'Glen, would you be so kind as to write the names of the Magellan people on this piece of paper? And any addresses and phone numbers. And don't worry about getting the numbers wrong. We're just examining your laptop and getting your phone records, so we'll be able to work it out if you make any little mistakes. Thanks.'

He starts to write. I dial control.

'Get that piece of paper copied and sent to Petra. Tell her I want a match with the handwriting on the messages.'

When Glen's finished, an officer takes it from him and leaves the room. Pat resumes.

'Right. We've already established that some of your Magellan associates might have taken the car. The car that was parked in central London containing ammonium nitrate, pure sodium and an assortment of other potentially explosive materials. You've yet to tell us the purpose of the contents of the car. And don't give me any shit about an experiment, Glen.'

His solicitor objects. 'You can't do that. You can't speak to him like that.'

Pat nods and Sally smiles and folds her arms. Pat directs his next question at the solicitor.

'Have you got children, Mr Forbes?'

The solicitor nods. It's obvious that he's scared to death of Pat.

'Right. A one-year-old child was taken out of her bed. She's been gone overnight and now it's coming up to five thirty and she's not been found. I'd like her back with her parents as soon as possible. Her father is a well-known businessman, Marc Lewis, and he's worried out of his mind.'

Glen's reaction is visible. Sally makes notes and Pat stares at Glen.

'Jogged your memory, has it, Glen?'

He's pale and shaken. I can hear Steve breathing hard, and Lauren bites her nails. They think we're near to our goal. They think Maisie is all but found and that Glen holds the key.

'It wasn't supposed to happen like this. We had a plan. Plan A. To hold the children of those executives who did most damage, to show them how the earth is feeling. How she hurts. How...'

Pat's laughing loudly now.

'Fucking hell, Glen, have you heard yourself? Take children; steal them away from their parents, in this case from

101

her bed, to show them how the earth feels. Jesus. It's one thing walking around with a placard, but that really is fucking bonkers, mate.' He suddenly bangs his fist on the table. 'What's the rest of the plan? Where were you going to take her?'

Glen starts to shout. His voice is high-pitched and hysterical and Sally looks surprised.

'It was fucking aborted. It was slammed. We never got that far. We had a list of kids, but we couldn't do it. We couldn't go through with it.'

'Why, Glen? Why?'

'Too risky. That's why. Too difficult.'

Pat fires back. 'Or maybe even Magellan thought it was too stupid. So, you all decided to blow something up. Is that it?'

Glen's head droops. His solicitor taps him on the shoulder.

'You don't have to answer anything, Glen. Remember what we said.'

Pat continues. He's not giving up. He never does. 'Go on, Glen. I'm good for this. What was Plan B then? Blow up a power station? A dam? Maybe one of their houses? All in the name of green trees and sunshine. Which by the way, doesn't decriminalise it, however many smiley faces you paint on it. Blowing something up is blowing something up, whatever you feel the reason is. So, go on. What's the plan?'

Steve dials his extended team. 'Stand by. Stand by for target.'

Glen's silent for a good minute, then he lolls his head to one side. He looks off into the distance and for a moment I think he's going to move to 'no comment'. But he doesn't.

'The visitor centre next to Sellafield. We were going to blow it up, just to scare people. The plan was to give them a warning first before we did anything.'

Pat leans forward. 'Did anything? Can you be more specific?'

Glen's lips move, but nothing comes out. Steve hurries out of the SMIT suite and into a nearby empty office. I can't hear him, but I know he's sealing off the area around the nuclear power station. Posting armed guards there. Lauren shoots me a worried look. Pat and Sally are waiting for Glen to speak. Pat finally loses it.

'Okay, Glen. Okay. So, what we've got here is a missing child and some chemicals in the back of a vehicle. Intention. To blow something up. Let me ask you this: who do you think has taken your vehicle? Who do you think is going to blow up a power plant? Best guess. Come on. A kid's life might depend on this. Maybe not just a kid's life if they reach their target. So, who's betrayed you, Glen? Who's the Magellan Judas?'

He shakes his head violently. 'I don't know. I don't know. It could be any of them. They're all as passionate as me about... it.'

Pat stands up and leans over the table. 'But you didn't drive to Manchester and kidnap a child, did you? So, who's the nutter, Glen? Which one of your Magellan friends is capable of this?'

Glen starts to cry again, this time hysterically. 'I don't fucking know. It could be Ian Kelly. He's been shouting his mouth off all over the place about teaching them a lesson. The big oil corps. You know? Making them think. Making them wake up.'

Pat laughs. 'Oh, Marc Lewis is awake all right. He's awake and wondering where his tiny daughter is. He knows what you and your Magellan crew are about, Glen. It's him who we got our information from. He knows about you, but he thought you were harmless. He thought you were a bit stupid, you know, all shouty about cutting energy generation, but driving to demos in cars. Throwing a brick through his office window, then jumping into your 4x4 to go home for a nice hot shower and to watch TV. He was laughing at you.'

Glen sits up straight and manages a grin. 'Not laughing now, though, is he?'

Pat lunges at him and Sally manages to catch his arm and pull him back. Even though I expected this, it still makes me jump. She rests her arm on Pat's shoulder and ushers him towards the door. She and Pat leave and the camera flashes off. Steve reappears.

'Right, everyone. I've put the power plants on high security. From 6am in the morning, through Monday rush hour, there'll be traffic streams and officers looking for the car in the city centre and beyond. In the meantime, a UK-wide alert remains for the vehicle. Pat's team are rounding up the suspects on Wright's list. Petra will have the handwriting sample back as soon as possible. In the meantime, everyone on the late shift must wait for instructions. Everyone else, get some rest, but be on call in case we need you to come in.'

The officers in the room disperse and Lauren shakes her head.

'Bloody hell. They could be anywhere. I took my mum and the twins to the coast next to that place last Saturday. Can you imagine...?'

We don't need a scenario painting right now so I shut her down. 'I can. Yes. I really can. But that car has got to be parked up somewhere. Someone would have seen it otherwise. We might have to go public.'

Steve's standing behind me. We both look at the press circus that's currently occupying every tiny piece of space outside the station. He moves his head from side to side, trying to release the tension that's built up in his body. He looks at me.

'I've got everything covered security wise, as much as it can be with someone driving a bomb round Manchester with a baby in the vehicle. We'll have to wait until Knowles gets the other guys in. That might take some time. Even if that does give us some idea who it is, we need to communicate with this person or persons. Jan, can you organise a press conference in the morning? Full on, with Amy and Marc Lewis.'

It's decision time. I've been here for a year now and it's time.

'Of course. I'll take charge of that.'

He stares at me. Steve doesn't know the full story of why I'm hiding here, but he knows enough.

'Lauren can head it up if you'd rather...'

'No. No. Thanks, Steve. But I've got to do it some time. This isn't about me. It's about Maisie.'

Lauren and Steve nod and smile. There's nothing more to say. I've got to face the outside world sometime, face what happened. And if I'm going to go on national TV I might as well do it properly. I turn to Keith.

'Can you let the networks know we're going to do this live at 9am? And that they need to start the broadcast five minutes before Amy and Marc come in. I want the full appeal broadcast, no cuts.'

Steve's shifting from foot to foot. Then he shrugs.

'Might as well. Give them the info about Maisie, obviously, and the car. Tell them all the details we have about the Range Rover. Pat's team have the registration documents, as it's on the system. They've scanned everything. And for God's sake, make it clear to the parents that there can be no mention of the explosives. That needs to be kept under wraps or there'll be national panic.'

He looks at the clock. 6.15pm.

'This might be a good time for everyone to go home and get some rest. Goes without saying to leave your phones on. Jan, if nothing happens overnight someone will pick you up at seven tomorrow morning.'

I don't want to go home. It's always like this. I want to stay, to be at the centre. But I know he's right.

'Okay. If anything happens, anything at all, comms will get in touch. Otherwise, see you tomorrow.'

He leaves, but only for the office next door. None of us want to go. Keith pulls up the Sky News webpage and starts to monitor it. Lauren is going through the list of evidence that Pat's team has scanned onto the intranet, even though she could work from home as she has a login.

No one wants to be the first to leave so I guess I'll have to take the lead. I dial the front desk.

'Can I get a car that's going towards Greenfield?'

There's usually a long wait but because of the activity around that area, a car drives up straight away. Even though it's like ripping a piece of skin away from the flesh, I pull myself away from the investigation and into the front foyer of the station. I stand well back so that no one spots me until the last minute. I've spent the last two years living in the shadows and I had hoped that it would last longer, until everyone forgets about me. But with a child's life at risk, I'll step out. Whatever the consequences.

CHAPTER ELEVEN

I t turns out that I'm not as anonymous as I think I am, even now. As I get out of the car and watch it wind its way down the country road away from my home, I see my nearest neighbour running up the back path. Kirby, my red setter, takes a running jump at me and nearly knocks me over just as Jean reaches me. Her husband Graham is just behind her. I owe them both an apology.

'Sorry. Sorry, Jean. I meant to phone. Thanks for having Kirby. Thanks.'

She's waving a newspaper at me. 'Ooh, Janet, love, you didn't tell us what you did for a living. Graham thought you were a nurse or something. You didn't tell us about this, did you, love?'

She looks worried. Graham has reached her now, and he stops and holds his knees, out of breath. He points at the hill, in the general direction of the Lewises' home.

'On that investigation, aren't you? Working for the police.'

Jean's hand goes to her mouth. Here in Greenfield, a cat stuck up a tree is big news.

'You should have told us, love. And we'll have Kirby

anytime you want. Any time. Just call it our contribution to national safety.'

I look at the newspaper. There's a large picture of me in the car leaving headquarters. I check the distribution. National. My name's all over it, but luckily, not my home address. It says Manchester. I don't live in Manchester. I survey the hilltops, and outward over the dusky moorland. There's a news helicopter fairly close, but I know it's hovering over the Lewises's house. I conduct a quick risk assessment in my mind as Jean tells me about Kirby's routine over the past two days. I think I'll be okay.

'We're very proud of you, Janet. Very proud. Have they... you found that poor little girl yet?'

Graham's arm goes around Jean's shoulder and their eyes widen as I tell them what I know will be repeated around the village as soon as I disappear.

'We're getting near. We have some very good leads. I feel for the parents. Lovely people they are.'

They nod for a while and just stare at me. Then Jean speaks.

'Well, we'd better be off. Seeing you in a new light now, Janet. We just thought you were a GP or something. Now we know, well, very impressed. Very impressed.'

They walk off, waving behind them, and Kirby dances round them. I wanted to tell them about my life, my training. My secret. But I don't want to spoil my friendship with Jean and Graham. They're the nearest thing I've had to parents for a long time. They'd do anything for me. When I had flu, Jean went to the chemist and bought me some Lemsip, and fed me chicken broth. I suddenly realise that I've got a warm feeling inside from them. They're proud of me.

I let myself in and Kirby settles on the sofa. The reason I bought this house, a detached cottage far enough away from anyone that they can't hear me, is that I love loud music. It helps me relax. I think it's something to do with my senses being so full up that I give myself a rest from the day. The louder the better, but I leave the volume on my CD player at eight. Even so, the bass thumps through the floor as I flick a Foo Fighters CD on.

Even though I slept in a cell last night, I'm not tired. The house smells of cinnamon and I immediately go on autopilot and start cooking. That's my great love, cooking. Well, it has been since I came to live here. Back in London, I lived on takeaways and pub food. But now it's what I call three or four pan dishes. The more difficult, the better. I've got a lever arch file full of loose-leaf recipes from all over the world. Following a complex recipe and eating the result is a double pleasure for me. I'm perfectly happy this way. Just me and Kirby, my rock music and my cooking. Perfection.

Don't get me wrong, the case never leaves me for one second. It's hanging in the background as I sing along and chop onions so finely that you can only taste them and not see them in the bolognaise-type sauce I'm making. Just the same, but at the end, instead of Italian herbs, I add fresh mint. Then I layer it with the penne pasta and pour over a cheese sauce, laced with mint and cinnamon. All the time I've been cooking it, I haven't been thinking about Glen Wright or Pat and Sally.

I haven't even thought about Maisie, until the second after I push the dish into the oven to bake. Then it comes back, and, as always, I notice what's front of the queue. What's most important? What stands out? And it's dolls. Paper dolls. Doll notes. Dolls holding hands. Doll scribbles. The chemical trail has linked the enquiry beautifully, but the dolls are running alongside it a close second. There seems to be an awful lot of paper dolls all of a sudden.

My phone's still inside my bra strap; I'm always ready. I take it out and scroll down the list of contacts, finding my old colleague from my PhD days, Catarina Young. If I ever need advice that doesn't have a police bias, I call Cat. As I dial, I sit down at my desk in the dining room and google dolls. Amid the porn and the lap dancing clubs there are some blogs about antique dolls and some dolls for sale on eBay. But none of the pictures fit the outline images in my mind. The shape of the doll messages. Cat answers.

'Jan. How's things?'

Cat's my mentor. She's been there for me since the beginning when I was a trainee. I trust her implicitly. Even enough to not hide my mobile number from her.

'Good. You?'

'I'm really well, Jan. Just got back from France with Phil. Been there for two weeks.'

I pause. All I ever seem to ring her for is advice about work. But I have no choice.

'Just ringing for some advice, really.'

'Mmm. About the child abduction case?'

I feel a shiver through my soul. Cat lives in Surrey. Even she's read about my involvement in it.

'Well, part of it. The abductor left some messages shaped like dolls. Then we identified some handwriting from pressure impressions, again, dolls. Then there was another reference to dolls, but I don't know how relevant it is. The problem is, the connection's been overlooked. There is other strong evidence, but I feel the investigation's going in the wrong direction, and that we're chasing the wrong people, even though they're involved. It's hard to explain. But the dolls?'

I can almost see her staring at some point in the distance as she thinks about what I say.

'Okay. If there's a doll theme running through this then it's a very strong symbol. People like dolls for different reasons. But usually it's family connection. Childhood. Fertility. They sometimes symbolise death. Or used as a likeness. What's the third reference?'

I swallow hard. It's so difficult to keep Cat in the dark after all she's done for me.

'I can't tell you, Cat. Sorry. It's part of the case that's not public as yet. Not that I...'

She's laughing. 'Chill, Jan. It's okay. I understand. But I can't advise you on something that I don't know about.'

I laugh too. I guess the past twenty-four hours have told on me. Laughing is the last thing I feel like doing, but it feels good. And I can feel myself opening up.

'The thing is, I feel like I've seen the doll shape before. Specific. The outline. But I can't think where for the life of me.'

'Probably something from childhood. Something very powerful. Buried deep. You know all this, Jan. Imprinting. It might be worth trying to connect with any places where you might have encountered dolls. Childhood stories. Or your mother. But quite often it's something in the background of an important event that you don't even notice. Like a painting on the wall of the house your grandfather died in. Or a badge on the lapel of someone who stole your mother's purse. Or a friend who wasn't so much a friend. Not much help. Sorry.'

I smile. It's an enormous help.

'No. It is a help. I'm convinced that the person who took Maisie is from round here. They know the area and if I recognise the paper doll then it must be from somewhere local. Thanks, Cat. I'll give you a call soon.'

She laughs, but then she speaks to me very clearly. 'Be careful, Jan. Be careful.'

I know what she means immediately. She's felt the same fear I'm feeling, and she knows I'm at risk. I can hear her breath, quick and deep.

'I will. I will. But it had to happen sometime.'

She snaps back. I know it's her way of helping but it catches me off guard.

'Did it? Is this what you want, Jan?'

I feel tears prick my eyes, but I won't let it through. I've got this far.

'Maybe not, but a child's life is at stake. And maybe more. So how can I not?'

She pauses. I know she's just worried.

'But you can't go back, Jan. Not after this.'

I look around the room. Blinds drawn to stop me thinking every movement outside is danger. Triple locks on all the doors. Much as I love Kirby, she's a dog that would maul anyone who broke in with me here. The state-of-the-art alarm system. CCTV, obviously, with a button on my TV remote to view each camera at will. The house itself is in a remote position with no house number. Generic name. The Farm. Safety. Real fear stays outside the thick wooden front door. I'll still have this. But she's right. I won't be able to go back. I'm visible now. I know Cat's worried, and I know why.

'No. I can't. But maybe it's time.'

'That's your call, Jan. You know where I am, kidda.'

She ends the call. I go to the oven and check if my macaronia is ready. It isn't. Even though I suspect Kirby's had several meals today, provided by Jean and Graham, I feed her again. She's happy and I turn the music back up and sing along with it as I stir my coffee. I sit on the sofa and Kirby nestles her oversized body on my lap and settles down. I put my hand on her flank and feel her breathing. It soothes me.

Putting Cat's obvious worry aside, I know what her advice about the dolls means. That I have to reach deep down into my psyche and try to pull out one memory, one individual image that has so far evaded me. Deeper down, even deeper. I know why this is bothering me so much. They're not just a couple of notes with the meaning in the text. Although that would be bad enough. They hold their own meaning. Someone has taken time to cut them out in a paper chain. They mean something to someone and form a pattern. I knew that somewhere within this case there would be a pattern, something the perpetrator hangs it on. In most cases, it's a matter of finding a pattern and understanding what motivates them.

I've worked cases where the patterns are trademark violence or items left near, on or in a victim's body. It can be something they leave at the scene of the crime. Sometimes even subconsciously. In some cases, the patterns aren't even at the scene of crime, they're symbols and signs marking the location of the perpetrator, often signposting them. That's where my expertise lies. In reaching to the bottom of my own psyche and putting myself in the place of the perpetrator. Why would they leave these symbols, these pointers? What do they mean to them?

It's become obvious during the course of this investigation what the Magellan symbolism is. The gang is a little unusual in that it's not drugs or money that are at stake. But they've progressed along the same path and ended up in a place where they have resorted to extreme means to get their voice heard. Their signposts are the tattoos and the Magellan signature on the posters and placards. They've even got an online signature, where they've managed to weave an air of mystery around themselves. Urban legends. Their symbolism amounting to more than the whole.

But the dolls are apart from this. They carry their own ragged-edged handwritten identity. I instinctively know that somewhere in the world there will be more of these dolls, that these will have been plucked from the inner life of someone and that this pattern has developed over the years. These dolls are part of someone's life. These dolls are something personal.

I spend some time looking at references for dolls locally and keep coming up with nothing. I pull out my phone from under my bra strap again and check for messages. No messages. No news on the car and no news from the Met. So, I return to searching my own consciousness for dolls.

The obvious trigger for this would be to revisit my childhood haunts but there isn't time. There was a time, before I moved back here, that I would have just rushed out and done it. Hard drinking and impulsive, I would have shunned the consequences. But I'm not that woman anymore. I'm me in moderation until I summon up the blood. I'm much calmer now, in control of the individual triggers that drive me. More concise. More calculating. I may be young, but I know myself inside out.

It's nine o'clock now. Twenty-four hours since Maisie Lewis went missing and although the rest of the team is confident that the abductor will be amongst the Magellan gang, who Pat and Sally are currently rounding up, I'm not so sure. I need to think about everything that hasn't yet been tied up with Glen Wright, or Magellan. My phone buzzes and I jump. It's Steve. He's obviously doing the same kind of resting as I am.

'Yep. What's the news?'

'No news. That's what I'm ringing to say. They've rounded up everyone on Wright's list.'

Something's not right.

'Everyone?'

'Yeah. Every single one of them has a watertight alibi. None of them have admitted to knowledge of the plan that Wright gave us either.'

I snort. They will. 'That's okay. Just let Pat loose on them for a while. You okay?'

He makes a deep sighing noise. 'I am. But I'm just

wondering about this appeal tomorrow. Are you sure you want to lead it? I can easily get Lauren to do it.'

It's tempting. Especially after what Cat said. But I know full well that it works both ways. I'm notorious, and that leaves me at risk. But it also makes me powerful, gives me gravitas. If I do the appeal, whoever has Maisie will know that we mean business.

'No. I'll do it. I'll step up.'

'Okay. I'll give the Lewises a call and ask Lorraine to prep them. Not the kind of folk to lose it on live TV, are they?'

I think about Marc and Amy, each coping in their own way. Amy by numbing the pain with medication, and Marc by playing amateur investigator and throwing himself into work. Both of them completely brokenhearted. I imagine them entering another night with no news of their missing daughter, only a baby, and out there with some maniac with a carload of dangerous chemicals.

That summons up the blood. My blood's almost boiling as I think about Glen Wright explaining about the earth and how it hurts, and that's why Maisie was taken. I fully understand what he feels about the environment, as I used to be a fully paid-up member of Greenpeace myself. But this is crazy.

'No. Neither of them. They know what's at risk.' In my mind's eye I see the picture of them with Maisie on a cupboard in her empty bedroom. Their proud smiles and the way Amy holds her up, so proud. 'They're good people, Steve.'

He blows air out in a long whistle. 'So, see you tomorrow. I don't think I'll sleep tonight. Thinking about that poor kid and them driving around in that loaded car. Driving round Manchester.'

It's then I remember why Steve has a limp. He was caught up in the Manchester bomb at the Arndale centre. One sunny afternoon in 1996 he'd set off to investigate a shoplifting and ended up with a piece of shutter stuck in his leg. The IRA had planted a 3300lb bomb on Corporation Street in Manchester city centre. There were no fatalities, because there was a ninety-minute warning and there was an evacuation, but hundreds of people were injured and nearby buildings were damaged so badly that they had to be demolished.

It's well known throughout the force that the huge bomb contained Semtex and ammonium nitrate. Steve was nearby when the bomb exploded. He was involved in the evacuation. He carried an injured woman and her child half a mile with a piece of shutter lodged in his calf, and went back to help more people until eventually he passed out. He's never talked to me about it, but everyone knows. That's how it is. We never talk about it. It's just business as usual every day.

'Manchester's watertight. You did a great job today. We'll get them, Steve. We'll get them. I'm following up some loose ends and I'll be ready in the morning. Get some rest.'

I end the call. He won't get any rest and neither will I. I download my emails and save the attachments to my hard drive. I load up the messages and the sheet that Petra said was the second sheet, nearest to the dolls. The one with the scribbles on it. Now I see what she meant. They're all dolls. One on top of another, overlapping and different sizes. The writing underneath is clearly a list, but only the clearest words jump out at me.

I cover them and see if anything else springs out, but have no luck. It's not a shopping list. Or a list of items. I list the words, to see if they mean anything.

My hair flows behind me as I turn right by Victoria Station into Belgravia. There's a record shop in a basement and I'm in there listening and smiling and tapping my feet. It's like summer in my heart as I drink in the feelings invoked by the songs. They make me feel alive, and remember the love I have for the people who matter most. Who I do it all for. It's confirmation of life.

All about feelings. All about love and maybe loss. Maybe joy. I put all the words into a Google search engine. I've no doubt in my mind that Petra's team have already tried this and come up with nothing. I'm thinking it's a love letter to someone. It's only when I look past the words and see the doodles I realise. Shoes. They're all shoes. Ballet shoes, boots, high heels. In my mind's eye I see the red feet of the paper dolls. Red shoes. These words are from a story.

My first thought is the *Wizard of Oz*. There's no place like home. I pick up my phone and almost dial Steve's number but then I realise that there's another *Red Shoes* story. One that's much more sinister. Where it doesn't end well. But I'm convinced that it's a story.

But how does this connect with a long drive up north to scare the shit out of a group of parents and abduct a small child? Whilst planning to bomb a nuclear power plant? It's almost obscene, and somehow much worse, because all the words are about feelings. I try to visualise someone who loves kid's stories but can, in the next moment, take a sleeping child from their bed. It doesn't come. The contradiction is so strong.

I go back to the screen and open up a browser. Tiny. Winter. Kind. Pretty. Lovely. I feed in the words, the ones between the dolls. I type in more partial words and search, but too many documents appear. So, I load the original story. I run my fingers across the screen and they are all there.

I stop and lean back in my desk chair. Why had no one seen this before? Surely Petra's technicians had googled the words? Looking at them again, if they were googled individually or all together the results would be too narrow or broad-based and meaningless. Like most logical searches there needs to be a context. And why would the lab contextualise the words as a fairy story when they are looking for a male abductor who may be a terrorist? There's a tendency to overthink textual evidence, assume it is a code or encryption. And sometimes it is. Sometimes it's a valuable signpost to the mind of the perpetrator, something they have taken the trouble to hide.

In this case, I'm starting to think that it's exactly what it says on the tin: addresses and a fairy story. That doesn't make it any less valuable. In many ways it clarifies what's going on in their mind. It tells me that whoever has Maisie isn't trying to conceal. Just like the crime scene, the impressions in the paper suggest that this is someone who isn't really concerned about being found. Which could work both ways – either they're completely confident about their mission, and are sure they'll get away with it, or simply unconcerned because they've got nothing to lose.

It's late, yet I still text Petra and Steve.

'It's a story. The words on the sheet. It's *The Red Shoes.*'

Then I realise that they tell us almost nothing about this perpetrator in particular. They tell us that they have read *The Red Shoes*. The focus on love and loss could point to a relationship. But the loss could mean that they've lost a lover. Or just lost love. That story has a deep, primal meaning. It's about someone with an obsession and the price they pay. They tell us that this person, the person who is driving around in a potential bomb with an abducted child is maybe bitter about a relationship, as well as having a grudge. A dangerous combination.

CHAPTER TWELVE

I couldn't sleep for thinking about it. I dozed in and out of dreams about dolls and shoes and Maisie until a slit of bright sunlight found a nick in my blackout blind and hit my bedroom floor.

During the night, I'd been woken by Kirby's low grumble. I'd checked to make sure that she wasn't sleep-growling, but she was awake and as soon as I moved she barked, loud and low. I went downstairs and checked the cameras around my house. They look up and down the road, to each side of my enclosed garden, and towards Jean and Graham's at the back. There was nothing obvious, only a wide-open space for my biggest fears to creep up on me when I am tired and stressed. It was then, as I stood in the middle of my kitchen in the early morning darkness, when I realised that my paranoia was back. I reset all the alarms and went back to bed, phone in hand in case I needed to make a quick call, and Kirby climbed on the bed with me.

By the time I'm washed and dressed, Jean's knocking on my kitchen window. I open the back door and Kirby bounds out. There's a small pang of jealousy when she nuzzles Jean's hand, but I don't have time for that. Jean hands me the morning paper. The headline chills me.

SILVER RANGE ROVER – Police search for silver Range Rover in Maisie Lewis abduction case.

I scan the rest of the article, but there are no specific details and no mention of the explosives. No mention of the registration number. I'm fuming about the details of the case being leaked, but I know that it's difficult to keep secrets with so many people involved.

Jean stands in front of me with her arms folded.

'Terrible business, lovey. How could anyone do that? How could that man take a child? It doesn't bear thinking about.'

I wish Jean didn't have to think about it. I wish none of us did.

'Thanks for looking after Kirby, Jean. I really appreciate it.'

She touches my arm gently. 'Well, you just catch him. He wants stringing up.'

She turns and walks away. Him. No matter what I think, the world has decided that whoever has taken Maisie is male. I watch as a car winds its way up towards my home, around the criss-cross corners and over the cattle grids. The backdrop is scenic today, with a low mist blurring the line between the moors and the sky. There's a steep slope at the other side of the lane opposite my front gate and I watch as two rabbits run through the scrub and stop as they hear the noise of the engine. The car comes closer and I peer through the windscreen to recognise the driver. When it draws closer, I see it's Terry Morris. No need to ask for ID. I know Terry. My jittery suspicion retreats as I get into the car.

In half an hour I'm back at headquarters. When I arrive, I go straight over to Petra's lab. I'd already had a text from Lorraine telling me that the Lewises would arrive at nine o'clock so there's plenty of time. I'm still niggled by the *Red Shoes* theory and my instincts about the abductor. I want to be absolutely sure before I make a final decision and go public. Petra's my sanity test.

The lab's almost empty and Petra is standing at the edge of a testing station in her white lab coat over a long bright red dress. She's lost in her own thoughts, but when she sees me she hurries over.

'Jan, so glad you're here. This got even more serious, if that's possible. Our opposite number at the Met just emailed me a list of the contents of the car, judging by the consignment notes and traces found in Glen's flat, it's not pretty.'

She's solemn and sad, a sign that she's very serious.

'None of this is. It's horrendous. It's so contradictory.'

She brushes her hair out of her eyes. She looks shattered.

'Yeah, so much evidence. So messy. Usually in cases like this there's barely anything. I got your text about the Red Shoes, by the way. Very interesting. And a little bit strange.'

'Why strange?'

'Well, not what you'd expect from someone who'd been storing chemicals and had a plan to abduct a child. But I guess everyone has an angle.'

It's a little bit unfair to test my theory on Petra. She places a lot of pride in her unbiased nature and her ability to stay neutral. But I need someone to confirm what I suspect. I think about my own preoccupation with loud rock music and how it fills my senses to the exclusion of all my worries and fears. It blocks it out for me. Does it mean anything to me? Yes. From long ago and far away. That's why I chose it. For the memories. Which brings me back to the *Red Shoes* and the paper dolls.

They were scribbled over a sentiment that whoever wrote it knows by heart, and doesn't really need to see written down. The writing of it reinforces it; just like me singing the words of the songs I play as they work their way into my memories like sticking plasters to close the wound. My list of favourite songs soothes me and helps me relax. Like a mantra.

'Hmm. I have to wonder, Petra, who this perpetrator is. Male or female.'

I watch her face for any sign of negativity, but she just raises her eyebrows.

'The dolls?'

'Yes. And the story. All devotional. Women's words. And the subject is love and loss. Obsession. Women like to talk about it, men keep it in. But on the other side of the evidence, there's a carload of bomb-making components and Maisie.'

She stares hard at me. 'Women are perfectly capable of abduction. Just like men. No reason to think not, Jan. But it is more statistically unlikely.'

It's true. The figures show fewer women abductors than men, but there are some. There are some women capable of abducting a small girl, causing their parents this kind of suffering.

'It's not just that. It's the looking around the bedroom, picking things up. I don't know. It's a gut feeling.'

She thinks for a moment.

'Well, time will tell. They've got to make demands sometime, Jan. Otherwise, why? Why do all this and not make demands?'

That's what's bugging me, and I know it's bugging Steve too. If this is Magellan, which is where all the chemical evidence is pointing, why leave it this long to claim responsibility and not state what they want? I change direction and let Petra off the hook.

'Yeah, like you say. Time will tell. We're making an appeal this morning. Is there anything else I should know?'

She reaches for a report. 'The soother found in the grass isn't Maisie's. Belongs to another child. For sure.'

I flick through the pages. Maybe it's one of Maisie's friends, someone from her nursery.

'Right. Thanks. Anything else?'

She shifts from foot to foot. 'I just want you to know how dangerous this is. Ammonium nitrate is one thing, and dangerous in large consignments. But pure sodium is another thing altogether. It explodes on contact with water. And they've got a lot of it.'

I stare at her. There's fear in her eyes.

'How the hell have they got hold of it?'

'Two of them have chemistry qualifications. So they'd know what to go for, and what to do with it. You don't need a special licence to buy any of these things, but you would need to know how to put it together. And this combination is lethal. Just a warning, Jan. It doesn't look good for Maisie if whoever's got her comes to the end of the line.'

'Understood. I think we'll get some positive results from this appeal. Thanks, Petra. Thanks.'

I hurry off and stand in the car park for a moment. What would I do if I was hiding a child? Where would I be? Somewhere I could hide a large vehicle, because there hasn't been one confirmed report of it anywhere.

Maybe Maisie is being kept in the car. If so, whoever has her won't have a TV and won't see the appeal. It needs to be wider. On the radio. I rush into the SMIT operations room and tap Keith on the shoulder.

'Keith, the appeal. It needs to go out on all national TV networks, but I also want radio coverage. On all the local and national stations. It needs to be all over everywhere, so, for once, let's start the rumour ourselves.'

He looks surprised. 'Great. It's usually the other way round. Keep it down. But whatever you say. You know what you're doing.'

I know what I'm doing and I know what I'm feeling. And I know what I'm going to do next will be a gamble for me, but it's the only way. If my hunch is right, it'll get results.

'Great. Oh, and one more thing. Can you get me a phone with an easy to remember SIM card number? Not connected to anything else as I'll be broadcasting the number.'

Keith stops tapping at his keyboard and swivels around to face me. 'You're going direct? Bloody hell, Jan, are you sure?'

I am sure. It's the only way I'm going to make contact with the perpetrator. By making it personal.

'I am sure. Can you put a live-time trace on everything that comes through that line, location, numbers, anything else you get?'

He taps the instructions into his console. 'No problem. If the phone's registered, it's easier. But if not we can still get the location in the cell network. It's easier if it's in a city, as the cells have to be smaller, the more people using the system the smaller the cell, and more of them. A few people in a rural area can get away with one large cell.'

He goes to get me the phone and I see Steve arrive, doors swinging in his wake. He looks twice as tired as when I saw him last night. He hurries over.

'Morning. All set?'

I smile. I am set, but he's not going to like what I have to say to him.

'Oh yes. I'm going to give a direct dial for the perp.'

He looks shocked to the core. He hadn't expected me to step up.

'No, Jan, not to you...'

'I know. I know all that. But I need to do it. I need to connect with whoever has Maisie.'

He knows I'm right, but he's weighing up the pros and cons.

'But they're a bunch of public schoolboys playing with fire. I don't know how successful it would be. And it compromises you. I don't think it's worth it, Jan.'

I know immediately that this is why I'm here. This moment, when difficult decisions have to be made, sometimes on a hair's breadth of evidence, on the tiniest fraction of instinct, defines everything about my job, and, I suppose, about me. I feel one way and Steve feels another way. He's doing a brilliant job, trying to find Maisie and protect the city he loves, and I'm doing the same. Different reasons, same goal.

'I don't think it's them. I don't think it's anyone on Glen's list. I think it's someone else, and I don't have a fully formed idea yet, but I just don't think it's Magellan.'

His face tells a story. A story of angry desperation and holding something in that I need to know.

'About that. They've all been rounded up overnight. Everyone Glen Wright mentioned and all their contacts. Every one of them in bed or at home or doing something they've got an alibi for. For the last week. They've searched all their properties. They've found all sorts. Drugs, counterfeit goods, weapons. But no sign of a one-year-old girl.'

'So why didn't you tell me all that last night?'

He should have. It was something I needed to know. I know why he didn't, though, because he doesn't want the case to fall into the chaos of having no suspects. Back into the mire of nothing.

'I told you earlier.'

He did tell me part of it. But not the whole. He was avoiding telling me because he knew we were out of options. He would have been hoping something else would turn up.

'You told me the guys had been brought in, not that there was no result. You should have told me. It's never too late for something like that. I text you about the story. *The Red Shoes*. What do you think? And the dolls? It's an individual. Come on, Steve, it's glaring at us. Too big to ignore. You know it is.'

He's red with frustration and he glances at the clock.

'It doesn't fit. We're going live in fifteen minutes and we haven't got anything. All that stuff up at the Lewises' place. And the paper. I know it's connected but I can't work out how. And there's so much at risk.'

He's staring at me, waiting for an answer. Waiting for me to suggest something to make it right. But all I've got is the same evidence as him, seen in a different light. I step to one side, ready to take the phone from Keith, who's returned to his desk.

'You're just going to have to trust me then, aren't you? Because if we're starting from nothing...'

'Just don't make it any worse, Jan. By putting yourself at risk.'

'I'm going to find Maisie. I'm going to connect with who's got her. We all need to work at that now, because the other line of enquiry has got us this far then come to a dead end. Until something else turns up in London, let's go with my gut feeling and the dolls.'

He shrugs and sighs. Double stressed. And I know how he feels. We're backed into a corner and now I have to bait the abductor. There are only a couple of options open to them. Carry out their plan. Or plans. Demand money or action. The third option doesn't bear thinking about, but I have to. They could decide that none of this was worth it and dump Maisie. Dead or alive.

They could have done that already, and this way we've got a

chance of finding out. Give them a line of communication; appear to be playing their game. Tempt them out to tell us what they want. It has to work. But then it has to be handled in the right way, and I'm going to do it.

Steve's shifting from foot to foot now. He's always nervous before an appeal.

'You do know that once this goes out on national TV it'll be a free-for-all. Everyone will have their two penn'orth. No sorting out the wheat from the chaff.'

'It's okay. Keith's got two officers specially trained to deal with it. And to find anything valuable amongst the general rubbish.'

'What I'm saying, Jan, is that it'll be visible. In the press. On TV. Everywhere. It'll be visible and you'll be visible. We all will.'

He meets my eye, but *I'm back there, in my car. Laughing and singing along to Green Day with the roof down. Loud as you like. Scattering pigeons and watching as cyclists scoot past me, heads down, bottoms in the air. All serious on a sunny day. Tapping my finger on the steering wheel to the beat. Stopping at another set of traffic lights and seeing a couple in the next car kiss. The other way, a woman pushes a double buggy up the road, her blonde-haired twins identical. Brushing my hair out of my eyes as the lights change to green...*

'I'll take my chances, Steve. I know what you're saying, and I appreciate it, but I've got a job to do.'

I look around and SMIT headquarters is perfectly still and quiet. Then I realise that I've been shouting. That's what stress does to people; it makes them behave in ways that they don't normally. It presses down on them until their emotions have to seep out through the edges and finally, misshapen, emerge.

I hurry over to Keith and grab the phone. I push it down my shirt and ping my bra strap over it.

'I've pre-loaded it with all our numbers so you can see if any of us call. We shouldn't have to, but in any case...'

'Thanks, Keith. Can you start the trace straight away? I want it activated as soon as the appeal is aired.'

I turn around and find the answerphone settings. I record a message.

'This is Janet Pearce. If you're calling to talk to me about Maisie Lewis, please leave a message and I promise I will get right back to you. For anything else, please call 101.'

Steve follows me up the corridor and into the room behind where the appeal will be held. I peep through the door and see the waiting press and cameras. The director hurries over.

'Any special instructions?'

I look at Steve. He shakes his head.

'Okay. If I make this signal,' I hold my hand high in the air, 'stop filming. I'll only do it if any sensitive information is revealed. If this is the case Mr and Mrs Lewis will be removed from the room quickly. And at the end, I would like a close-up shot of my face as I give my message to the perpetrator. I'd like this to be distributed as the header for the piece, the main sound bite. I'd also like the whole appeal and the separate sound bite to be issued to radio stations, both national and local, for immediate release.'

Steve joins in. He's understanding where I'm coming from now.

'Nice and even all the way through. Give the parents some respect, no close-up shots, nothing too choppy. Just a steady image until Jan gives you the nod for her piece.'

The director writes down the instructions. 'Got it. I'll let you see what we have before it goes out. You could always record it again, separately.'

'No. It has to be in the context of the appeal. Emotional overload. One thing after another. I want to make a connection with the perpetrator, and I need it all to look spontaneous. Any hint of being staged and who knows what might happen. We need to get the bastard in one go.'

I realise I've been a little over-assertive, and he backs off slowly. He needs to know that this is a one-shot set-up. The only chance we have to connect with Maisie. It's nine o'clock and thirty-six hours after Maisie Lewis was abducted. Time's running out.

CHAPTER THIRTEEN

The door behind me opens and Lorraine leads Amy and Marc Lewis into the room. Out of their own environment they look forlorn and, as I always am at this point when the parents beg for the return of their beloved child, I am shocked by the rawness of it all.

Amy looks drawn and tired and her eyes look more sunken than even yesterday when I saw her last. She feels her way around the backs of the chairs, so lost in the trauma of her missing daughter. Marc looks around the room, hands in pockets, then on his wife's back, guiding her towards me. With each of their steps toward me I feel more and more determined to find Maisie by whatever means I have.

As Amy approaches me, I see she has brought the photograph, the one from Maisie's bedroom. I'm glad she did. It shows the strength of them together, the happy scene before whoever did this cruelly ripped them apart. Marc's grey skin and dark under-eye circles tell me he hasn't slept. Eventually, after what seems like an age for me, and what must feel like a century to them, they reach me.

I've worked on cases in London where children have been

abducted and, when they are safely home, the parents have told me that time seemed to stop at first, then move very slowly, then become elastic. Moments of thinking about their child that lasted seconds in real time were etched into their consciousness as if they were days.

Those parents who hadn't had their child returned reported that after this stage there are two sets of time rules. Normal time, where life inevitably must carry on, and missing time, where there is an underlying slow-flowing river of emotions, separate from normal life, and increasingly more hidden. Hidden because people forget. People grow bored with hearing about other people's pain. So, it's pushed under normal life, a parallel universe of inexplicable hurt.

Parents never forget. Although the remembering might get less frequent, any little thing can trigger it. A smell, a taste, a touch, a sound. Anything. And the pain is back, just as strong as before. As strong as Amy and Marc's pain is now, pushing them forward from the brink of nervous and physical exhaustion so that they can represent it for the nation to analyse through their TV screens. Lorraine hurries over and steps between them.

'All set? Jan, can you give Amy and Marc the rundown?'

I look at their expectant eyes and summon up the blood. For me and on their behalf.

'Right. Keith will introduce the case. Just the bare minimum outline. Then I'd like you to speak. You first, Marc, then you, Amy. Have you prepared something?'

Lorraine shows me two sheets, neatly written in her hand. 'I've written it down for them and checked it.'

Marc looks at me earnestly. 'Don't worry. We're not going to do anything rash. We're doing exactly what you told us to.'

'Great. Thanks for that. And before we go out there, I need to tell you that after you speak, I will be making my own appeal and giving a dedicated telephone number, as well as the usual numbers. This is to gain trust. Get a connection.'

I can almost sense what Marc's next question will be.

'Have they said what they want yet? Is there anything else at all?'

I see Steve looking at me from the other side of the room.

'No. There hasn't been any contact yet. But we're confident there will be after this. As you know, we've got ongoing enquiries in London.'

I desperately want to blurt out the whole story, along with my new perspective on the case, but I know it's not the time to throw even more into that slow-flowing river developing underneath Marc's normal life. It's not the time to hug Amy and rub her back, fetch her a cup of sweet tea. We all have to play it cool for now, play the game and make sure that the appeal makes the most of the opportunity we have to break through to the person who has Maisie.

The door opens and we feel the buzz on the other side. The director nods and Steve leads us through. There's a row of standard catering tables covered with white cloths, and behind us a huge Greater Manchester Police logo on a pull-down backdrop. The room is crammed full of reporters, most of them regulars, and there are four cameras. Keith is standing at the back of the room and makes the letter T with his fingers, taps into a phone and I feel the gentle hum of the second phone under my T-shirt. I give him the thumbs-up and we're ready to go. Steve begins.

'Thank you all for attending. I'm DCI Steven Ralston. We're here today to appeal for the safe return of Maisie Lewis, the daughter of Amy and Marc Lewis.'

I'm sitting next to Amy. I look at her and her scared wide-eyed face, unused to being on camera. I take her hand under the table and she squeezes mine.

'I'll give you some details and then Marc and Amy will make an appeal, followed by a few words from Dr Janet Pearce. We'll take a few questions at the end. Maisie Lewis was abducted from her home at nine o'clock in the evening on Saturday the 27th May. We have made some progress and we've traced the vehicle that Maisie was taken away from the property in. The vehicle is a silver Range Rover registration number HT2 4SG. We're conducting a country-wide search for this vehicle. If you have seen this vehicle, or if you see it, do not approach. Call 999 immediately. Maisie Lewis is just one-year-old.' A huge picture of Maisie holding her favourite teddy bear replaces the logo behind us. 'Her parents want her safely back home. Her father, Marc, will say a few words.'

The room is silent. Marc stares out. He's obviously media-trained and knows how to present himself, hands flat on the desk, chin out. But words fail him. The red light on the camera blinks and I see him fighting with his emotions. Amy turns her head slowly to look at him just as a single tear runs down his cheek. Amy looks at me and I nod. She speaks in a low, shaky voice.

'Marc and I tried for ten years for a baby. Ten years. We're lucky people, good jobs, a lovely home, but our lives were complete when our little girl was born. She's the most precious thing in our lives, so please, please give her back. Let us know she is okay. Anything. Please be nice to Maisie, and please give her back to us.'

The reporters have stopped scribbling and are hypnotised by Amy and her sweet-natured plea. Marc still stares ahead. I see the lens of the camera nearest to me move and I know it's my turn. I stare at it hard and hope that every emotion is evident. I know what people look for, how they are affected by other people, big eyes and a slight smile. Empathy.

'Thank you, Marc. Thank you, Amy. I'd just like to appeal

to the person who has Maisie. We're here to listen to you. We have a direct contact number you can call if you want to speak to me. I will personally take your call. The number is 079255522552. I'm here to help resolve this matter as quickly as possible. If you are the person who took Maisie, please call me on that number. Again, 079265522552. Anyone with any other information, call Crimestoppers or 101. All we want is to make sure Maisie is returned to her parents.'

The lens retreats and the room erupts into noise. Amy and Marc are led out and Steve moves closer to me to answer questions. Perry Soames, a local journalist gets first call.

'Are there any suspects as yet? Have you any idea who took Maisie, Jan?'

Steve answers this one. 'There are ongoing enquiries but I can confirm that we have a definite route of enquiry that we are following.'

Another journalist now. National this time.

'Have you been seconded from the Met onto this case, DC Pearce, and if so, is there something underlying that we aren't being told? Something about Mr Lewis's involvement?'

I bounce back quickly. 'No. I've been working in this area for a while now on different projects. This information we have given you about Maisie being abducted is all you need to know, isn't it? We rarely go into details about any enquiry.'

'So, there is something?'

I stare directly at him. It's amazing that they don't want to help us. Every answer we give is never enough.

'No. There's a missing child and a vehicle we're asking for help finding.'

Steve winds it up. 'One more question.'

A tall man in a black leather jacket stands up. 'Jeff Lewis. *Manchester Echo*. Is it true that this enquiry is linked to arrests over the past twenty-four hours in London?'

Steve tenses beside me. The camera's still rolling. I jump in.

'As DCI Ralston said, we don't go into detail about ongoing enquiries.'

Jeff looks directly at me. He doesn't know it, but the words he utters next promise to seal my fate.

'So, the London arrests, is this something to do with Lando, DC Pearce? Is it linked? Is that why you're here?'

I can almost sense the attention of a group of London gangsters suddenly focus on this case, and consequently, me. I can almost feel their heads turn towards their TVs and radio at the mention of the Lando case and my name. Suddenly I'm completely visible. No tricking my paranoia that maybe they hadn't seen the report or my appeal at the end. Maybe they have no interest in a missing child from Manchester, so little interest that they zoned out and missed my involvement. But I keep my focus.

'No. No involvement with Lando. This is a completely separate investigation. Operation Lando is closed.'

Lando. Lando. Lando. I've suppressed the name for so long that it feels strange saying it over and over again. Jeff Lewis sits and seems satisfied with the answer. Steve rises and thanks them for coming. I see Keith and the director talking about the immediate release of the footage to all TV, radio and internet sources.

I hurry back to Marc and Amy who are standing with Lorraine in the corner of the back room sipping tea. Marc looks wiped out. He moves forward to greet me.

'Thanks, Jan. Thanks. Hopefully we'll get some joy with that number. Does it actually come straight through to you?'

His desperation is almost radiating from him. Amy is hanging on to his arm and looking around the room.

'Yes. I'm going to take any calls. I'm going to manage any contact there is. But I have to warn you that it's not a given.'

He nods his head sadly. 'No. Of course. Look, I'm sorry about yesterday. I was angry. I just wanted to do something. But I guess I can't do anything. Not even speak up for my own daughter.'

I feel so sorry for him. A powerful man, but defeated in the light of his only child being at the mercy of an anonymous abductor. I want to hug him and tell him that it will eventually be okay, but I have to hold it together.

'It's a common reaction, Marc. Lots of people, even me, freeze sometimes. You're under a lot of pressure. And you gave us some very useful information yesterday. I think we'll make some progress now.'

Marc looks away. I can see how despondent he is. And who could blame him?

'I don't know. I don't feel optimistic. I just don't understand what they want. Why they haven't told us yet what they want. I don't understand why they'd take her if they didn't want money or us to do something.'

I assume that 'they' are Magellan. I expect Steve has kept him informed on the progress and he's convinced that one of the Magellan gang have Maisie still. That Steve hasn't told him about the shopping centre plan or that everyone from Magellan is currently in a cell in a variety of London police stations. Probably best for now. It'll stop him thinking that anything worse has happened to her. Even in his fragile state he's still scenario building. It won't be long until he figures out that we still have no suspect.

'Hopefully, now we've opened a line of communication, they'll tell us what they want. And you and Amy will be the first to know.'

Lorraine arrives to drive them back home. They nod their acknowledgement and I watch as they disappear through the exit. I walk back slowly to the SMIT suite, and grab a cup of tea on the way. I stop at one of the high windows and look out onto the world. Two years ago, my world shifted on its axis and, in the last fifteen minutes, it's shifted again. My beloved city, my safe place in the world, has now become dangerous for me again. I'm out on a limb, reminded of the days when I first left home. Scared, tired, and separated from everything I loved, except this is a million times worse.

I gulp down the tea and go to find Keith. He's sitting at a desk in SMIT where forum messages are scrolling down a large screen. He sees me and points at the screen.

'See this, Jan. All this after just one appeal. Mainly about the vehicle. Find Maisie pages going up on every forum. I'll have to get Frank and Jamie onto this to monitor. That's the problem, isn't it? You've got the phone, Jan, but they could send it in anyway. It could come by bloody carrier pigeon for all we know.'

He's right. Computers make our lives a lot easier in many ways. Instead of having to look for criminals, they're often right there, on forums. Pictures of stolen goods for sale, posts revealing violent and abusive natures. But it can also work the other way. It's another fairly anonymous communication route. One which helps people to feel secure giving information, but it's so disorganised that we could miss it if we're not completely on the ball. And we need to be.

'True. Very true. But the original messages were handwritten on a piece of jotter. That doesn't strike me as very high-tech. Even so, bring in an extra four people. I want every channel watched twenty-four seven, and outwards communications. I want all the UK looking for that car. It's got to be somewhere.'

I go over to the secure office area and sit on my own. Somehow life feels different, as if I've detached from everything and I'm even more focused than I was before. Focused on a little girl out there with strangers, and a missing car. I'm still sitting with my arms folded, staring out of a window overlooking the city when Lauren knocks on the door. She opens it a fraction.

'Can I come in?'

I wave her in and she sits opposite. When I don't say anything she continues.

'I suppose we just have to sit and wait now, don't we?'

'Yes. And try to work out where that car is. Whoever has her has taken her to make a point. Or why the threats, and why take the car? A big point. Either that or to actually carry out Plan B.'

Lauren taps her fingers on the desk. It's a habit she has, and it irritates me. Her fingernails are always painted, thick and red.

'They won't get near Sellafield, though. Steve's got it locked down. And it's only a matter of time until someone sees the car.'

'Unless it's somewhere out of the way. Somewhere out of the city. I still think Maisie isn't too far from home.'

Lauren looks surprised. Probably surprised that I've let her in on my line of thought.

'Even with the London link?'

'Mmm. Yes. I think the car was driven from London to Saddleworth on Thursday, the notes distributed on Friday and Saturday and Maisie taken on Saturday night. If the car had returned to London, it would have been picked up by now on the motorway registration plate recognition. Or on the congestion charge register. Or on any number of CCTV. That leaves the rest of the country, but no one's seen it driving around. I reckon it's still here.'

'So, you think they're holding her nearby?'

I think *she's* holding her nearby. But I don't say this to Lauren. She'll know by now that all the Magellan gang are in custody and that Pat has persuaded Glen Wright to spill the beans about everything. The amount of pressure Pat would have piled on him would have meant that no stone would have gone unturned. Pat would have the names of everyone who Glen thought had even the slightest association with the Magellan plan. But this has to be someone who knows about it. A woman who knows about both plan a, and plan b. I pick up the phone and call Pat Knowles. Somehow, I dredge up his mobile number from the mire of my suppressed memory. He answers on one ring.

'Jan. Okay?'

'Yep. Look, Pat, did you ask Glen everything? About everyone who knew about Magellan. Even associates?'

He pauses. I know what's wrong. I know he wants me to chat with him, to acknowledge him. When I don't, he gets onto the business in hand.

'I did. He gave me a list of anyone who had any knowledge of Magellan. We've got them all in. But I expect you know that.'

'I do. Thanks, Pat. Were there any women on the list?'

I imagine him running his nicotine-stained forefinger down the line of suspects.

'Nope. No women. No women on the intelligence photos either. Do you think a woman would do that? You know... Maisie?'

'It's what I've been wondering. Petra thinks it's possible, but not probable. I don't see why not? And the dolls, I don't know, Pat. Seems like there's more to this.'

There's silence for longer than there should be. I know that he's reading the file.

'Right. Yep. I can see where you're coming from. I'm just over Wandsworth way on another case at the moment. I'll have another go at him when I get back in a couple of hours. But I think he's empty, Jan. I think he's empty.'

I end the call and look at Lauren.

'He'll ask Glen again. Ask him if there's anyone else who knew about Magellan. Anyone at all.'

She's still tapping her fingernails on the desk.

'So, we'll wait.'

I was going to say that it's a big part of the job, but the little silver comms phone, the one Keith gave me, buzzes and I grab it from under my T-shirt. I was hoping for a call, but it's a text.

Found you, Jan. Now we're coming to get you.

CHAPTER FOURTEEN

I almost expected it, but not so soon. My body launches into protection mode, but I'm an old hand at this. I'm used to counteracting the fight-or-flight alert that tells me to conserve my energy for the battle ahead. I know that the feeling of panic, the draining of blood and the urge to hide or run only lasts a maximum of five minutes because that's all the body can sustain. So, I wait. Deep breaths. Bring back the oxygen. Summon up the blood. Summon up the blood.

Keith doesn't look so calm. He rushes towards me.

'Central London. Unregistered phone.'

News travels fast and Steve and Lauren appear.

'Of course it is. It's only what I would expect from them.'

Steve, who is usually calm and full of sighs, is red faced. 'We'll make sure nothing happens. You'll be all right with us, Jan.'

They're not used to this. Although I'm sure that officers here have received threats before, the provenance of this one takes it out of their league. They look more worried than before, if that's possible.

I feel my blood pressure return to normal and the cloudy

thinking retreat. It's so long since I've felt like this, and I've missed it. I'm shocked that, after all that's happened, I feel this way. I've missed it because it means I'm back in the game. I ran, but I'm back. I've enjoyed my time in the back of beyond, in my cottage in the countryside, but I suddenly don't know where home is. I can't go back there now until this has been resolved.

I think about Kirby and realise that Jean and Graham will care for her. The inside of my house will tick along as usual, gathering tiny fragments of dust in layers over all my belongings that suddenly don't belong with me anymore. I worry about the remnants of last night's dinner left in the fridge, which is a good sign that my fear is backing away to make room for resilience. I survived last time. I'll survive again.

I want to tell Steve that I'll be fine on my own. I know what to do, because I've done it before. There's no need for them to watch out for me. But we're a team and even in these circumstances we stand together.

'Thanks. I appreciate it. Don't worry. They're all bark and no bite. I'm still here, aren't I?'

Lauren goes to speak. 'But, Jan, last time–'

Steve quickly interrupts. 'Okay. But make sure you're with one of us at all times. Keith will monitor the phone; it might be best to isolate that number now.'

That won't help. It's gone too far.

'No. It's too late for that. It'll have been broadcast by now. I still want to go with my plan. I'm a big girl and I've got the whole of the Met and you lot looking out for me. Maisie comes first. We need to keep that line open for the perpetrator to call.'

They all stare hard at me. Keith speaks first.

'Jan. You don't have to do this, you know. You can work covertly. You know we can hide you, arrange for...'

'Been there, done that. Like I said, my major concern is finding that car and finding Maisie. Maybe it's time for me to stop pussyfooting around and come out of my little hidey hole, where they probably think I'll run back to. I'm never going to be able to hide away and still live a life. So, this is the only way. But I don't want to put you guys at risk, so if you think I'm a risk, take me off the case.'

Lauren folds her arms and shakes her head. Steve looks shocked.

'My God, Jan, we all want to help you. You're a great officer and profiler, the best. We need you here. And besides, this is what we do. Protect people. If we can't do it, who can? Right?'

He looks at Lauren and Keith. They both nod.

'So, don't even think about it. We're a team.'

I search their faces for any sign of doubt, any trace of them wanting out. Steve and Keith are flushed and emotional, but Lauren is poker-faced as usual.

'Okay. But this is my battle, at the first sign of anything call for support, don't make yourself a sitting duck. And anyway, they'll have to find me first. So back to Maisie. The main plan now is to wait for any communication. I've asked Pat to interview Glen Wright again about anyone else who had knowledge of Magellan. But we can't stop. We need to monitor every single piece of information that comes in via 999 and Crimestoppers.'

Keith gives us his input.

'Yeah, I've got a comms team onto it now. All we've got so far is abandoned Range Rovers. Hundreds of them. All over the UK. We've got an all-forces alert to investigate anything that comes in and check it through DVLA.'

I'm still a little shaky, but I fight through it.

'So, we're looking for someone who has knowledge of Magellan's plan, someone close to them. We've got the initial messages, the list of addresses and names, and a playlist. We've got the chemical trail and it all ties in with Glen Wright.'

Steve takes over. 'That's progress. But we need to find this vehicle quickly. I don't need to tell you that. I've got the whole of Manchester locked down, and so far we've managed to avoid telling the public the real dangers. But the more people know about it, the more risk of it being leaked. So, we need to act fast. We're relying on the public to find that vehicle. Jan, how confident are you that Pat Knowles has got everything out of Glen Wright? What are the chances of him giving us anything else?'

I think about it. Pat Knowles. I'm guessing that he has exerted maximum pressure on Glen. I know his methods. Cruel and calculating, but effective. Pat says his methods are 100 per cent successful. It certainly seemed to work on Glen. He divulged almost immediately and even gave us the addresses of the Magellan gang. Pat would have asked him a specific question, but I know that they would have included asking him for everyone who knew about the plans, the chemicals, who he got bomb-making advice from. It's certainly plausible that this could have all been done within the gang, but had Glen missed anyone?

Gangs are led by people who are strategists, and have foot soldiers. Pat and Sally will be busy working out who is who and logging it all for future intelligence. This investigation has turned up trumps for them, identifying a major threat on their patch. But gangs have bystanders. People in the background who are privy to their workings. Mothers, brothers, fathers, sisters, partners. All of them invested with just enough emotional weighting to make them stay silent about their loved one's criminal activity.

'Very confident we'll get more out of Glen. But to be sure, I'm going to go over Glen Wright's file and the other interviews myself. Just to make sure. And I've asked Pat to re-interview him.'

Steve looks more motivated now. 'Right. Back to it. I'm going to check on the security arrangements. Lauren, can you supervise the all-forces collation of intelligence. Keith, half-hourly reports.'

He strides off and Lauren leaves. Keith remains and hangs around for a few minutes before he approaches me.

'Okay?'

I'm not okay. Far from it. But that's inside. On the outside, I remain calm.

'No choice. I either do it or I don't.'

He turns to go but stops. 'For what it's worth, I think you did the right thing at the appeal. Opening it out. It's a risk, you know, inciting media panic if they find out about the bomb, but it's the only way.'

He leaves and I'm relieved to be alone, because an idea is forming. It's often what's not said that tells the bigger part of the story. People omit facts for various reasons. We haven't told the public about the potential explosives because it would cause mass hysteria and that wouldn't help find Maisie. But people also omit information for other reasons.

I've seen it before in eyewitness accounts. Quite often people leave out huge chunks of description because they don't think it's relevant. This can be for many reasons; the perception of what they think is relevant to a particular crime, their personal preference, even biases and cultural influences. They don't do it on purpose to be obstructive. And the reason they do this is so deeply ingrained in their self that it's carried out subconsciously.

I imagine Pat in the station, in an interview room, pushing Glen to the limit with guarded threats Pat may or may not be able to carry out. Glen, searching his memory for information relevant to Magellan and the plan he so willingly told us about earlier. But what if there's something important, hidden in his psyche, that he doesn't think is relevant? Someone on the periphery of his life who he knows won't blab. Someone so invested that he doesn't even give them a second thought.

I trawl through the interview transcripts. Nothing in Glen's, so I read carefully through all the Magellan gang's interviews on the screen in front of me. Everyone they mentioned has been brought in, all indexed and catalogued carefully on the familiar Met templates. Nothing in Glen's background. Only child, elderly parents living together in Buckinghamshire, both at home at the time Maisie was abducted.

The young woman from the flat, Jane, knew nothing. Her statement confirmed Glen's whereabouts and his copious use of cocaine. She hadn't known him long and knew nothing about Magellan. She's become hysterical when told about the chemicals in the flat and had asked Sally to say she was sorry to Maisie's parents. They are still holding her, mainly because she knows so much about the case.

I phone Pat again. He answers in half a ring.

'Pat. Any joy?'

'No. He's in a right state. Spewing everywhere. Doc says he's not fit to be interviewed.'

I feel my body tense with anger.

'Probably withdrawals. I've read the reports. Plenty of drugs inside the flat. And probably inside him.'

'Yeah, he was looking dodgy overnight. I looked in on him a couple of times. Reminded him what would happen if he didn't talk.'

I bet he did. He wouldn't leave Glen alone until he'd drained him of any information and the case was closed. I talk to Pat softly.

'You need to try again as soon as possible.' I've got a feeling that there's something else. Someone involved in his life who I've got to be careful of. Pat's good at his job and I don't want to insult him. 'Something buried deep that only your, er, methods, can bring up.'

Pat sighs heavily. It's his way of being sarcastic. 'You know my hands are tied, Jan. You know what I can and can't do.'

'I'm not asking you to do anything outside the rules. Just open up the range of people who might have been near him. Has he got a cleaner? Someone he sees on a regular basis? His dealer? I don't know. It's got to be someone he thinks isn't important. Did you get any impression of what he's like, you know, biases, preferences?'

There's a pause. I can hear Pat light a cigarette.

'Yeah, he's a prick who likes his cocaine a little bit too much.'

'A prick?'

'Yeah, he tried to lie at every turn. Thinking he could do one over on me and Sal. But we explained the consequences to him on the way to the interview room, what would happen to him inside if he's convicted for trying to blow a kid up. You know. He's got no respect for himself or anyone else. Completely self-centred little twat.'

He takes another drag of his cigarette.

'My first port of call was his parents, and I explained to him how we'd tell them everything and what it would do to them. All he cared about was them bankrolling him and this fucking Magellan operation. What I can't understand is why this Marc Lewis character didn't report them in the first place. It could have saved all this. Anyway, I showed him the intelligence we already had and Sally said he showed signs of actually fucking approving of how he looked in the videos. Touching his hair and face, nodding and smiling. Vain little fucker. Not much else. Oh. The girl said he was shit in bed.'

Self-obsessed. Convinced he's right. Fits my profile.

'Thing is, Pat, I think he knows who this is really. I think he knows, but he doesn't know he does. He's discounted a set of circumstances.'

'Like what?'

'Anyone at all who came in and out of the flat in the last month. Anyone. Impress upon him that we mean everyone, not just who he thinks is important.'

Pat sighs again. This time it isn't sarcasm. 'Fucking hell, Jan, I wish you were here.'

I end the call quickly. That's not what I want to hear. Obviously the news about my heightened visibility hasn't reached Pat.

I go through the evidence one more time. I look again at the dolls, desperately trying to place the shape. I'm seeing it all the time now, at the back of the colour field images when I close my eyes. I know it. It's there somewhere and I just need a trigger to drag it upwards. I speak the words of the story into my phone. Then I put my earphones in and listen to it.

I'm struggling to contain my tears. I don't know if it's the fact that I can no longer go home, once again I don't belong anywhere, or the growing sadness of the words, but my emotions are gurgling up from a hard-pressed down place inside. The person who's written those words on the jotter is obviously desperately sad. Has lost something. Something precious to them.

They're devastated and are writing to soothe whatever pain they are feeling. They know it by heart, and it's like a soft old blanket or a favourite coat, sitting close to their torment in order to numb it. I look at a picture of Maisie and at the dolls. How could anyone who knows so much pain inflict it on someone else? Unless it was revenge.

I check my own mobile, but Pat hasn't rung back. I scan around the SMIT suite and everyone is busy on the phones, taking information, scanning screens, waiting for the one snippet of information that will move the case forward. It's astounding that no one has seen the car. Unless it's parked up somewhere remote.

I go back to the maps and try to figure out a route based on which way the vehicle went. It was traced out of Greenfield but once it reached more populated areas it disappeared where it left the main roads and entered areas with no cameras. No sightings at all after nine fifteen on Saturday night. It's quarter past one now. Forty hours since Maisie was taken. Forty hours since that little girl has seen her mother and father. Forty hours with someone who, according to the evidence, appears increasingly unbalanced.

I go to call Jean and Graham. Jean answers.

'Oh, hello, love.'

I swallow hard. This isn't going to be easy.

'Jean. I'm not going to be home for a while.'

'Oh. Oh dear. Going away?'

I can hear Kirby in the background, squeaking a toy. I keep my breathing steady, stay calm.

'Yeah. Going away.'

'Any idea how long for, love? Only we can take care of Kirby until you get back, and check on the house. If you like.'

I stare out of the window onto Manchester Centre. There's a steady stream of cars travelling up and down the road outside. Any one of them could be whoever is coming for me.

'No. I don't know how long. I'll send you some money for Kirby's food.'

'No need for that, love. You can give it to me when you get back. Will you drop the key off?'

I know that I won't be dropping the key off. I know that my home will sit empty until it's safe to go back there. If it ever is.

'There's a key under the right-hand flowerpot, right of the front door as you face it.' All my plants and careful gardening, it'll all grow wild now. No one to care for it. No one to pick the fruit that'll ripen on the trees and no one to harvest the vegetables I planted in the spring. I choke when I think about how clinical I am when I'm storing seeds, all in evidence bags, neatly stored in the dark. How much I'll miss it. 'Thanks, Jean. Sorry to trouble you with this. And if anyone asks...'

'Mum's the word. I'll tell Graham.'

I'm just about to go into detail about Kirby's flea spray and how she's allergic to certain ones when I feel a gentle vibration against my chest. It's a different tone from the earlier text and I immediately look at Keith who holds up his hand to signal a call. I drop my own phone and pull out the other one.

'Hello. This is Janet Pearce. Thank you very much for calling. I'm here to help you.'

I keep my eyes focused on Keith, who makes a winding signal that tells me to keep the call open while he traces it. I listen carefully. Backgrounds hold heavy secrets, a collage of signals and signs to the nature of the call. This one is silent. I strain to hear sounds and there are passing cars in the distance, and someone reading a story. I press the phone as close as it will go to my ear. Even though Keith will be recording, I need to get an immediate impression.

CHAPTER FIFTEEN

The whole SMIT suite falls silent as the call is relayed with a two-second delay through the huge speakers. *The Red Shoes.* The rhythmic reading, a deep male voice continues, and I try again.

'Is there anything you want to tell me? The little girl, Maisie, is she with you? She's called Maisie.'

But it's just cars passing by and the occasional rattle of a lorry.

'Don't be afraid. We'll help you all we can. We just want to get Maisie back to her mum.'

The call is ended and there's a scramble to analyse it. Lauren hurries over.

'Do you think that was him? Do you think that was the perp?'

I spin around. 'Him? Why him?'

She narrows her eyes. 'Well, I don't believe a woman would take a child. The probability is that it's a man. And the chemicals. And Magellan. It all points to...'

'A man? Fuck off, Lauren. You're being too subjective. Just because you wouldn't do it doesn't mean any woman wouldn't.'

She stands her ground. 'Would you? Well, would you, Jan? Even though you're not a mother and you could never understand, no matter how much you say you do, how it feels to hold your own child.'

I'm back in the car park with my brown suitcase. The car is empty. My hand is on the car door handle and I push myself to open it and throw the suitcase onto the seat. Instead of starting the car and driving away I get out and stretch. I stare at the suitcase through the window for a long time, then lock the car and walk away.

I stare at her, my breath shallow. I know my skin will be flushed and my pupils will have narrowed to pinpricks. My body temperature will have raised a fraction and my pulse is quickening. Depending on how perceptive Lauren is, she will see this too and, depending on what her real motive is, she will stop baiting me with this line. I don't want to talk about my personal life to anyone on the team. It weakens you, makes you vulnerable. It gives anyone who has the slightest inkling of a disliking for you ammunition. I know that other women see me, even at my young age, single and childless, as some kind of poor lonely soul, but it suits me. The freedom, the ability to take off when I feel like it. I have my reasons. Lauren will never understand this. So, I decide to take another direction.

'Like I said before, yesterday at the Lewises', it doesn't matter what you and I think. It's dangerous ground, that subjective position. Whether I would or you would abduct a child is not the issue. The issue is what the evidence tells us and if it is remotely possible. And if you want to get personal, I'll explain to you once again how I do my work. I'm a trained profiler. I'm trained in reflexivity. I know my own biases and push them into the background when I make decisions.'

I realise every eye in the room is on me. But Lauren comes back at me.

'But you're always going on about following your instinct. Gut feeling. And my gut feeling is that this is a man. There's no real evidence that it's a woman. Men can read stories and cut-out dolls.'

I raise my hands in mock horror. 'Okay. Let's see, Lauren. One thing we know for sure now is whoever has Maisie has made contact. Man or woman, which means she's most probably safe. Otherwise, they wouldn't bother, would they? Of course, it could all be some massive coincidence that the main evidence is a chain of dolls. And if you and the bloody press have their way it's your stereotypical builder in a four by four, which doesn't fit my profile at all. But we'll soon see, because they'll make contact again. This case is finally moving.'

She backs down. We're still eye to eye when Steve intervenes. He rushes into SMIT, alerted to the call.

'Did we get a trace?'

Keith rubs his hand over his head. 'Pay as you go mobile on the Vodaphone network. It's somewhere in the cell network between Central Oldham, Royton and Chadderton. We're working to get more details from the network operator about the chip, the phone and the call.'

Lauren's glaring at me and Steve intervenes. 'Look, Lauren. Jan knows what she's doing. She's done this before.'

She turns around to face him. 'But all my training's been on negotiating on child kidnap cases and abuse cases. And I've got the empathy angle as I've got kids of my own. I don't see why Jan has to lead on this when she hasn't.'

Steve stares at her. He doesn't need this. None of us do. I close it down quickly.

'Right. We'll work on it together, Lauren. We'll use your training and my experience. Just don't tell me I don't know what I'm doing and we'll get on just fine. Just respect my right to have my view, children or not, yeah?'

I can tell she's still not happy, but what choice does she have? She's young and ambitious, but it would serve her better to hang around and gain experience. But the look in her eyes now reads that she's thinking I might be gone soon, anyway. Maybe she's right.

I realise I haven't eaten lunch and I head for the café. I'm only halfway down the glass corridor when I hear Lauren's voice behind me.

'Jan. Jan. Come back.'

I turn around just enough to see her but avoid eye contact.

'Don't bother apologising. Let's just get on with things. I've got enough on my plate.'

She's shaking her head. 'No. It's not that. It's a phone call. Some information.'

We hurry back and Keith plays the call over the loudspeakers. It's a woman's voice.

'I'm ringing to report a baby crying. I've heard it crying for hours now, and I saw a woman leave this morning. I'm at the Travelodge at Chadderton. I've told the staff but they don't believe me. Poor little mite, in that room on its own.'

The emergency services operator speaks. 'Can you give me your exact location?'

'I'm at the Travelodge at the roundabout near the M62 junction. The one with the Toby Carvery on the side. Just in front of the shopping centre.'

We grab our belongings and rush to the car park. Lauren drives me to the Travelodge and just as we arrive, she finally speaks.

'You know, Jan, I'm not being difficult. You might not always be right.'

No time for discussions. We get out of the car and go into reception. Steve's right behind us with two SMIT officers and a woman from social services.

'We've had a call about a baby crying. Mother left this morning.'

The blonde receptionist doesn't look up. 'She came back. Told the woman who phoned. Wastin' yer time.'

I lean over the desk. 'Which room?'

She looks up now, but it's too late. Her attitude has pissed me off and there's no time to waste.

'Twenty-six. But yer wastin' yer time.'

'I'll take my chances. Give me the key card for that room. Please.'

She pushes a key card into the machine. 'There you go. Have you got a warrant?'

'Just open the doors so we can go upstairs. Please.'

We hurry upstairs and open the door. The room is bare except for a little girl sitting on the floor beside the bed. She isn't crying now, but her shoulders move up and down with the deep sobs she makes every now and again. She's clutching a teddy bear. I pull out my ever-present protective gloves from my pocket and pull them on. The television has been left on the news channel and I see a close-up of myself and hear my voice loudly echo through the Travelodge corridors.

'Get Petra's team up here.'

Lauren calls Petra and I look at the girl. She's about one-year-old and she starts to cry again as I pick her up. Steve comes over.

'Thank God for that. I thought we weren't going to find her.'

I look at him. The little girl grabs hold of my hair and pulls it hard.

'Steve, this isn't Maisie.'

He visibly pales. 'Who the fuck is it then?'

I hand the little girl to Lauren and reach inside my handbag for a cotton bud. I wipe the bud on the side of her mouth where her soother has left a smear of saliva. I unwrap the plastic cup from the side of the sink in the room and use the plastic bag that covers it to contain the bud.

'I'm going back to Central Park to get this tested. This little girl needs to be checked over in hospital. Lauren, can you arrange for that, please? This room needs to be sealed off. Where's the woman who phoned this in?'

One of the officers leads Steve and I to the next room. A middle-aged woman and a younger man are sitting on the bed.

'Is it her? Is it that little Maisie?'

'Unfortunately not. But we'll need some information from you to find her mother. She tells us that she heard the door slam at around ten o'clock this morning and heard footsteps outside her door, then a fire door shutting farther up the corridor. Then the baby had started to cry. She had only seen the back of the woman the evening before as she went into the room. She was short and thin with a light blond ponytail.'

We go to the reception next.

'So, what did the girl say when she left?'

The receptionist is no more helpful than when we arrived. 'Didn't say anything. Just gave me the card.'

'How did she pay?'

'Cash. Upfront. For two more nights.'

Steve looks out through the side window at the car park. 'What car was she driving?'

She looks up now and stares at us. 'How do I know?'

He leans over the desk. 'Because you have a camera on the car park. Wind it back.'

'I don't know how. Not my job.'

He loses it. He jumps over the desk and she stumbles backwards. He's operating the CCTV, running it backwards. A minute, two minutes go by and the woman picks up her phone. I face her off.

'Put it down. Just leave it alone. Can't you see how important this is?'

She puts the phone down and Steve beckons to me to come behind the counter. He runs the CCTV forwards and we see a woman carrying a child climb into the front seat of a silver Range Rover. The car's parked under some trees, out of sight of the road. No one would see it there. He zooms in but we can only see the back of her, or, as she climbs into the car, her face sideways on, and there, in her arms, Maisie. It's clear from the footage that she's crying. It's also clear that the woman can't hear her as she's wearing earphones. She straps Maisie into the front seat, then gets out and opens the back doors. We both lean closer. She's checking something that we can't see.

We watch as she starts the car and every nerve in my body is on edge as she almost crashes into a bollard in the car park. It wouldn't take much to cause a chemical reaction in the back of the car and Steve's face contorts as she turns the car sharply in the car park. We watch as she follows the road to the roundabout, and then turns off and drives towards Oldham town centre. I get out my phone and call Keith.

'It's not Maisie. But we've seen the perpetrator. It's a woman. Aged approximately twenty-five to thirty years old. She's in the car with Maisie on the move. She travelled towards Oldham at around ten fifteen this morning but she was still in the area we observed her in when she called us. She's on the move so easier to find. Can you tell operations to focus their search, please?'

'Roger that, Jan.'

'And can you get someone down here to get this CCTV. Apparently, the staff don't know how to work it.'

I end the call and go outside with Steve. One of the officers is guarding the door now, and he briefs him on the position of the car in the car park for when the SOCOs turns up. The woman from social services leaves with the little girl and Lauren accompanies her. As she passes me, I see the trace of a smile on her lips, but she can't meet my eyes.

Steve goes outside and lights a cigarette. *I'm immediately back in my old life, where I drank expensive whiskey in expensive bars and smoked twenty a day. Where my motto was to always wake up and go to bed on different days. Where I light a cigarette at the traffic lights, sucking in the smoke as I throw my lighter on the dashboard. More traffic now, the air turns acrid and I drive a little faster to get home quicker, laughing at my concern over the London air quality when I'm smoking and rocking backwards and forwards to Red Hot Chili Peppers' 'Give it Away'. It's me, though. Through and through. Late nights, loud music, cigarettes and alcohol. I remember thinking that I'd hold on to it as long as I could, no matter what happened.* I try to hold on to the decaying memory by breathing in the smoke from Steve's cigarette but, like everything else, it drifts away and I'm left alone with my new life.

Steve's paler than before, even, and his hand shakes slightly. It's not nerves. I've seen him like this before. It's frustration. We all feel it when cases become more and more complex and every step closer means two steps farther away from the solution.

'Who is she? Who is she, Jan?'

I've been asking myself the same question. Who is she and who is the little girl in the room? Surely she hadn't left her own child?

'My best guess is she's someone who knows about Magellan. Someone's sister? Girlfriend? But why would she attempt this on her own? It doesn't make sense, Steve. But I've asked Pat to interview Glen Wright again. Maybe he'll come up with something.'

Steve drives me back to headquarters and drops me off outside the lab building.

'Give us a call when you're ready to come back. I don't want you walking around on your own.'

I nod and slam the door. I know he's watching me until I pass the reception area. Until I'm safe. Like a dad dropping his daughter off at a disco, making sure she gets in okay, and no harm comes to her. But he can't protect me. The people who are after me now are ruthless. I already know the lengths they'll go to. And their reasoning isn't like ours. Its different goalposts, a rationale based on badness and point-scoring revenge rather than justice and fairness.

I carry on towards Petra's lab and she's waiting for me. I produce the cotton bud.

'How long to compare it with the soother found at the scene?'

She takes the bag from me.

'Couple of hours. Two, maybe three. I'll mark it as extremely urgent.'

'I already know the results. But we'll need this to close the circle. Your team are up there, looking at the room. It's a woman, Petra. With a baby. She's ditched her baby in the hotel. A little girl.'

Petra puts her hand on my arm. She knows me well. She knows when my carefully pressed-down undercurrent of sadness is about to burst out. She tilts her head to one side.

'It's okay, Jan. The little girl is safe with us. Now we must find the other little girl. The original one. Maisie. Be brave, Jan.'

I'm trying. I really am. I leave the lab and stand in the hallway outside, wondering about the woman and Maisie. She was holding her tight, like she would her own child. There is no sign of cruelty. She appeared to put her in a child seat in the front of the car. I find myself wondering about the fumes from the chemicals and if they could affect someone so much that they made a rash decision like abandoning their child. Then it strikes me that the child in the hotel might not be her child. She could easily be another child she has abducted.

I'm shocked to realise that I've made an assumption. I've let my emotions rule me, probably because of my disagreement with Lauren. I've worked on an unproven premise. I've no proof at all that the child is related to the woman who has Maisie. I walk out of the lab building and onto the concrete frontage to Central Park. It's a sunny day and I'm telling myself that I have to keep my eye on the ball, stick to the evidence I'm building. I see the press vans in the distance with their huge satellite dishes and the news anchors leaning against the lamp posts, smoking and drinking coffee from Styrofoam cups.

I carry on walking and think how Styrofoam cups are bad for people and how it would be better to serve coffee in paper cups when I suddenly realise I'm fully exposed in an open space. I see the clear blue sky above me and the line of trees in the distance and make for the main building. As I step onto the tarmac and go to cross the Gateway road, I feel the whoosh of a car moving very quickly behind me and I jump backwards, toppling onto a grass verge at the side of the road.

I look up and see a black BMW speeding towards the Manchester Road. I get up and run to the main building, coasting past the news vans and fielding any queries. Once inside, I pull out the comms phone to silence the urgent buzzing and read the inevitable text message waiting for me.

That's a warning, Janet. Kill you next time.

Keith appears in the reception area, all red and out of breath. 'You okay?'

I try to recover. I'm not okay, but I have to carry on.

'Yes. Just give me a minute.'

'We got the reg. The text was from central London again.'

My breathing slows a little. 'They'll just change cars. Nothing will stop them.'

He looks worried now. 'Wouldn't it be better, you know, safer for you, if you went off the case?'

I stand up straight. Like the Japanese proverb says: Fall down seven times, get up eight.

'But where would I go? Last time they thought they'd got me. This time it won't be over until it's done. They'd just find me. So I might as well stay here.'

I see it slowly dawn on him what has happened and what I have to do now. He's imagining being unable to go anywhere for fear of attack, of being unable to go home. In that split second, I look out of the window and over the hills towards the moors. The purple stretches of heather and the craggy outcrops that create sinister shadows at night. On the other side, the city I love.

It's a varied landscape of my life. And although I can't go out there now, not with total freedom, for fear of attack, I can still do my job as long as the team feel safe with me and fight my battle to the end. I think to myself, as I watch the tall clouds move over the hills and towards the city ever-famous for its rainy days that I can't think of a better place to die.

CHAPTER SIXTEEN

W e go upstairs and, before we even have time to assess what just happened, Pat calls.

'I'm just about to start interviewing Glen Wright. Seems he's feeling a bit better. But before I do, I heard...'

I move into a side room. I know what Pat is going to say.

'Yes. You heard right. But it was inevitable, wasn't it?'

There's a long pause.

'Look, Jan, I...'

'Don't, Pat, just don't. It was a total fuck up. We've had two years to think about it. I've come to the conclusion that it'll all play out one way or another. So, leave it. Yeah?'

A pause again. So I fill in for him.

'The job, Pat. The job. That's what's important, isn't it? We've got to find Maisie Lewis. Believe me, if this hadn't originated in London and gone national I'd still be safe. Well, relatively safe.' I know I'm rubbing salt into an old wound, so I change direction. 'You got the latest case info?'

'Yep. Found a kid but not the kid we want. Yep.'

'Great. So, either Glen Wright or any of the other Magellan must know who that someone on the edge of their lives, and their motivation. What this is about. Then we'll have some idea what they intend to do.'

This is the bit where he usually argues that it's not his field, motivation. That he's not a fucking mind reader. He doesn't have a crystal ball. But instead he says just one word.

'Sorry.'

I end the call. It's too late for sorry. It's too late for anything. I need to focus on what happened in the hotel to the exclusion of Pat and his walk down memory lane. It's becoming clear that this isn't what we thought it was. It isn't someone from Magellan with an environmental grudge kidnapping the child of a drilling exec and threatening to blow up a visitor centre.

Instead, it's a woman with a child driving a stolen car full of volatile materials. It's unclear if she knows what's in the back of the car and why she took a one-year-old from her bed. I leave the side room and find Steve.

'Pat's going to interview Glen Wright in a minute. Do you want it on the main screen or...?'

He stares hard at me and pulls me to one side.

'Keith told me what happened. You okay?'

'Yes. I just need to get on with things. I just want to get on with the case.'

He's turning his phone around in his hands, processing something in his brain. He looks stressed and tired. We all do.

'You can't just ignore what's happening, Jan. We can only protect you to a certain point, you know.'

I speak clearly and quietly. 'I'm not ignoring it. But there's nothing I can do to stop it now. Nothing. From past experience they won't take chances, won't do anything drastic. Nothing to draw attention to themselves. No guns or huge gestures.' I step closer to him. 'Everything they do looks like a tragic accident. A robbery gone wrong. A fall from a balcony. A terrible...'

He holds his hand up. 'I get the picture, Jan. But what about you?'

'You mean is it going to affect my performance? No. Obviously there'll be some changes to my personal life, but I won't put the team in danger. The guys from Lando. They're clever. They just want me, not you. Not Lauren. Just me. They'll wait until I'm alone, until I'm vulnerable.'

He looks shocked, probably shocked that I'm waiting around, knowing what to expect, and there's little I can do to curb it.

'Bloody hell. So, what'll you do after this? After we find Maisie?'

I smile. He still wants me on the team. He said, 'we'. I'm still on board.

'Come on. Let's go and watch Pat grill Glen Wright. Then we'd better go and update the Lewises in case someone from the Travelodge phones the tabloids.'

Before we reach the main screen, where Pat and Sally will feature in a second, Lauren appears.

'The little girl's been assessed. She's come to no harm; she was just hungry. Hasn't been harmed. I ran a check for missing reports but there's nothing. I'm betting she's the woman's child.'

I look at her. She's moved straight onto my theory and you can't even see the apologetic seams.

'Mmm. The woman has Maisie. We saw her on the CCTV. We've concentrated local resources in the area to look for the car.'

She stares straight ahead at the screen. Her facial muscles are tight and there's a thumping pulse in her temple. She's angry.

'What's wrong with people, Jan? What's wrong with them? How could she leave her child like that? Every morning when I leave the house I worry about my kids, being separated from them, anything happening to them. And when I get home I'm so grateful. I know, in the end, this job indirectly keeps them safe. That's why I carry on.'

I touch her arm. It's the nearest to an apology I'm going to get. The screen flashes into life. Pat and Sally are in the same interview room with Glen and his solicitor. Glen's left hand holds a cup of tea and his right arm is in a sling. He's no longer cocky and grinning. He slumps over, head lolling to one side. I see Sally look at Pat, who's staring at Glen, and smile slightly. Of course. Why would they not be together?

Pat waits four minutes for effect, then begins by naming everyone for the purposes of the recording. Glen looks up, glassy-eyed.

'So, Glen. We need some more information from you.'

Glen interrupts. His speech is broken, fragmented. 'I don't have any. I told you everything. Just charge me so I can get bail.'

Pat sniggers. 'Bail? You're kidding. We need to know who else has been in your pad in the last month. In particular, any females. Anyone, Glen. We need to know everyone.'

He leans back on his chair and tilts it backwards. 'Just Jane. And she's fucking clueless. No one else. Just Frank Jones and Cary Miller. And you've got them.'

Pat thinks for a moment. 'We've got them and they're not women, are they, Glen?' He pulls out two prints. 'For the record, these photographs are of the woman who has taken Maisie Lewis from her home and who has been driving your car around. I'm showing the pictures to Glen Wright. Glen, do you know who this woman is?'

Glen picks up the first sheet. His face changes immediately. His jaw goes slack and eventually his mouth closes. He looks closely at the picture and then at the other one. He places them back on the table.

'Fucking hell. Oh my fucking God.'

Pat nods again. Sally is watching Glen and writes some notes.

'So, you know her then?'

Glen puts his good hand up to his eyes. He's clearly exhausted. He rubs his eyes and looks again at the pictures. 'I know her all right. And you're in fucking trouble, mate. If you think you'd hit the jackpot with Magellan, Jesus Christ. That's Tina Durose.'

'Address, Glen. And how do you know her?'

Glen looks increasingly agitated. 'I... I've got a kid with her. That'll be the kid in the picture. Jennifer. My daughter.'

Sally intervenes. 'No, Glen. That's Maisie in the picture.'

'So, where's Jenny then?'

Pat smiles his evil smile. 'Can you tell us when you last saw Tina Durose and in what situation?'

'Last Wednesday. She's living in Ancoats now, near her mum, so she brings Jenny down here every month or so. She turned up at my place, something about her car broken down and she needed some cash, and Jane was here.'

'Did she know anything about the plans you had? Or Magellan?'

He starts to laugh. Then he becomes very serious. 'Know about Magellan? It was her idea. It was her idea to raid offices and get addresses so that we could harass the bastards. But when she got pregnant, she kept going into hospital, then she couldn't come on demos. When she had Jennifer, she went fucking loco. Crazy. So we sidelined her. But she knows all about it.' He shakes his head. 'She knows fucking everything.'

'So why didn't you tell us she was there last week? Or involved with Magellan when I asked you? Is there anyone else you need to tell us about, Glen?'

'Tina's not involved anymore. How can she be? She's a mum.'

WHAT I LEFT BEHIND

'That doesn't stop her knowing about it though, does it? And I asked you for the names of anyone who knew about it.'

The look on Glen's face makes me think that Pat's promised him something in return for this information and he's realising that he might not receive it now.

'What's was she going to do? With a baby?'

'Not very bright, are you? She hasn't had a memory transplant at birth, you know. She still knows what she knows and now she's in charge, isn't she? Whether she's got a baby or not, she's in charge. Looks like you made one big miscalculation here, Glen.'

Sally shuts her notebook and rests her arms on the table.

'So, Glen, what I need to know from you is her intention. Is it more likely that she would carry out the Magellan plan or not?'

Glen flashes a grin, but it's suddenly lost its effectiveness. Sally and Pat don't react, they just wait. He looks at his solicitor who's writing, and ignores him. Then he jumps up, crashing his chair backwards.

'She's fucking crazy. Crying and screaming, then not speaking for days. I was looking after Jennifer and trying to keep it together. Then she started moaning about stuff, stuff I did around Jennifer. Jennifer, Jennifer fucking Jennifer. I never wanted a kid. I love her now, but I never wanted Tina to get pregnant. I told her she was on her own, but she was trying to make me into fucking Super Dad or something. So I ended it. She tried to live in London, but it didn't work. So she moved into some flat in Ancoats. I don't know where it is.'

Sally continues. 'Okay. What's her mother's name?'

'Laurie Durose. She moved in with Tina's stepdad about nine years ago, that's why Tina moved to London.'

I pick up the comms phone and speak directly to Pat. 'Ask him where Tina comes from. Originally.'

Pat nods and Sally suddenly looks annoyed and glances at the camera.

'Do you know where Tina was born? Where she comes from?'

Glen shakes his head. 'Manchester. She's got a northern accent. Broad. She never really told me. All she did was moan about her mum and her stepdad.'

Pat takes the initiative. 'Was she interested in dolls?'

He starts to laugh manically. 'Interested? She's fucking obsessed. Dresses Jennifer as a doll. She just thinks they're lucky for her. Something about her childhood. Never had any, or something. Oh, and those fucking shoes. Red fucking shoes. Obsessed with them, too.'

Pat stands up. 'Right. That's all for now.'

Glen sinks into his chair. 'Hang on. What about my charge? What about Jennifer? Where is she?'

Pat leans over the desk. The solicitor leans backwards.

'Social services have your kid, Glen. And with her mother on the run with someone else's child and you in custody, that's where she's staying.' He leans closer. 'You know, there are people walking this earth who would do anything to have a kid.' I can see Pat's spittle hit Glen's face. He's red and angry and I know he's losing it. 'And you and your girlfriend can't even look after yours between you.'

Sally pulls at Pat's jacket and puts a comforting hand on his arm. I lean back and watch it play out. The screen flashes off and Keith hands me Tina's mother's address in Ancoats.

'Can't get Tina Durose's address as she isn't on the electoral register. It'll take me a while to get it off the benefits office or infrastructure. But as far as I can see she's twenty-five, no previous.' He pulls up a set of intelligence photos from the Met files. 'But she's been identified by intelligence. Here, in the background.'

She's right behind Glen in some of the pictures, and farther in the background in others. Small, compact. Quite pretty, really, in a grungy kind of way. All wild hair and combats, but the close-up shows carefully applied make-up and professionally applied false nails. Angry, shouting, and, in the last two, pregnant. She's wearing red shoes or boots in every picture. I grab my bag and jacket.

'Steve. Can you go and update the Lewises? Tell them Maisie is safe, at least for the time being. Me and Lauren will go and see Tina's mum.' I turn around and face the operations room. 'Okay. We need to step up the search for that car now it's on the move. Let me know immediately if it's spotted. Get the CCTV on all routes from that Travelodge and track it as far as you can.'

Keith shouts after me. 'Shall we update the media? You know, silver Range Rover? Public looking for a guy? With Jennifer in the hospital and the Travelodge sealed off, lots of people will know there are some developments.'

I think for a moment. What can we tell them?

'Just tell them that then. Some developments and we're closer to finding Maisie. Nothing specific. Nothing to spook Tina Durose. Let me know.'

Lauren follows me to the back doors of the building. When we get there, she tries to stop me and speak to me. I don't know if she's going to apologise or voice her concerns about working with me under the circumstances, but I take control.

'Bring your car round here, Lauren. I'll get in the back without being seen and lie on the back seat until we're out of the immediate vicinity. Okay?'

She nods and looks relieved. In a few minutes she turns and parks beside the door. I crawl onto the back seat and lie flat. There's a Lego on the floor of her car, and a blue rubber Smurf stuffed underneath the back seat. I remember her kids and how concerned she must be to have me in the car. But there's no time. We're out of the car park and travelling towards the city.

'Anyone following? Just nod yes or no.'

She nods.

'Okay. Drive towards the big Tesco on Oldham Road. Park up and go inside. Get three sets of underwear size 14. Get two black T-shirts and a hooded top, and two pairs of black jeans. Quick as you can. Let me know when the car following gives up.'

Halfway up Oldham Road, and just as she pulls into the Tesco car park the car turns off. She gets the clothes and in fifteen minutes we're pulling up outside Tina's mum's house. I get out of the back and straighten my clothes. Lauren knocks on the door and an older woman, peroxide blonde, opens it. Lauren shows her warrant card.

'Mrs Durose. We're here to have a word about your daughter, Tina. Can we come in?'

She rolls her eyes and opens the door. Once in the lounge she motions for us to sit. The room is small and smells faintly of cannabis. She knows this and stands by the electric fire, bolt upright with her arms folded.

'What's she done?'

I get my notebook out.

'You don't sound surprised she's done something. Jan Pearce, by the way. I'm a Detective Constable with Greater Manchester Police.' I go to shake her hand but she backs off. 'Okay. We've got reason to believe that Tina has kidnapped a child. You may have seen it on the news. We need to get access to Tina's flat in order to understand what's made her do it and to see if we can find any evidence.'

Lauren holds up a warrant. Mrs Durose stares at us blankly.

'You mean that kid up Saddleworth? Bloody hell. Where's Jennifer?'

'She had Jennifer with her. We think she went to London and drove back in a car which we need to trace. Then she booked into a Travelodge and left Jennifer there. She took Maisie.'

She explodes. 'She did go down to bloody London to visit that wet streak of piss. But believe me she's not behind the bloody door herself. She was crackers before she had Jennifer but she's worse now. Thinking up crazy schemes to get that bloody Glen to come up North. And she wouldn't take those bleeding headphones out. Not for a single minute. So, I'm not surprised she's done something off the radar.'

I look at Lauren. She's looking around the room and sniffing.

'Why does she wear the earphones all the time?'

Mrs Durose lights a cigarette. 'So she can't hear Jennifer. She can't stand the sound of Jennifer crying. Instead of doing things to stop her crying, she just plays the same thing over and over again. Some bloody soppy words. Muttering all the time under her breath. Says it keeps the pain out. It's a wonder someone hasn't reported her.'

The story. I calculate my next question carefully.

'Do you think she'd ever hurt Jennifer?'

She pauses for longer than she should. She takes several drags of her cigarette and blows the smoke out of the side of her mouth.

'I don't think she'd mean to. But she's not well. She's always going on about dolls and Glen. It's like she's obsessed. Jennifer could be crying and she's still drawing dolls on bits of paper and telling me how Glen will do this, Glen will do that.'

'Dolls. Okay. So, what's that about?'

She shrugs and flakes of heavy dandruff fall from her shoulders.

'She's always liked them. Pictures as a kid.'

'Is she religious? Is it to do with any particular beliefs?'

171

She eyes me carefully. 'I don't really know. We were close when she was a little kid, but then I had my own problems. I haven't really asked her. Couldn't see anything wrong with it. Dolls. Harmless, aren't they?'

'So, you don't know where this particular fixation came from?'

She rolls her eyes. It makes her look even more stoned than she already does. 'No idea. None whatsoever. She was always out. Roamin' round on her own. A proper loner. What's this got to do with that kid?'

'Did you read to her when she was a child? Fairy stories? Hans Christian Andersen? *The Red Shoes.*'

She snorts and looks puzzled. 'Are you fucking kidding? Not my thing, readin'. Not at all. She liked to watch telly.'

'Did she ever mention anything called Magellan?'

'Oh yes! That's all she used to go on about before. How the bloody planet was being destroyed and how she was going to make them pay. That's how she met him, isn't it? Through that. Him, with his posh mum and dad and his money. He gives her money for Jennifer, you know. So where is Jennifer? Is she with Tina?'

Lauren jumps in. 'No. She's at the hospital being checked over. I'll give you the social worker's number and you can arrange something with her.'

Mrs Durose gets a pen and paper and scribbles Tina's address.

'Here you are, this is Tina's address. It'll be a mess. I don't go round there, but I can tell you it'll be a tip. Last time I went round there it smelled like she hadn't put the bins out for weeks. Dirty, it was. No place for Jennifer. Bloody hell. That poor kid and her parents. I'll bloody kill Tina when I get my hands on her.'

'Have you got a key? To Tina's place?'

She shakes her head slowly. 'You're joking. She wouldn't let me in most of the time.'

Lauren takes the address and radios through for support. No key, so we'll probably have to use force. We get up ready to go. I give her my business card.

'If she gets in touch, contact us, please. Straight away. Someone else will be round very soon to take your statement. Oh. One more thing. Have you always lived in Manchester?'

She starts to laugh. It's a manic kind of laugh, the hysteria of someone who has endured trauma that has changed their lives.

'Nah. Lived up Uppermill since I was a kid. Priory Farm. Just behind Dovestone. My parents had a farm just outside the village. My husband and I, Tina's dad, took it over, but he was an alkie. He drank all the money away and we had to sell it. Moved here when I met my partner.' Her eyes momentarily flicker upwards and I know he's upstairs listening. 'I've been trapped here ever since. No kind of life, this. No wonder Tina's gone tapped.'

She shows us to the door and I make a point of raising my voice.

'I'd be grateful if you didn't repeat our conversation to anyone. Particularly the press. It could harm the investigation if you do and put Tina in danger.'

She nods and glances upstairs again. When we're outside, Lauren takes a deep breath.

'Thank God for that. I'm always paranoid about breathing that stuff in. Addles your mind. And that's no place for Jennifer.'

I'm just about to give her a lecture about being with people who love her is better than being in a children's unit when the comms phone rings.

CHAPTER SEVENTEEN

I pull the phone out and fumble with the green button to switch it on. We're standing on a Manchester street, concrete pavements and terraced houses with the not-so-distant sound of traffic echoing through. But the world falls silent because we both know what any contact with Tina means. I push the speaker button so Lauren can listen in.

'Jan Pearce. Is that you, Tina? If you let me know how you are and where you are, I can help you.'

We stand under a grey sky speckled with clouds and a single crow squawks in the distance. We both lean closer to the phone to pick out background noise and hear the forlorn cry of a young child in the background. In the empty spaces where Maisie is silent, gasping air for her next cry. She cries again. It's strong and fills me with hope that she might yet be returned.

'Tina. Look. Whatever it is, we can help you. Whatever's wrong, we can help put it right. You just need to give Maisie back to us. Your mum is looking after Jennifer and she's fine. Just tell us where you are.'

I'm silent and counting down the minutes until Keith buzzes my personal mobile to tell me her location. Maisie carries on crying. A car passes and we move even closer to the phone's speaker. I consider going back into the house and asking Mrs Durose to appeal to her daughter, but that could go both ways. She could persuade her to bring Maisie back, or scare her into doing whatever she intends to do more quickly.

My phone buzzes again and I pull it out with my free hand. It's a text from Keith and I pass the phone to Lauren.

'She's heading for Saddleworth. She's up on the Huddersfield Road, somewhere between Scouthead and Greenfield. Difficult to triangulate, because the cells are more distant out there. Can't pinpoint it exactly.'

We're still listening to Maisie crying. The yelling has turned to a whimper now. We hear her murmur and can just make out one word. Mummy.

'Look, Tina, whatever has happened, we just want Maisie to be back with her mum. She's...'

The call ends and we stand in the street. It's started to rain, but neither of us move for a minute or so. Then Lauren speaks.

'This doesn't look good, does it?'

I've been thinking the same. It's confirmed many of the initial hunches I had, but I don't feel triumphant. I feel more concerned. We're no longer looking for someone who's going to demand a ransom. This isn't something Marc Lewis can blame on his job. This is something completely different.

'No, it doesn't. We've got two witnesses saying she's disturbed. She's got knowledge of the contents of the car, but I don't think her intention is to blow up the power plant anymore. Otherwise, she'd be heading north. There's no real pattern to this. Except she can't stand a baby crying. She's dumped her own child and now she's blanking Maisie out. The good thing is that she's phoned us. That shows us that she's got a flicker of hope.'

Lauren snorts. 'She's got a flicker of hope? From where I'm standing, she's holding all the cards.'

'Maybe. But what about from where she's standing? We know she's driven down to London in her own car to see Glen with Jennifer. She's caught him with Jane and driven off in his car because he wouldn't give her the money to fix her car. She's driven back north and posted the dolls to the first recipients. Then she's gone to the Lewises', likely to do the same and, for some reason, decided to take Maisie. They found what I think is Jennifer's soother in the grounds, so she was probably carrying Jennifer with her.'

Lauren looks puzzled and asks the key question. 'But why take Maisie? If she's not going to demand anything?'

I focus on Maisie's bedroom. The picture, the fingerprints. The paper doll.

'She was in the room a while. Looking around. Then she took Maisie and drove to a Travelodge. The car wasn't particularly hidden, just lucky that it was under some trees. She didn't hide the children, but she paid cash. Then she left her own daughter in the room and drove to Saddleworth.'

I search for the reason, the purpose, for taking Maisie but I can't find it in this information. None of it makes sense. Unless this isn't what we think it is. There hasn't been a demand despite two phone calls. No code word or drop-off point. Not even a cryptic request for an exchange – Maisie for cash. Nothing at all. I cast my mind back to my conversation with Petra. We're dealing with an amateur, not a professional. Everything in the abduction points to this, and so does the lack of a demand. But that still leaves the reason she took her. If not for money or power, then why?

Lauren sighs and stretches. We walk up the street to her car and I think about my grandmother. She lived in a terraced house like this, in Ashton. I used to stay with her when my parents were arguing, when times were bad, which meant more and more as my childhood progressed. I loved it there, cosy and warm. It's what I think about when I can't sleep; my grandmother's lounge.

The police car is already parked outside when we reach the flat. Four officers get out as Lauren parks up. Before we get out of the car, she turns to me with a worried look on her face.

'Tina's mum didn't seem bothered, did she? Not really shocked or surprised that her daughter had taken someone else's child. No offers to rush round or to talk to her or anything?'

It's been bothering me, too. She was angry about Tina's relationship with Glen and how she treated Jennifer, but she hardly mentioned the fact that her daughter was on the run with a kidnapped one-year-old. No real sign of worry or surprise. I slump back into my seat.

'Yeah. Makes me wonder if she knew something. Knew there was something wrong and was used to it. She mentioned Tina's flat. We might find something there.'

We walk over to the flat. It's a ground floor, one-bedroomed standard council accommodation. The neighbours are already out and I ask two of the officers to take any statements that are forthcoming, but not to mention why we're here. Lauren shows the warrant to enter to one of the officers and he promptly rams through the door.

The first thing that hits us is the noise. It's *The Red Shoes*, booming out loudly. I go to the stereo player to turn it down and see it is on a loop. It must have been playing over and over for four days or so. Everyone covers their ears except me. I know only too well the decibels required to numb the brain into submission.

The second thing that hits us is the smell. It's an overpowering smell of bleach and lemons. Tina's mum said that it would be a mess, but it's the opposite. It's more than clean. It's practically sterilised. Every inch of this flat has been scrubbed. There are tell-tale dried bleach marks on the tiled kitchen floor, the kind you usually see in the autopsy room after hours. I check the bedroom. The bedding smells fresh and clean and the bed is expertly made. Jennifer's cot is pristine and her toys stacked neatly in a box.

The only thing that makes this place look any different from any other flat are the hundreds of dolls. They're everywhere. Chains of little dolls hanging from the ceiling like all-year-round Christmas decorations. All the dolls are white and look like they have been cut from sheets of notepaper. There are some larger cardboard versions sitting on the mantelpiece, different shapes this time and quite well formed. And their feet are all painted red. Tina's obviously had a lot of practice.

The noise is quieter in the background now and we settle into searching the flat. I pull on my gloves and sort through two black bin bags in the kitchen. There's a single cup on the draining board, and I pick it up. It smells strongly of bleach. The usual supplies of basics in the fridge are stacked in extremely neat piles. Every tin in the cupboard has its label turned outwards. It all gives the appearance of something unreal. And it is. I've seen it before. It's someone putting things straight before they go away for good. Tina's mother said that the flat was a mess, but Tina knew that someone would come here and she wanted to leave a good impression. Be in control. I turn to Lauren. She's opening drawers and examining the contents. She holds up a jotter.

'This could be the pad that the dolls were made from.'

I go into the bedroom and open a cupboard. I already know what will be inside, but my stomach still lurches when I see them. Dozens of pairs of red shoes. All lined up in neat rows. Boots, Wellingtons, slippers. All red.

I phone into SMIT and ask for SOCOs to attend.

'Not much more we can do here, Lauren.'

She tuts and folds her arms. 'This isn't what I was expecting at all. I thought there'd be half-eaten pizza and shitty nappies everywhere.'

I hear the doubt in her mind, the slight suspicion that Tina might not be as unbalanced as we think.

'No. It's not what I was expecting either. It's worse.' I pick up a picture of Tina and Jennifer. It reminds me of the picture in Maisie's bedroom. All smiles and cuddles. But when I look more closely, Tina is wearing earphones. Even in a posed photograph she's listening to the morbid words of the story. She looks different in this picture. Carefully curled hair, her make-up less bold and her nails bitten to the quick. But the anger is still in her eyes. She's wearing a plain T-shirt and I can just about see the start of a tattoo on her shoulder. Even the multiple earrings she wore on the Magellan intelligence photographs have been replaced by neat pearls.

I look around the flat. Beyond the clean facade she's created for us, through the distraction of the music and behind even the guardian paper dolls, I can feel her. Tina. Someone whose life has changed beyond all recognition. Someone whose environment and everyday has morphed into something she cannot bear, for whatever reason. She's here. Somewhere, underneath a top layer of obsessive cleaning, she's bound to have left clues.

I open bedroom drawers and sort through. No diary. No notebooks. Just a pile of bills. All paid up. I look through everything and, as usual, what's not there is more obvious than what is. There is no paperwork to indicate Jennifer was ever here. No birth certificate or hospital tags, no first locks of hair or first-size baby clothes. Just a baby capsule wardrobe for a one-year-old, a cot and some toys. It's as if Jennifer's existence has been frozen in a slice of time.

My thinking is interrupted by my personal mobile ringing. I check the display and it's Jean. I can hear Kirby barking in the background and my heart jolts.

'Oh, hello, Janet love. I just wanted you to know that there's been a man asking after you. He just asked where you lived. I told him I didn't know. Is that all right, love?'

Bastards. I know they won't harm Jean or Graham. It's not their style.

'Yes. It's all right, Jean. Don't worry.'

'Only the other thing is, I thought I saw your bathroom light go on and off about half an hour after he came round. I wanted to phone the police, but I phoned you instead because, well, you are the police.'

She sounds confused and I'm devastated that she has to go through this.

'Don't worry, Jean. You did the right thing. We'll deal with this now. Just don't go near the house. I'll send someone up there.'

I end the call and Keith calls me before I can call him.

'I heard all that, Jan. This is getting serious now.'

I think hard. We're so near to finding Tina but I need to protect Jean and Graham.

'Can you send someone inconspicuous to sit with Jean, please? House behind mine. Perps will be long gone now so don't bother to send anyone into my house. And please log all this to do with me in a separate file to the Maisie Lewis case. I'd like a transcript of everything in that file.'

It's true. They'd be long gone before anyone got near. Someone would be watching every approach route. They're experts at it. Keith's quiet except for the tapping of his keyboard. I listen to the story, on its fourth loop by now, turned down to a reasonable volume, and try to blank out the image of someone sneaking around in my house, touching my possessions. Looking at my photographs. Wishing I had brought my most precious things with me. Like Tina must have done. Unlike me, she's made sure that she has everything she needs with her. Her ID, Jennifer's ID and papers, anything that is remotely personalised. As I wait for Keith to reply, I casually open drawers and cupboards. No photographs, except the carefully posed, framed one.

It's always in moments like this, when I have a lot on my mind I see deep into the soul of the world and understand. As I stand in the ordered chaos of Tina's stage-managed flat, I glance into her bedroom and see a series of what were eight pictures hanging on the wall opposite Tina's bed. There are seven pictures left. Three of them are framed photographs of Tina outside her secondary school. Another is a framed photograph of Tina and her mother and father outside what I recognise as a farm in Uppermill. The next photograph is missing and my eyes scan quickly along the next three.

My worst fears are not borne out, because the next three pictures are of her outside her mother's current home, and with Glen and Jennifer in Trafalgar Square and on The Mall. She hasn't taken any of them. My eyes stray back to the space on the wall, the empty hammered-in tack where the missing picture used to hang. These pictures are in chronological order. A timeline of her life, with all the things that are important to her. Whatever that missing picture shows is very important to Tina at a time between being a small child and moving to Ancoats.

But no one else would know what it is as Tina appeared to have no one to turn to. Her mother clearly hasn't been here for some time and seemed unconcerned that Glen had another lover. No one seemed very forthcoming outside the flat when asked for a statement. It seems Tina is all alone at a time when she hardly knows who she is. And I can empathise with that. Keith finally speaks, interrupting my train of thought.

'Okay. All done. Completely separate. Someone's on their way up there now. I've got someone to look in on your place, too.'

'That's okay. They'll see anyone approach and vacate. Then go back when they've gone. They'll expect me to go home at some point. Everyone has to go home, don't they? They usually send one team to do the job. And they don't give up until it's finished. But thanks anyway.'

I can hear him breathing on the other end of the line. 'Fucking hell, Jan.'

'Yeah. Well. Let's see what happens.'

I end the call and get back to Lauren. She's looking at Tina's stereo player.

'A music player and no CDs.'

I stop the track and everyone turns around. The story was calming and hypnotic and I can see why Tina listened to it. I open the CD drawer and pluck out the disc.

'One CD. All she needs. On a loop.' I pick up the picture. 'She's listening to this all day and night. Blocking out the world. Blocking out Jennifer. And now blocking out Maisie.'

Lauren sniffs and grimaces. 'I still can't get over this flat. It's so clean. Unnaturally clean. I was expecting a right dump, like her mother said. Doesn't fit with someone who's depressed, does it, Jan? Doesn't profile onto someone unbalanced and unable to manage their lives?'

I look at her. She's not critiquing me, but theorising.

'No. But what if she's done this for a reason? What if this place was a culmination of all her depression and being overwhelmed and suddenly she had the solution? What if she knew that she wasn't coming back, and she decided to leave the place like she found it? Damage limitation in her own mind. A way to redeem herself? She's taken all her personal belongings.'

Lauren stares at me. 'Well, where do you think she was

going then? Back to Glen? Did she drive to London thinking she could get back with him?'

I look around the room at the dolls. Each one has a smiley face drawn on it, all cheerful, holding hands across Tina's flat. The cardboard cut-out ones sit with their legs hanging over the edge of the mantel, hands under chins.

'I don't think so. I think she went to give Jennifer to Glen. I think she went to London to give Jennifer to her father. She's taken most of Jennifer's clothes and all her baby things. It's like she's lifted Jennifer and all her history out of this place. But Tina wasn't coming back here. And she knew we'd come looking for her. This clean-up was her way of saying goodbye.'

CHAPTER EIGHTEEN

I lie in the back of Lauren's car again and she drives to the station. When we arrive, she opens the side door and the boot and gets my shopping out as I crawl back through the side door. The door where criminals are often taken for their own protection. As we reach the SMIT suite, I see Petra. She nods and smiles at us.

'I got your results for the soother, Jan. It has DNA in common with the child you found in the hotel room.'

I feel a surge of optimism. At least this closes the circle and places Tina and Jennifer at the crime scene.

'And there were traces of the chemicals found in the hotel room, too. We're just testing Jennifer's clothes for them.'

'Thank you, Petra. That's really helpful. I sent you the notes to bring you up to date, but this just confirms things.'

Her expression suddenly changes. 'What about you, Jan? Where will you stay? You can gladly stay with me. Anytime.'

Lauren reciprocates. 'Or me. Although with the kids we don't have much room.'

It's good of them to offer me a place to stay. They're willing to put their own lives at risk to help me. I know Lauren doesn't want me there of course, but she still offered. But there's no need. I know what I have to do. Petra puts her head on one side, the way she does when she's deeply concerned.

'But you can't go home on your own, Jan. You can't. Your neighbours will look after Kirby, I know, but you can't stay in a hotel on your own either. And not indefinitely.'

'I know. But while I'm working on this investigation, I'll be fine. When that ends, well, I'll think again. Things have a funny way of changing very quickly.'

Lauren laughs nervously. She's clearly worried for me.

'But when there's a contract out on you it doesn't go away, does it? You need to do something, Jan, in the short term.'

Petra knows this is dangerous ground for me and tries to defuse the fire she saw ignite in me.

'Just as you were getting settled from last time. But you managed it then and you will manage it again.'

Lauren gives up and moves over to operations to see what social media is saying about the case. I feel the burning of my situation and Lauren's assessment doesn't help. I know this has to end somewhere, but I don't know where that end point is. They can chase me forever, but I can't hide forever. Not if I want to carry on doing the job I love.

I go into a side room and review the case notes. All resources have been sent up to a ten-mile area around Greenfield. I picture the narrow roads and the open moorland that scowls over the deep valley dips. Most of the area is very open and, even from a distance. It would be easy to spot a big silver Range Rover on the moor.

But I know as well as anyone else who comes from that area that if you want to hide you can. If you know where to go. There are abandoned barns and huge rocky outcrops that Tina would know about, as well as the planted pine forests that are dense at the top, but negotiable at the bottom. They'd been planted that way so that the men who go there each year to hack them down for Christmas could reach them easily, even at the centre.

Even so, it's with one eye on my phone that I think about Tina and who she is. I'd gone through the details with Lauren, but something else that her mother said stuck in my mind. Her mother had said that she couldn't let go of Glen. That she'd strategised to get him back. That she's been disturbed ever since she had Jennifer. So much so that her mother noticed. And the headphones. She couldn't face her baby crying so she blocked it out. If she was anything like me, she blocked out her pain with loud comfort music. But she wasn't like me. She was obsessed with *The Red Shoes*. The overzealous cleaning. And her fascination with dolls becoming an obsession.

I know where it all points. She's unbalanced. Maybe in denial. Or depressed. It can happen after a lot of change. She'd had a baby that stopped her being who she was and her boyfriend had dumped her. Had she resented Jennifer so much that she'd used the story to pretend she wasn't there? If so, why take another baby? Surely not to swap her? For another child? But what if the other child was the same? Then what?

My heart sinks. Then what? What did she plan to do with Maisie now? In my psychology undergraduate classes, we'd studied post-natal depression, but I hadn't encountered it until one of my school friends, one of the girls at the wedding the other day, Anna, had left her baby outside a shop one day and gone home. Everyone had laughed it off as an accident, just careless, until two members of her family saw her shopping alone in Selfridges in Manchester on a Tuesday lunchtime. When they asked where Jackson, her son, was, she calmly said that she had left him at home asleep. He'd be fine until she got back. She'd done it before.

She'd been leaving him for one day every week just to survive. She literally couldn't face spending every minute of the day with her baby. In the end, she got help and she and Jackson are close. She told me that she had never stopped loving Jackson. It was more that she felt that she couldn't be close to him, because she wasn't good enough. So, she reasoned with herself and did what she could to cope, however irrational it seems to the rest of us.

Everything points to this. Tina leaving Jennifer, her unreasonable focus on Glen. But where did her taking Maisie fit in? I look at the comms phone. Nothing more since the last call. I know that Keith's got it on a five-second delay to screen out anyone who's going to abuse the number. The question is, do I confront Tina with this? Do I face her with what she has done, tell her what I think and then tell her I can help her? Maybe it will resonate enough with her to bring Maisie back unharmed.

The alternatives are unthinkable. I don't even know if Steve and the rest of the team are going to buy this. Steve doesn't have a lot of sympathy for mental illness – a crime's a crime to him. He reckons that even if people are mentally ill, they still have a sense of what's right and what's wrong, unless they are a psychopath. He's more likely to treat Tina like the terrorist he thinks she is.

I completely understand where he's coming from on this, especially with her background, but it's seldom black or white. Steve's 'if... then' formula gets us so far, then I often have to fill in the details. That's why we work so well together, to a point. But on this one, our basic principles come into play. His experience with the Manchester bomb and the catastrophic damage done to the city that he loves, and my understanding of the human condition.

It's difficult to see where they will meet in the middle. I can see it in his eyes, the determination that this won't slip through the net. That the car won't be allowed anywhere near the city. That what happened to him and thousands of unsuspecting shoppers will never happen again. I don't expect any softening of his principles to accommodate a young woman with problems. All he's seeing is the components of a bomb being driven around by someone unstable, and the best way to halt the process is to remove the threat. By any means.

I look at the case notes. He's already got armed officers on standby and a swat team combing the area for Tina. He may be a quiet man, but he's always calculating, weighing up what the next move is, and the one after that. Check Steve's strategy and he'll have everything carefully planned with a number of different options. The only thing that it doesn't leave room for is instinct. He dislikes instinct just as much as he hates anything being described as personal. He likes to keep it all detached, all clean cuts and divides.

I know it's not that simple. For all I know, Tina's intention, misguided or not, may be to carry out the Magellan plan to prove she's part of the gang. Or she may be completely confused and so out of touch with reality, because of her post-natal depression or whatever she's suffering from, that she's not thinking straight. Or she goes to Sellafield and she'll most likely be detained on the way there. Or worse. I try to consider a worst-case scenario, but they're all as bad as each other. She clearly has an end game, otherwise she would just hand herself in. Either way, Maisie is still suffering.

The only ray of hope is the line of communication. I check the phone over and over again. We have a set procedure for contacting perpetrators in this situation. We have her number and Keith would have tried to call her back the first time she called. But he won't call over and over again, because that might cause her to ditch the phone. But he will call every couple of hours from a withheld number, so we're not completely relying on her to call us. If she answered he would have patched it through to me in seconds. But she hasn't.

So, I keep checking. Even though it has a loud ring I check that there are no missed calls. I look at the case log, rolling up the screen as people report no progress. On the face of it there's a lot of activity, but all in all we still don't know where Maisie is.

I look through the huge window of the office into the SMIT suite and everyone is buzzing around urgently. Steve's arrived now. He's studying the network feeds from Keith, then he picks up the newspapers and runs his fingers through his hair. His slumped shoulders give him a desperate air and his crumpled suit matches his slouch. A communications officer approaches him and beckons to him. They hurry to a screen, only for him to go back to Keith. All this and we're getting nowhere. All these resources dedicated to hunting Tina down, certain that she's intent on some criminal activity. Maybe she is. Or maybe she's a mixed-up woman seeking a solution to her dilemma, in her own way, and it's just spiralled out of control.

Steve eventually looks around and sees me. He comes into the office and shuts the door. His forehead is shiny with perspiration and his eyes red-rimmed. He sits down heavily.

'I've been up to see the parents. They're a lot more upbeat than I am.'

I push the phones around in front of me.

'Because their daughter is alive.' It comes out as a statement, but I meant it as a question. 'We'll find her soon, Steve. We're making progress. Closing in.'

I see his eyes rest on the standard issue comms phone.

'Yeah. We'll find her. But it's what'll happen first that worries me.'

Now would be a good time to raise my theory about Tina's state of mind but it's tricky. Steve's a brilliant police officer, but he's subject to the usual stigma about people's mental health. Crazy. Nuts. Demented. He uses all these words to mean anything slightly outside the norm he has set for people who are law-abiding citizens.

I consider the situation carefully. I might spend all my time chasing criminals now, but during my profile training I learnt that the basic opinion of the public on people who commit crime is either bad or mad. Bad in terms of evil and mad in terms of not in charge of their faculties. It's just not as clear cut as this. Of course people who make criminal decisions based on their lack of morals should be punished. They've purposely done something bad. But mental health problems can skew that sense of right and wrong. At one end of the scale there's desperation fuelled by all sorts of cultural problems. Depression can seriously affect someone's view of the world, as can schizophrenia. At the other end of the scale are psychopaths.

I think again about the difference between my own view and Steve's. He believes that people know right from wrong and goes entirely on that basis, until they are in court and then reports are obtained. I prefer to try to understand the psyche of the perpetrator, imagine how they may be feeling. This can predict their next move.

The end result using Steve's method and my own method is clear. Chase a single scenario and there's a bigger chance of the perpetrator getting away. Try to pre-empt them and there's a better chance of catching them. Mapped onto Maisie's abduction, both of us know the stakes. Chase Tina all over Saddleworth as per Steve's current plan and she can either feel cornered and do the unthinkable or she can simply drive through to Huddersfield and dump the car, taking Maisie with her. My approach would be to carry on communications and gain trust. That way we can get everyone out of this alive.

We sit looking at each other and I know he's waiting for me to soften his stance, suggest a way to dissolve his harsh scenario into something more manageable, more pliable. More understandable. I know the script as well as he does. That's why we're sitting in the room. It's the turning point. There'll be tantrums and tears but eventually we'll make a decision now as to how this will end. He starts the dance.

'So, what you got, Jan?'

'On top of Glen's statement about Tina, I went to see her mother.' He rolls his eyes. He already sees where this is going. 'She mentioned that Tina had been acting strangely since Jennifer's birth. Lauren and I went to Tina's address, and it was scrubbed clean. I don't think she intends to come back.'

A vein in his temple begins to throb. His pupils recede and his skin flushes slightly. 'Scrubbed clean?'

'Yes. Most personal belongings removed and the whole place deep cleaned. She knew we'd be there, and she didn't want to leave a mess. But she was going somewhere with Jennifer.' I look at the desk. Steve's stress levels are sky high now and what I say next is not going to help at all. 'My best guess is that she has post-natal depression.'

He stares at me for a moment. Then he bangs his fist hard on the table. 'Post-natal fucking depression? Is that some kind of excuse for taking a child? Taking a one-year-old from their bed? Stealing a car full of explosives? You haven't even spoken to her yet and you're pinning some namby-pamby label on her. Jesus, Jan.'

I've seen him like this before. Lots of times. I hold my nerve.

'All I'm saying is that her state of mind may be troubled.'

He jumps up and knocks the police issue plastic chair flying. 'Troubled? Troubled? I'd say it was more than troubled. She needs to be stopped. She's driving that car around the city. My city and–'

I raise my voice just enough to counter him. 'Our city, Steve. And this isn't primarily about the car. Or the explosives. Like Petra says, they're unlikely to be primed to explode. Glen said they were stored separately in their raw form.' I look him in the eye. 'It's not as if someone has parked a bomb up under a bridge in the city centre, is it?'

He opens his mouth to say something but closes it again. He probably hadn't even realised that he was projecting his own agenda onto the case, but he's in no doubt now. I continue.

'This is about Maisie Lewis. Running Tina into a corner isn't going to make things any better for Maisie. You've heard the recording of the phone calls. She's in the front of the car crying, with deafening noise playing. Things are already bad, Steve, and putting Tina under more pressure by sending SWAT after her isn't going to turn out well.'

I can completely understand how he connects this case with his past, and how he predicts the same outcome. I saw his whole expression contort when ammonium nitrate was first mentioned. He wasn't the only one. Anyone involved in Greater Manchester Police at that time would have the same reaction. But this isn't the same. Not exactly, anyway. That bomb was primed, had a trigger. As far as we know, this one doesn't. He rubs his face.

'But what if she heads for the nuclear plant? To carry out the Magellan plan?'

'I don't think she will. She had some pictures in her flat, family stuff from the past. She took it with her. I think it might be a photograph from her childhood, it was in a series. It seems like she has a chronology of the things that were important in her life. Linked to places. Linked to home. And she took the one after her early childhood. Look, Steve, if she heads for the city, then I'll leave it to you. But while she's still up on the moors, let me try to talk to her.'

He sits down. 'I don't like it, Jan. If it were just the kid. Now you're talking about some crazy woman who can use this to get her off the hook. And we're helping her do that.'

I stand up. I know in my heart that I'm going to do it my way.

'No. I'm not trying to excuse her. What I'm trying to say is that if she has post-natal depression, she could do anything. Anything, Steve. We initially thought that she had a couple of options, a decision-making process based on Magellan. If I'm right, it means the situation is even more dangerous.'

CHAPTER NINETEEN

Steve leans forward as it slowly sinks in. Everything we previously strategised for is thrown out now, and a new game comes into play. The realisation that I'm not trying to be a do-gooder and make excuses for someone transforms his features, and he crumbles.

'So, what do you think she'll do, Jan?'

I turn the comms phone round and round between my fingers while I think of an answer.

'Not sure. It's not clear cut. It's pretty clear that she's not thinking straight. It's why she took Maisie that's stumping me. She could do anything, planned or unplanned. She could even intend to carry out the Magellan plan. Or she might just decide to. That's the nature of it. She'll be feeling confused and off the scale. The situation is unpredictable. But on the positive side, if she's got a problem and I can convince her that I can help her, she might deliver Maisie right to us.'

He still looks unsure. It's a long shot, but it's a safer option for Maisie.

'Okay. Give it a go. But there has to be a compromise. That we carry on looking for her while you try to make contact. I'll call off the SWAT team but keep the cordon around the city. And I'm going to escalate the search. We've only been using road vehicles at the moment. I'm going to deploy the helicopter. Optimise the heat-seeking element. If she's hiding somewhere, then it's the best chance we've got.'

He's right. The darkness of the moor at night makes it difficult to see a foot in front of you, even with a full moon. I can think of more than twenty places that Tina could be hiding, even with a silver Range Rover. The helicopter would be able to find her even if she was amongst the dense canopy of the fir trees or had driven into a derelict barn. I nod my agreement.

'That's sounds like the best plan. I'll escalate efforts to make contact and next time I have her on the line I'll up the ante. She wouldn't be calling if she didn't want to co-operate.'

'Let's hope so. For everyone's sake.'

We're interrupted by Keith, who opens the door a little and leans through. 'Pat Knowles on the meeting screen for you.'

I push a button and Pat's face appears. He's checking his phone and is caught off guard.

'Oh. Jan. Good to see you. And you Steve. Just checking in for an update.'

I let Steve fill him in.

'Still tough, Pat. We've got a comms link on and off with Tina Durose and we've heard Maisie Lewis in the car. Alive and well. Jennifer's at the hospital and we're just interviewing Tina's mother. Anything your end?'

Pat's tapping his pen on the desk. He's tapping out a drum and bass tune and I realise that he's still hanging out at the same haunts.

'We're waiting to charge Glen Wright, but I want to know what's in that car first and what state it's in. If it's just components, like he says, it's tricky. But if there's a detonator included, then it's a different story. We've applied for an extension, but at some point, we have to charge him. Nothing pertaining to this case from anyone else, but lots of stuff to go on. This Magellan stuff, it ties in with our previous intelligence. Nice work. Gives us lots to go on.'

I watch him, all animated. His hands moving to illustrate his point, and resting in front of him, neatly, as always. I take a breath and join in. 'Good. So, we're going to crack on. I'll be trying to gain Tina's trust and Steve's going to try to track her.'

Pat doesn't speak for a long second. He clears his throat. 'Good luck. If there's anything we can do at this end, just let me know. We'll collate all the case notes and share them with you, the ones we haven't already. Erm, Jan, is it possible to have a private word?'

Steve stands up. 'Yeah, thanks, Pat. Nice one. We'll let you know what happens when we find the car.'

He leaves and I'm faced with Pat on my own. I didn't want this scenario. But here we are. He's looking at me, his green eyes clear and alert. No obvious sign of stress, but he has that under control. He used to joke that he could pass any lie detector test. I wait for him to speak, but he doesn't at first. Then he licks his lips and inclines his head, the way he does outside work, when he's bothered by something.

'Jan, hope you don't mind me doing this, but I read the case notes. I... we were worried about you.'

That's exactly why I had them separated, so no one would worry. No one would try to take me off the case. Or dig up the past.

'No need. I've got it.'

He nods slowly. 'I'm sure you have, but after what–'

'Don't go there, Pat. And I do mind you doing this. Let's leave it there.'

He looks at me for a minute longer and I see his hurt, his sadness. It's like staring into his soul and I don't want to.

'Okay. If that's how you want it, but be careful, Jan.'

I fold my arms. I will be careful. I'm always careful now.

'Goes without saying, Pat.'

I press the button that ends the call, and he's gone. *I'm back in the open-top car, my long hair blowing in the wind. One hand on the wheel and the other hand holding a cigarette, which I flick into the breeze. Laughing as I drive through Euston and towards Bloomsbury. Tapping the wheel as 'Dub Be Good to Me' blasts out. People pulling bags along, tugging at their children's hands. Horns beeping, but I don't care. I just go with the traffic flow. I've nothing to hurry for. Relaxed on a busy Saturday afternoon in London. The smell of pub food making me hungry for the Chinese takeaway I bought, thirsty for the harshness of the neat whiskey as it hits my throat.*

I snap out of it quickly. I'd kill for a cigarette right now, but I ignore my cravings and think about my strategy with Tina. I need to get inside her head. The one thing I know Tina and I have in common is blanking things out with a distraction. My personal distraction is music. It does it for me. It's a hangover from my teenage rock chick days before life became complicated and serious. There's still an echo of it left in me, I guess it reaffirms my determination not to let the weeds of sentimentality choke me.

Tina's distraction is all emotion. All loss and goodbyes. All wrapped up in death, of course, and quite devastating. She's dancing, dancing towards the inevitable, confused and hurt and convinced that she's the girl in *The Red Shoes*. She's suffering. She's trying to break free from a life that's out of control and her only way of doing it is by running.

All the physical clues make sense now. The clumsiness at the crime scene. The ragged dolls. Why would she be worried about them? She would be long gone. Was she taking Jennifer to London to leave her with Glen? Leaving Jennifer in the hotel room might seem a callous thing to do, but perhaps she was trying to spare her. Or give her a better life by giving her up. But why not adoption?

Because post-natal depression doesn't give you those kinds of sensible options. It eats you up inside, bringing you to the edge of insecurity at what should be the happiest time of your life. Puts a partition between you and your baby and other people. Magnifies your emotions by a million until you can't stop crying. Strips your self-esteem until the needle rests on fat and ugly. All this when your baby isn't sleeping and cries every couple of hours for food.

And it doesn't stop after a few weeks. It gets worse and worse unless you get help, it throws you off the cliff of reason and begins to invent its own bizarre coping strategies. It makes you feel like another person, strange and unbelonging. It makes you unable to ask for help, because you are too insecure. It makes you want to run away from the baby you wanted so much.

I know this because of the testimonies of thousands of women that are everywhere, maybe even in your own family. Yet it's still a taboo, still frowned upon, and still unbelieved. Still perceived as an excuse because, who, after all, can't love their own baby? What kind of woman would that be? Tina is feeling all these things now. They are all tied up with her own situation.

Glen Wright was her only hope. It's clear that she was part of Magellan. She has full knowledge of the plans; she knew about the plan to blow up the art gallery and the pictures that would be there – she even had prints of them. Maybe it was her idea. On the intelligence pictures she was always in the background, watching, plotting. Was Tina the mastermind like Glen claims? Then, when she was pregnant and no longer able to join them on their guerrilla warfare she was pushed out. Pushed into the role of girlfriend and mother when she really wanted to be out there with Glen and the others, fighting the cause.

So she came up north to start again. To try to get help from her mother. But it's clear that her mother is already helping her boyfriend smoke all the drugs in the world. From her attitude, Laurie Durose stopped helping Tina a long time ago at the first sign of trouble and found her own way to dumb down the intolerable life she found herself living. Tina would have had to struggle on her own, day to day, no job. Monthly journeys to central London to watch Glen living it up with his cocaine and his girlfriend. Watching as he stole her life. Although the Magellan gang carried out criminal activity, it formed Tina's life and defined her. Like my rock chick former persona, she would have been a rebel. There's not much rebel-like about dirty nappies and midnight feeds.

A clear picture's beginning to form now. But if I'm going to communicate with Tina, I'm going to have to meet her on her own level with the full information. Today's level. I'm going to have to step into her red shoes for a while and try to see what she's thinking. What's stopping me doing that is Maisie. In all the excitement of uncovering Magellan and its activity, all the analysis following about this being a kidnap and expecting a ransom, we've lost sight of the possible reason for taking a child.

She'd been to the other addresses on Glen's list and posted the paper dolls. I look at the message again. 'Hold Mummy's hand tight. Don't run off with strangers. Because you never know what those strangers might do to you.' At first it seemed like a sinister threat, especially in the light of Maisie's abduction. Even then I read it as a warning but discounted it. Could it be that she was warning the parent of the children on the list? In her own increasingly twisted world, was she trying to stop Glen and Magellan? Did she know what was about to happen? Is that why she stole the car, in order to stop them driving it to Manchester?

But if all this is true, why didn't she just tell someone? Why did she risk driving Jennifer around in the car if she knew about its contents? Is that why she left Jennifer in the hotel, to protect her?

I look outside myself now, into the SMIT suite. Steve is briefing the helicopter pilot and Lauren is getting her coat on. She looks at me, stony faced and dog tired, and waves. I glance at the clock. It's nine o'clock. Forty-eight hours after Tina took Maisie. I think about the Lewises and how they face another night without their daughter. They know she is close by but they can't do anything.

I think about Tina and Maisie in the car. Will she stay in Saddleworth, stay put until tomorrow morning? Will she let Maisie sleep? Will she sleep herself, or will she listen to *The Red Shoes* over and over?

There's a shift change now and Steve is giving a changeover briefing. The night-time crowd will be monitoring all communications and social networking and watching the results from the road searches and helicopter searches. I see hands raised to ask questions at the end of the briefing, and Steve's pointing at me. Heads turn and incredulous faces stare into the glass-panelled room. I go and stand amongst them. Steve rallies.

'Ah, Jan. We've got a couple of questions about the perpetrator that you may be able to answer.'

I look at the night shift. All are officers at the top of their field, the peak of their career. They are used to critically dangerous situations and handle them with skill and a professional attitude. A young man in part uniform part stab vest puts his hand up again.

'DC Pearce. DCI Ralston has told us that if we come across

the perpetrator, we need to not approach her. We've been told to wait until you arrive.'

He's all charm and cockiness and I see his purpose before he continues. But I let him go on with it.

'And?'

'Well, she's an unarmed young woman with a baby. I understand the care that has to be taken around the explosives, but DCI Ralston says we have to wait even if we recover the car. Why's this?' He glances around the room at the other officers. 'I mean, she's a tiny thing. It's not as if she's going to cause us much of a problem, is it?'

He's smiling at me and I understand that his job is simply to catch Tina and retrieve Maisie. But my job goes deeper than that.

'Maybe not. But this is for Maisie's protection. Tina might not cause you much of a problem, but I suspect she's suffering from post-natal depression and Maisie isn't her own child. God knows what she'll do. So, I think, as someone trained to deal with these matters, it might be the better option. We don't want Maisie hurt. If she hasn't been already.'

His smile fades and there don't appear to be any more questions for me. I go over to the window and look up and down the road. There's a black BMW in the Fujitsu car park across the road and I see the dim light of a cigarette ember. They won't risk waiting here much longer. They'll think I've been spirited back to my house. Probably don't even know we're onto them. No point sending anyone as they haven't done anything yet. And after they do, we won't find them, anyway. That's the way they work. The comms phone beeps a text.

> You can run, but you can't hide, Janet. We're coming to get you.

Keith turns around but I hold my hand up as I watch the

BMW pull out of the car park and drive towards Oldham. Heading for the hills. Heading for where Tina will become more desperate by the minute and even more unstable. With no support, no friends and a broken relationship she was unlikely ever to ask for help. I just hope that she accepts it from me.

CHAPTER TWENTY

Ten o'clock passes, then eleven. I dip in and out of the SMIT suite, waiting for news of the helicopter search finding Tina and Maisie. It has a camera on the underside and a spotlight, and projected onto the large screen I see the moorland. From high up it looks like a patchwork quilt. The dry-stone walls and the different textures of vegetation define the patches, with the shadows thrown by the hills and valleys forming deep creases. Every now and then the light reflects on the long stretches of water, reservoirs that fill the deepest crevices of the Pennines.

Keith eats a McDonald's burger and chips at his desk and rhythmically shakes the ice in his Coca-Cola. He'd brought me the same earlier, but I could only pick at it and imagine what was going on up in the dark hills. Twice I decide to go up there, once even calling a car. But then I remember that the entire area is crawling with officers, all searching for Tina in a landscape she knows better than any of them.

I look out of the windows towards the city and its twinkling lights. The black BMW hasn't reappeared. Even though its presence keeps me a prisoner I wish it was still there. While it's gone, I'm scenario building. My tired mind is catastrophising and dredging up the past. Lando was a nasty business that spiralled out of control. It started small enough, but like the current investigation, uncovered a whole lot of wrongdoing. All of a sudden, intelligence whisperings came to life and wound themselves around the criminals who surfaced.

They were cruel, but clever. They'd evaded our eye for so long, because they never took chances. Clinical in their operations and enduring in their perseverance. If you were waiting for the Lando crew to forget about you, you'd be waiting a long time. A lifetime. We knew this because some of their work was revenge attacks for ancient grudges, old debts. Bought from other long-crumbled criminal empires. We struggled to pin anything on them because they always left the scene of the crime looking like it wasn't a crime scene. It was carefully stage-managed, and impeccably carried out.

But we'd picked away at the scab of their weakness. One of their operatives hated the police, and we drove him to the hair trigger of his temper, and eventually he blew. We'd been regularly bringing him in, holding him for exactly twenty-four hours, then letting him go, only to pick him up twenty-four hours later. We knew he had kids, and we always went to his home to get him. Like most gangsters, he didn't want his mother or his children to know who he was.

But it was becoming clear who he was, and it pissed him off. It pissed him off so much that instead of playing the long game, waiting it out, finding the right time, he acted alone on the spur of the moment. He created enough of a diversion, turned enough Lando heads that we were able to retrieve two girls they were holding. I was in the right place at the right time and faced him off. As he waved a gun at me, I saw in his eyes that we had out-waited Lando. Played them at their own game. Pushed them until they had nowhere else to go, and he was the very visible manic manifestation of their failure.

But I know that was the exception to the rule. They wait in dark corners, waiting for the opportunity to strike. They're cold, calm executioners, carrying out orders and never giving up. They could be anywhere now, and that's what bothers me. In the cold light of day, I would never let these thoughts overtake me, but now, tired and on edge, I see them knocking on Jean's door and terrorising her. Finding my school friends and scaring them. Taking their grudges out on fellow officers, while I sit here in the station, safe. They're out there. Waiting for me.

I mull over the possible scenarios and then admit to myself that I'm exhausted and that I have to sleep. I check on the search progress, but there's nothing to report. The helicopter has returned to base and will set out again at first light. There's a skeleton crew patrolling the roads in and out of Saddleworth, making sure that Tina's going nowhere. I take my handbag and the shopping, which is all I possess in the world as I can't go home, to the staff shower rooms and step into the warm flow. I wash my hair with soap and rinse it. I'm lucky to have naturally wavy hair so, even though I like it straight, I can leave it to dry naturally and still look semi-presentable. But in a professional environment I always straighten it. As I am spending another night in the cells, I leave it wet.

When I'm dressed again, I ring operations and book a room. Because it's Monday night it's quieter, no lurid screams and drunken wails from the neighbouring cells. An officer called Terry shows me to number fifteen, nicer than before. He brings me a laptop and tells me the password to the wifi signal. This way I can catch up on the media perspective on the case.

It's just as I thought. Still focusing on finding the male silver Range Rover driver. The entire country out looking for a silver Range Rover with a male driver and female child passenger.

Two of the tabloids have even come up with a description for silver Range Rover Man. Six feet one, stocky build, wearing a white T-shirt. One even has a photofit picture telling us what he might look like, with the caption 'this is not a police photofit' underneath. I check my emails and there's nothing to worry about. A mortgage statement for a house that I can no longer live in. A reminder to upload my gas and electric readings.

I can't bear to think about them going through my things. My music. Opening cupboards. I just hope that they don't see any photographs of Kirby and realise that Jean is looking after her. I choke up when I think about them taking her away. But if they did, there's nothing I could do. Rather than inflame the situation, I'd just have to let her go. I'd never give in to their demands. Never.

If all this does ever end, I'll go back for her, of course. I'll find somewhere else for us to stay. Like Petra said, I did it before and I'll do it again. But I can't keep doing it. Something will have to give, one way or another. I know that. I also know that it won't be me doing the giving. I haven't figured out what I'm going to do to stop it, but I know myself. In the end I'll go the whole hog and make sure it ends. In a way, this is what I've been waiting for. Unsettling though it is, it's the endgame and I'm ready.

What I'm not ready for is my phone to ring and for it to be Pete, Kerry's husband. I let it go to voicemail and wait until the notification text hits my inbox before I reluctantly listen to it. Pete sounds panicky.

'Jan, look, Kerry's gone into labour. I'm in Belfast and I'm getting the next flight home. She's a bit early, but they said she will be okay. And baby will be okay. Can you get there as soon as possible? St Mary's. Thanks, Jan. See you there.'

I stare at the blank walls of the cell. I'd promised to be there at my friend's baby's birth. Birthing partner, because her husband faints at the sight of blood. I feel my stomach sink and I feel sick. I can't do it. A promise is a promise, but not when my life is in danger.

Kerry had been so supportive since my move back to Manchester. They all had. They'd forgiven my complete silence for years. They'd forgiven the fact that I changed my phone number and didn't tell them, that I hadn't written to them or made any kind of contact. That I'd sent the letters they wrote back to them, unopened. That I'd started a new life in the bright lights of the capital without them.

When I'd turned up out of the blue, devastated and broken, they'd called around with soup and wine, their patience at my shocked silence endless. None of them mentioned my trademark auburn curls had been cropped into a short bob. None of them had ever demanded an explanation, and I hadn't offered. They nursed me back to as normal as I could ever be after what I'd been through with nights out and cosy nights in. When I'd bought my cottage and settled down, they'd arrived with a little bundle of joy. Kirby. Kirby Red, they'd called her. Like me. Same colour. Kerry had said that tiny, helpless Kirby had reminded her of me when I'd first appeared, a mass of regrown red hair and sorrowful eyes. I'd told her I was eternally grateful and as the days passed and Kirby, became my joy, I'd promised her that I would do anything to repay the blessing.

And now I was going to let her down. My heart is already out of the door and halfway across Manchester, but my head says stay put. They'll be waiting. They'll find me either going out or coming back. They're in no hurry. Besides, it's unfair to lead them to my vulnerable friend and her new baby. It's a lever they can press in the future if they miss this time. I know what they do. They wait until you aren't expecting it. They strike when you are on the edge of consciousness, doing something you are concentrating on so you can never quite recall the face or the hair colour, or the car.

I even know when they would strike this time. In the delivery room, just after Kerry's baby is born and my love and emotions are overflowing so much that it's impossible not to laugh. Then, in the only moment in the past three and a bit years I haven't been completely vigilant. Then. Like always it would look like an accident. A slip, a fall, some kind of unavoidable happening. So, it's not fair on anyone. The way it is now, just me and them, that's the best way. We all know where we are and no one else suffers.

I compose a text to Kerry and Pete.

> Really sorry. I'm out of the country, too. I didn't expect this for a couple of weeks. Sorry.

They'll know it's a lie. Kerry knew I had no plans to go anywhere. She'll ring my phone and find it's been switched off. But in the single ringtone before it goes to answerphone, she'll realise it's not a foreign ring. She might try it again just to make sure. Then she'll know I'm lying. But Kerry's nice. She'll leave some kind of forgiving message telling me not to worry. That Pete will be there soon and he won't miss the birth. She'll promise to see me soon, when I get back.

And she's so nice that she'll mean it. Yet a little bit of trust will be eroded. She won't ask me to babysit because I might let her down. There'll be no family invitations and no christening invite. And I'll have lost another important person in my life. I have acquaintances, but Kerry's my only remaining real friend outside the force. I have Petra and Lorraine to moan about general things to. I told Petra a little bit about my past, but I can't weigh anyone down with it. It's too much.

It's times like this you take stock. Here I am sitting in a cell, completely alone. Don't get me wrong, I love being alone. Alone with Kirby and all my home comforts. My music. Some good cooking. A glass of malt whiskey, but only the one. Alone but surrounded by familiar things. The smell of my garden and my favourite perfume. Right now, I'm completely alone. It takes years for things to become familiar. When I first bought the cottage I felt at home, but it wasn't home.

I still missed my apartment in London. My shabby chic furniture and the Persian cat who lived next door. She never went out. The beautiful polished walnut floors and the way that, when you looked out of the window, your vision was level with the tops of the trees on the street below. The musical cocktail cabinet and the ringing laughter of the happiness there. The way I could walk less than a mile in any direction and find an excellent restaurant. That place had my stamp on it and the shock of leaving left its mark, on top of everything else.

But I love Manchester and I had to return. I couldn't go back to my apartment, so I had to find another home. I was on autopilot and my soul was telling me to go back to what I know. The rolling hills and the craggy outcrops that, in the darkness, look like monsters. The dark purple moorland that I am sure is the colour of my heart on the inside. The smell of the mint my grandfather let grow wild across the end of his garden. The sound of beating wings and scuttling feet with every footstep through the brittle heather. So, I ran back home and hid away. I ran back to my former friends who I hoped would take me back. I made the cottage my home not by replicating my London heart, but by riding the tides of discomfort until one day it welcomed me.

I'd gradually begun to love it and its garden. I furnished it from instinct instead of choosing the matching pieces the rote of my mind told me to. Mustards and green, deep browns and burgundy, the colours of the countryside. I forced myself to get to know the neighbours and to shop in the village so that my home widened and eventually joined hands with the city. The resulting bridge had served me well. Still ever vigilant, I'd found a way I could be comfortable at the same time. I ran back to somewhere safe and secure, where I'd sprung from. Where I'd roamed the hills alone in my childhood and I knew. Knowing. Home. I'd roamed again with Kirby to reacquaint myself with the subconscious maps I'd built as a child, to connect with the steadfast trust of the never-changing landscape.

I toss and turn, trying to sleep and listen for the buzz of the comms phone all at once. There's a text from Salvador, Sal for short, an Italian chef I met a few months ago and I'd been out with a couple of times. I doze in and out of half sleep, thinking about a raven I rescued and helped to mend its broken leg. On the day I'd set it free, up on the black crags of Indian's Head, I'd realised what would happen to me one day. That I'd be an adult and free to fly like the raven. I'd watched it soar high above the hills and then disappear to the west.

I must have dreamt about Maisie and Tina, and them setting out across the moor on foot. Tina holding Maisie's hand tight and the heather snapping under their feet as they run faster and faster. Maisie looking back towards her parents' house and crying for her mummy. Amy and Marc reaching into the darkness and grabbing at the shadows as their daughter slips away from them. Then Kirby is running with them, looking back at me for her stick like she does when we're playing on the moors. They're ever running and when my dream changes perspective, it's me running. Running for my life. Tripping through the dust and cobwebs, birds scattering in front of me. I must have dreamt all this just before waking, because the first thought I had when I awoke was the remnants of a dream.

The second thought I had was much clearer. I know where Tina is going. I know where her desperate journey is taking her. She's going home.

CHAPTER TWENTY-ONE

I get up and dress. As I hurry to the shower room, I check both phones in case I've slept so deeply that I haven't heard them. Nothing. It's seven forty-five when I arrive in the SMIT suite room. The day shift has arrived and Steve is watching Keith's screen as he gives him a rundown on the search that took place last night. Lauren is sitting at her desk reading the case report and updating the files so that the Met has a two-way data conversation with us and we can learn about new developments quickly.

I nod in acknowledgement of several senior officers who have just met with Steve. He looks up as I hurry through the suite.

'Morning, Jan. Stay at Petra's, did you?'

I don't want to lie to him. But at the moment the fewer people who know about my sleeping arrangements the better. So, I throw him a curve ball.

'I've got an idea, Steve. We need to contact Tina. She's called us, but we haven't called her.'

Keith pulls up a log from the past two days. 'I've called her on the hour every hour between nine and six yesterday. Nada.'

They both look dead beat. Keith's desk is littered with Coke Zero cans. Caffeine to keep him awake. I expect he's been here all night.

'So, my theory is that she can't hear the phone. Not with that damn story on full blast through those earphones she always wears. She probably looks at her phone every now and again. She'll see the calls, but the moment's gone. So, I'll text her.'

Steve's face clouds with worry. 'On dangerous ground there, Jan. You know the directives on communications. Speak to them first.'

We're supposed to get any text we send by any means cleared first to make sure it doesn't break any entrapment rules, especially if the recipient is vulnerable. So, we usually don't bother.

'But I'm just going to offer her help. A way to put things right. She wants to make contact otherwise she wouldn't have phoned.'

He thinks for a moment. He has to consider all the options. 'Unless she's taking the piss. Silent phone calls. She could be just making us sweat.'

He's right. Tina could be on the edge of her nerves, waiting for the right time to blow up the car or hurt Maisie. But my gut feeling tells me that she isn't. Keith intervenes.

'But if she's listening to the story on the car's CD player then she'd hear the call. Maybe she just doesn't want to answer.'

Again, a good point. She may just like to be in control. This could be what it's all about, the need to be in charge. But again, I doubt it. Her life has slipped too far the other way, where she has dissolved so far into her situation that she is grasping onto who she is by a hair's breadth.

'Or she may be listening on a portable CD player. Mmm.

Let me try. We need a way to directly appeal to her, get her to trust me.'

It's a dangerous scenario. She's so volatile that any mistake could cost us the case, and Maisie. Steve's right to be cautious, but I don't see what options we have. To me, it's all about getting on a one-to-one basis with Tina, making her feel like I care and that she can talk to me. I've had all the negotiation training. We all have. But it's more than that. It's about the words you say and the control in your voice. Too much and the perpetrator will immediately sense that it's a set-up. Too little and they'll know you're trying to be their best mate.

In my experience it's better to try to be as truthful as possible. No massive false promises that are going to seem outlandish, although this route is sometimes tempting when a case looks desperate. No over-friendly banter. It's not lulling the perp into a sense of false security, it's making them think that you don't mean what you say and, consequently, they discount it. All the calls are recorded and anyone who's negotiating knows that any hint of entrapment could affect the final outcome of the case. We can make bargains, but we can't push them too far.

We're taking a big risk with Tina because the situation is so unpredictable. By talking to her we could alienate her even more. Her hatred of the police and most other forms of authority are more than evident in the intelligence pictures and the last thing I want to do is build on that until she feels like she's trapped. Or desperate. If I push her and push her, she might begin to feel cornered. And that's when people make rash decisions. When they can see no other way out. But what choice do we have?

The only way I can see to handle this is to open a line of communication and talk to her about what's going on. Open and honest. Point out that she has options. Try to show her that harming Maisie will make it worse for her in the long term. And if it gets critical, where Tina sees no long term for herself, revert to Steve's original plan. But we'll only know all this by talking to her. Steve nods his agreement. I type out a text message on the comms phone and show it to him.

> Tina, it's Jan here. You called me yesterday.
> Look, I can help you sort this out. Just you and
> me. Call me x

He stares at it for a long second. He shifts from foot to foot a few times then nods again. I can tell that his entire police career is passing before his eyes. I've had moments when I know what a split-second decision can cost. It nearly cost me everything. But if I'm right on this one it could help me get some dialogue with Tina. Help me to get her to at least drop Maisie somewhere unharmed. We all hesitate for a little longer, then I press send.

In fifteen minutes, a read receipt flashes onto the phone. We'd all sat in silence. Waiting for a call. Now at least we knew that she has read the message.

'Still the same position. Up between the Lewises and Uppermill. Possibly Denshaw.'

I scour my memory for all the places that she could be hiding, but there are so many. Boat sheds on the side of the reservoirs, ruins of ancient farmhouses, hidden from the roads. Shelters built for cattle and sheep. High dry-stone walls, built to stop the land slipping, half toppled, but enough left to hide a car behind. We'd looked at the same cameras at the same junctions as when Maisie first went missing until they ran out on the unlit high peak crossings.

She knows we're looking for her, so she's kept to the narrow lanes. Some of them would be only just wide enough to pass in the big silver Range Rover, but she would have known to slow down and negotiate the width and the turns. High up there, dirt tracks and lanes lead to old houses that could only be seen from the air basking in the mist settling in dips. So beautiful and surprising to see as you top the brink of a hill. But for Tina, the perfect hidey hole. I think about the gap in the calls and the time before she read the text. She would have to find phone reception.

Keith is setting up an earphone feed in case a member of the team observes anything in the conversation or needs to direct me. I smile. He believes in me. He believes that Tina will call.

I wonder how Kerry is, if she and Pete have met their baby yet. I wish I'd been there, but it's an impossible situation. I think about Jean and Graham and how they would have fussed over the officer sent to sit with them. How that officer would have been itching to go over to my house and see if my pursuers were there. Chances are that they've left someone there and returned here. Someone hiding in my bedroom. Waiting for me to come home from work, all unsuspecting, or behind the back door. While they watch for me here.

I watch for a while, certain that they will appear on the road where they were parked yesterday, but nothing as yet. I pace up and down, waiting, waiting. Steve calls Marc Lewis to update him and I watch as he waves his arms about, trying to explain why we haven't found Maisie and how Marc's company can't fund a twenty-four-hour helicopter search. When the call ends, he comes over.

'It's getting critical up there now. Marc Lewis is starting to think about taking action. It's only a matter of time before this gets out.'

It's a constant worry that people involved in the case take matters into their own hands. Marc's a powerful man and I realised right from the first moment I spoke to him that the calm exterior held in a calculating mind, which even under the extreme trauma of his daughter being abducted, would work out routes to solve the situation.

'Who could blame him? It's horrendous. He's under a lot of pressure. And we can't really stop him talking to people.'

We both know what that means. We'll have lost control of the case and Marc will just pay any ransom demanded, thinking that it will get Maisie back. Unfortunately, it's rarely that simple. They just demand more time, more money and when their demands aren't met, kill their detainee anyway. We go through the daily newspapers, thick with accusation about unknown car man. They've already been scanned for any reference to the explosives or Magellan. There are a few snapshots of Lauren, but thankfully, none of me. Although it might have been better if a few had appeared. This way it looks like I've run away. But nothing could be farther from the truth.

The comms phone rings at ten forty-seven. It buzzes against my chest and makes me jump. I pull it out and back into a side room so the echo from the broadcast of the call can't be heard. On the third ring, and Keith's signal, I answer.

'Hi. This is Jan. Is that Tina?'

I can hear birds in the background. A few seconds pass and I start to think that this is going to be another silent call, a taunt. But eventually she speaks.

'Yeah. It's Tina.'

'Good to speak to you. You okay?'

I hear a rustle and a sob.

'Not really.'

'Right. Do you want to tell me a bit about what's wrong?'

She's definitely crying. I can hear it in her voice. Like Glen said, she speaks with a northern accent, too Manchester for Lancashire. Lower vowels than Steve, closer to my own twang.

'Is this just you or is half the fucking police force listening in?'

I stare out at the completely silent SMIT suite. I hate lying. But in this case, it's necessary.

'Just me, Tina. Just me. I can help you.'

I hear twigs breaking under her feet. She's outside and walking.

'Where's Jennifer? Is she okay?'

I panic a little. More lies.

'Your mum's looking after her. She's fine. What about Maisie? Is she okay?'

Trade an answer for an answer.

'Yeah. I suppose.'

'Where is she, Tina? Where's Maisie?'

More sobs.

'In the car. She's in the car. I needed to get some time alone. I can't stand it.'

'What? What can't you stand?'

'That feeling. Like you can't do owt for 'em. Screaming. Screaming. So, I went to the woods for a bit, you know, to phone you and see what I can do. I never fucking wanted this, you know.'

I look at Steve. I see the relief wash over him. At least she's saying that none of this was intentional. None of it was Magellan. It's personal.

'Okay. Tell me what happened. As you can imagine, Tina, we know part of what's happened. The doll messages and Maisie. Why did you take Maisie? That's what I don't get.'

She's sobbing hard now. And running. Her heavy breath resounds through the SMIT suite.

'I went to see him. Glen. I was going to ask him to look after Jennifer while I got me head sorted but he was with that Jane. My car was broke and he wouldn't give me any money so I took the car keys. I knew what he was going to do. I knew what they were planning. So, I warned 'em. All of 'em. Then when I got to that big house on the tops, I took Jennifer and I was going to leave her there.'

I feel my stomach turn over. Leave Jennifer there?

'So, you were going to leave Jennifer there?'

'Yeah. Posh like, so she'd be looked after.' More sobs, then her voice raises several decibels. 'Because I can't do that, can I? I can't look after her. Not on my own. When she starts crying, I can't stop her. I can't touch her sometimes. I just want to run away from her. But she's my baby and I miss her.'

Alarm bells are ringing loud and clear for me now. Leave Jennifer? Only someone desperate and not thinking clearly would resort to this. Tina's an intelligent girl. If she was thinking clearly, she would know that the Lewises, no matter how wealthy they were, couldn't just 'look after' Jennifer. It isn't that simple. Unless you are at the end of your tether and need a quick solution to tell yourself. She's sobbing loudly and needs a break. And I need to change her direction back to Maisie.

'Is that how you feel, Tina? But Jennifer's well looked after. Anyone can see that.'

'What's wrong with me? I can't be like other mums. I can't be happy. All I want is the night and Glen and my life in London. He gave me all this shit about being there for me and I bought a load of baby clothes with his drug money. My daughter was going to have the best. But it didn't stop her crying, did it?'

Her heart is breaking and I feel for her. I know only too well what it's like to want your old life back. But I need her to talk about Maisie.

'But how did you come to have Maisie?'

She calms a little. I hope beyond hope that I've engaged her, gained her trust.

'I was going to leave Jennifer in a bedroom, and then the kid woke up. The little girl. She started to cry, and I lost my bottle. That's right. I can't even get leaving my own kid right. So, I picked her up and before I knew it, I was in the car. Then driving off. Two crying babies. So, I blocked it out. If I don't, I can't stand it.'

It doesn't seem like she wants to hurt Maisie. I take a deep breath.

'Tina. Maisie's parents love her. They'd like to have her home...'

'No... I know what you bastards are like. I've seen you in fucking action. You know my background. Magellan. You know. And I've seen what you do to people like me.'

'Tina, wait. What if I could promise you safety? If you just leave Maisie in an agreed place, or I'll meet you on my own.'

She's thinking. I try again.

'Her mum and dad are heartbroken, Tina. You could just hand her over and then you're free to go.'

I hear Steve's voice in my ear and look up. 'The car. Ask her if she knows what's in the car.'

'Besides, it's dangerous driving around in that car. Come on, Tina. It's over. This can't go on indefinitely.'

She snorts and laughs loudly. 'No, it can't. I never meant it to go on indefinitely. It has to have an end, doesn't it? And what's left for me? Where do I fit into it all? I'm nowhere. No one.'

'So, what's your plan, Tina? You obviously know why it's dangerous, yes?'

She chokes and coughs and catches her breath now. I hear water in the distance and a bird calling loudly.

'Of course I fucking know. I know all about what's in that car. I know what Glen was going to do with it, because it was my idea. Before I actually gave a shit about anything. Blow up a few shops, a few rich fucking Mancunians. Collateral damage. Who cares? Kidnap a few kids. All for a good cause. Until I first set eyes on Jennifer. Then it all changes. Then I can see how fucking stupid it all is. How futile and it'll change nothing. And how it's all about Jennifer. And how she doesn't like me. How she likes Glen, laughing with him. Gurgling. Then sleeping next to him. He wouldn't have done it, you know. He hasn't got the balls. But I had to be sure.'

'But you ended up taking one of the kids. And you can put that right.'

She's crying again. She's really up and down and that worries me.

'But I won't see Jennifer, will I?'

I can't promise her that. I just can't. She sniffles some more and begins running again, branches snapping around her. I watch as Keith scans the maps for possible locations and issues direction to waiting patrols. When I don't answer she speaks again.

'No. Thought not. This is a fucking mess. But it's best for her I'm gone.'

'What do you mean, Tina? Gone? Just bring Maisie to me and we'll sort something out. I promise.'

She's silent for a long time and I can hear the sound of passing cars in the distance. Then the line goes dead.

CHAPTER TWENTY-TWO

I rush into the SMIT suite. I need to get Tina back on the line.

'Keith, get her back. Get her back now.'

The call connects and the tone rings out in the silence. The whole operational staff listen as it rings and rings. He cuts it off and tries again. Steve paces around, stopping only to look over Keith's shoulder. It rings and rings again and then she cuts it off.

Suddenly there's a loud ping and I feel the comms phone buzz in my hand. A text message flashes onto the screen and we all stare at it.

> Meet me at The Summit in an hour. On your
> own. No police. I'll drop the kid off with you.

We all stare at the screen for a moment longer. I jump up and my eyes meet Lauren's. We run for the door, Steve just behind us. I race down the stairs towards the front doors, but Steve grabs my arm and swings me around.

'Wait. Wait a minute. We need a plan. And you need to be careful.'

I pull myself free. I've never liked to be held down.

'No. We just need to get to Saddleworth. You go up in the ops car with the backup. Lauren will drive me up there. She'll drop me off at the bottom of the road. You stay at the Lewises' and I'll keep you informed via Keith.'

We're nose to nose and he's not giving up.

'It's risky. You going on your own.'

'Well, I *am* going on my own. It's our only chance. God knows what she'll do if we don't do this.' It's a stand-off and I know what the deal breaker is. 'And Steve, promise me you won't get them to intercept her. Think about Maisie first. This way we'll get Maisie first and Tina and the car later.'

I turn and hurry out to Lauren's car. I glance up the road and the BMW's back. But there's no time for lying on back seats now. No time for sneaking around. Lauren speeds up the road and as we pass the black car, I try to peer through the windows to see the shady figures inside. Lauren indicates right to take the Oldham Road and I look over my shoulder. They aren't following.

Once in Saddleworth, Steve and the others turn off at Greenfield and head towards the Lewises'. Lauren and I carry on through until we're climbing. Up and up, almost into the dense clouds that hang over the hilltops. I know that it'll be easy to apprehend Tina afterward because there is one way here and one way out. Once she travels this road and reaches the highest point in the area, she has to continue on the same road, or turn round and go back.

I look up and down the road and I fully expect that, by now, Steve has someone at each end. The problem is that they would be quite distant, as The Summit has a panoramic view. Tina would be able to see anyone waiting nearby from this point. I get out of the car and look around. Lauren sits in the car, gripping the wheel. I expect her to drive off, but she gets out.

'Funny place to meet.'

I lean on the dry-stone wall. Not such a funny place if you know the area. It's a vantage point, almost a tourist attraction, and the road is reasonably busy. A few cars have passed us already. High up so you can see everything. Yet not remote enough to be ambushed. It makes me think that maybe Tina does want to escape. Everything she said in the phone conversation pointed to someone so unhappy and desperate that they want an end to it. I have a sudden uncomfortable feeling. She's mixed up. A little bit out of control. Telling us that she took Maisie and found herself in the car. Unreliable. Unbalanced.

'Mmm. Let's see. You go back now. She won't come up here unless she's sure that I'm here alone.' Lauren looks sad. She's staring at her shoes. 'What? What, Lauren?'

She steps forward and for a minute I think she's going to hug me. 'I feel bad leaving you here. You know, with what's going on. You're a sitting target, all on your own.'

'Don't worry. It'll all work out.'

She touches my arm and then she does hug me. I smell a faint scent of her perfume and hair products. I suddenly miss my bathroom and my morning routine. When she lets go, she walks to the car and drives back down the road.

What I was going to say to her was that it will all work out the way it's meant to. But that sounds too fatalistic. She knows as well as I do that I'll fight to the death. We all would. I've worked with the SMIT team long enough now to know that although we have our differences, we have a lot in common. The main thing is commitment. Commitment to a case. Commitment to each other. Even with my life at risk, I couldn't even think about ducking out. In every case each team member carries a burden of trust, and someone leaving would be a chink in the armour. So even in my situation, even though they'd all understand, I'm going nowhere.

My situation isn't about fighting so much as about waiting. It's a battle of attrition. All about them taking opportunities when they can. About being undetected, yet everyone being perfectly clear about what they are capable of. It's the opposite of Magellan and their almost exhibitionist behaviour. That's real terror. The unknown.

So, I wait. I pull myself up onto the wall and watch a peregrine falcon hunting in a field below me. I'm so high up, about four hundred metres above sea level, the falcon hovers almost level with me. In the distance, I can see the moorland for miles and miles, shrouded in grey clouds, sometimes dipping into the valleys. Despite the dullness and the endless bracken and heather, every now and again there is an outcrop of bright yellow furze or the whites and blues of wildflowers. I've been up here at this time of year for most of my life, and the wildlife is staggering.

Even when I lived in London, I would drive up here in the summer. I'd pretend that I was going somewhere, that this was a convenient route for me to follow. I'd travel through different areas of Britain and pretend that their lush greenness and breath-taking scenery was a substitute for the moody bleakness of my moors. It's hard to describe the appeal of the acres of marshes and scrub. It's a corner of myself, hiding away in the recess of my soul. Embedded in my dreamscape so that everything subconscious takes place here and is connected. I'd drive from London telling myself all the way that it was the outlines of the hills and dips of the valleys I wanted. That it was the familiar roads and pathways that my childhood feet had walked over.

Underneath, I suspected that it was something much more intangible. Like all children I'd spun my own stories around my local environment. The old woman who might or might not have been a witch. The garland of flowers left hanging in a tree

– innocent enough, but somewhere inside I knew that it meant more than this. The rose petals I picked from my grandfather's garden because, to me, they were perfect, but when he scolded me, I learned early the meaning of being ready. I still remember their perfume to this day. The robin that came each day to see my mother and I, and the idea he was my grandfather's spirit. Deep-rooted symbols that left an imprint on my being, and connected me back to the half-light of the evening as I sat on the wall at the back of our house watching the swallows.

But in reality, I was coming back for the love. It was as if as I drove out of Oldham and the red brick turned to stone, I could sense the comfort of my childhood hanging over me. The nearer to my childhood home and haunts I got, the stronger the sense of love and care. Even though those people are long gone, my mother and father long dead and my grandparents before them, it's as if everything they ever felt about me has been left here in layers.

And it isn't just the people. I can understand why Tina came back here with Jennifer. She probably knew that her mother wouldn't be entirely present for her. But she came back all the same, just as I did. Either of us could have gone anywhere in the whole world, but we came back here, where we had been children and run free across the moorland. Standing here now, I get a sense of myself as a young teenager, walking for miles across the desolate spaces, ducking behind walls as cars passed me on the narrow roads.

I just wanted to be alone. I suppose that's never left me. Any relationships I've had have either fizzled out or ended dramatically, for them anyway, because I have just carried on in the isolated world I made for myself and preserved, despite being with someone. I'd always hoped that one day I'd find someone to smash that shell, to make me want to stay with them.

To run to their love and care instead of hurrying back here to the layers of my past.

I nearly did find it. But in the end, it was the same betrayal, the same unbalanced amount of give and take with me doing all the giving. In this case, the ultimate giving. At one point I thought I'd found a whole island of love, someone who cared, but I was wrong. So, I stayed in my shell and it's not so bad.

I look up and down the road. No sign of her yet. It might be a long wait, but I'm used to it. If I'm honest with myself, leaving London was never an answer to my dilemma. The Lando case never really went away, it just simmered in the distance until the time was right. I don't think it ever will go away. I'm shocked at this admission to myself, yet I know in my heart it's more of a matter of managing it. I'll never be free. I'll always be waiting for someone to jump out of the shadows when I least expect it, when I'm distracted or laughing or drunk. That's when they'll strike.

I kick up the dust at the side of the road and walk a few yards. I can see my childhood home, Uppermill, from here. It's huddled around a crossroads, the older part of the village at the edge of the road with the newer, more luxurious homes built for Manchester commuters set farther back. I've stood up here on Saturday nights with various boyfriends looking down at the lights of the villages, sitting in between the hills like a string of Christmas lights, with the brighter lights of Oldham and Manchester in the distance.

There's very little light pollution up here and even prettier than the twinkles that people make are the stars above us. I've lost count of the times I've walked up here, most recently with Kirby, and stared in wonder at the Milky Way. It's a real leveller to see it all from this height, because you really feel like you can touch heaven. I wonder if Tina had experienced all this, just the same as I have. She knows this point well, so sure of it, or she wouldn't have arranged to meet here.

I wonder if she'd ever laid on her back in the bracken and the moss, ignoring the insects and birds and stared at the sky. If she'd swum naked in the reservoirs, thinking that your heart will stop because it's so cold. If she'd watched the lambs in spring and sworn never to eat lamb again. If she'd rescued the baby animals and kept them secretly in the back shed until they were well enough to let go. If she had any love layers to come back to. If she really has the bottle to kill herself, because if she has, we're in trouble.

I already know she's in a bad way. Blaming herself for wanting her old life back. Thinking that she's a bad mother. Feelings of hopelessness and desperation so bad that she's already left her daughter, because she thought she would have a better chance without her. I feel sorry for her. Sorry that no one noticed how she was feeling. Sorry that she couldn't tell anyone, not even her mother. Sorry that she considered leaving her child with Glen Wright. Sorry that she's so messed up that she doesn't know which way to turn.

If she drops Maisie with me now and co-operates, there's a chance that she'll get some treatment for the post-natal depression. She'll be referred for mental health reports and my case notes will flag it up. It's a terrible thing, and so common. Like most kinds of depression, it's hard for people to report because you don't realise you've got it. Your world slowly sinks into darkness and the warped thoughts and desperation become normalised.

By Tina's own admission she'd regretted having Jennifer. Yet by her own admission she loved her and was prepared to make a go of it with Glen. Even without the depression her life would be difficult. She was making an enormous but unplanned leap from front-line activist to mother. From coked-up lover to sleepless nights with a crying baby. But she'd done it for love. She'd even moved Jennifer away from Glen to try to bring her up on her own. But it would have been an uphill struggle in a life she was unprepared for.

It's sad, but the courts won't see it like this. Her background will be dredged up and she'll be pushed into a single-parent-on-drugs stereotype. And her part in Magellan. Tina knows only too well what will happen. She knows that all this, as well as abducting Maisie, will cost her Jennifer. She knows this and she's trying to put it right by meeting me and dropping Maisie off. As much as I'm trying to gain her trust, she's trying to gain mine. But I've got a bad feeling about this. I don't know if it's the obsession with the dolls or the way she's so unpredictable. The way she scrubbed her flat down as if she wasn't coming back. How she left her own child, but not Maisie. Is that because she loves Jennifer and now love is all that matters? But she doesn't love Maisie. She doesn't even know her. And all this depends on how far gone she is; how much affect her condition having on her.

I look at my phone. It's just coming up to the hour. A few cars have passed me and I wonder if Steve's got people driving backwards and forwards up and down the road. I calculate that it would take about fifteen minutes to drive the full length before reaching a turnoff that wouldn't be seen from up here, and turning around. Depending on where she's coming from, I'll be able to see the silver Range Rover long before she got here. I look down the road towards the Lewises' property. Steve would have told them what was happening. He has a policy of keeping all parties informed; that way they don't go off and seek information on their own.

Amy and Marc have coped so well, been so co-operative. I shudder to think what I would be like in their shoes. I can picture Steve pacing around for ages at the house, waiting for my intelligence. Lauren would be sitting perfectly still, poker-faced on the outside, but as I'm coming to know her better, seething inside. She's got a lot of stray feelings to tame before she's top of her game. And Marc and Amy. Out of their minds with the terror they feel. Having to survive whilst every minute the underlying river of fear eats away at them.

It's an hour now. I look down the road again. And up. Maybe she'll come from the Huddersfield Road. Maybe she was hiding on that side, up by the abandoned farmhouses that dot the desolate area as the A635 winds out of Lancashire and into Yorkshire. Nothing. I can't even see any cars coming either way now and I vaguely wonder if there's a roadblock in place. I'm debating whether to ring Steve and ask him when the comms phone rings. It's Tina.

CHAPTER TWENTY-THREE

I let it ring three times before I answer it to give Keith a chance to activate the trace. I'm heady and a little bit giddy with the fresh air and the cold breeze numbs the bridge of my nose.

'Tina, nearly here, are you?' Silence. Well, almost silence. I can hear muffled noises in the background mixed with a baby crying and Tina's sobs. 'Tina, I'm up at The Summit now waiting for you to drop Maisie off. I'm on my own.'

She coughs and clears her throat. 'Liar.'

My mind races to the surrounding roads. I swing around the panoramic view. Had Steve done something I didn't know about? Has she seen a cordon or a line of police cars waiting to snare her?

'Sorry, Tina? I don't know what you mean. I'm up here at The Sum—'

She suddenly screams. 'Liar. Liar. You're all liars. This isn't how it's supposed to be.'

I need to get her to talk. My personal phone beeps and I read the message from Keith.

No movement. Same place, somewhere between Greenfield and Scouthead.

I text him back with my free hand.

Get a car up here. She's not coming.

'What isn't, Tina? Look, you can trust me. You can tell me what's going on. It's between me and you. But you need to give Maisie back. Please, Tina, she wants her mum.'

She's crying hard now, sobbing. 'And what about me? And Jennifer? Jennifer needs her mum, too.'

I have to lie to her. It's not my style, but I've got an ever-growing bad feeling about this.

'And as soon as this is over Jennifer will see you, won't she? Look, Tina, something's gone wrong here. Something's gone wrong. You're not well, Tina, otherwise you would never have taken Maisie, would you?'

She's quiet for a moment and I can hear the music again. And Maisie.

'I would. I planned it, didn't I? But it's different now.'

'Yes, different. You didn't mean to take her. It's because you're out of sorts. You know, it can happen to some women when they've had a baby.'

She snorts loudly. 'Baby? Jennifer's one.'

'Yes. And it's been getting worse, hasn't it? Been feeling worse, have you, Tina? Until you didn't know what you were doing?'

She starts to laugh. It grates against me. It's not even a manic laugh. It's someone who is at the very end of their tether and they don't know whether to laugh or cry.

'Yeah. I suppose it has affected me. But you know, I was a bitch before I had Jennifer. A real evil bitch. I planned to blow things up, you know. And I was going to take one of their children. I was. So, don't hang all this on some poor Tina story. I know what you're like. You're just one of them, trying to make me think I'm off my head, so you can just catch me and throw me in prison. I know that's the fucking endgame here. What did you say your name was? Jan? Jan Pearce? I know who you are. I fucking know who you are. You worked for the Met.'

'I did. But that doesn't mean anything now. I'm trying to help you, Tina. Here and now. I'm standing here on my own at The Summit waiting for you.'

She's laughing louder. I can feel my blood pumping hard as I try to control my voice.

'Good. Wait up there. I bet you've got everyone in place, haven't you? To trap the mad girl with the kid? To make sure you get the kid and the chems but who gives a fuck about what happens to me?'

I can't help it. I've always wondered what makes people do it. What makes them do extreme things? I'm always looking for the reason why people have done things, the rationale. The human. But Tina's said it herself. She was always going to make a bomb. It's just that now her love for her daughter had got in the way. She's like every other person who decides that they will, for whatever reason, take out another person, or people, to make a point, to highlight their cause. But it's deeper than that. What I want to know is why Tina herself wanted to do it. Why does someone strap a suicide bomb to themselves? Why would Tina drive around in a car full of explosives? Not from the Magellan perspective, the plans, the group think. But from her point of view. I can't help it. I have to ask.

'Why, Tina?'

'Why what?'

'Why did you want to make a bomb? Why? What made you do it?'

There's a long silence and my personal mobile rings. I know it will be Steve or Keith telling me to lay off. I cancel the call quickly.

'Magellan. Glen and I. Glen's a chemist and he knew what to get. He knew how to make it. We were going to do it together. Hit them where it hurts. In the pocket. Those businesses are worth billions.'

'But what about the people, Tina? And what about you? You must have known you couldn't get away with it.'

'Yeah. The people. We would have warned them first. Course we would. We had it all planned. And I didn't care back then. But like I said. Jennifer. And I couldn't do it now, anyway. I had her, didn't I? And what would she do without me?' She's sobbing again and I wonder if I've pushed her too far. 'But Glen would. He said he was still going to do it. He didn't care about Jennifer, about what would happen if... well, not if, when. Let's just say he wasn't going to leave the car outside. We weren't. We were going to... to...'

'It's okay, Tina. It's okay. None of that's going to happen now, is it?'

'I did it because of me. Because of who I am. Was? Started off as just some kid from a broken home living in London, but then when I got more into it and met Glen it was a competition. Us against them. The big corps. And it seemed like the right thing to do. Sacrifice myself 'cos who am I, anyway? Just some girl. Glen didn't even want me really. Wanted an open relationship. And when I couldn't do the drugs and the rallies he dropped me like a brick. I nearly did it then.'

'What? What did you nearly do?'

'Drove the car up north and did it. Took the plant out. And me.'

'Was that the plan, Tina? But you didn't, and that means

something, doesn't it? So, the chemicals have been there all that time? In the car? Outside Glen's house?'

'Yeah. Well, not all of them. We weren't going to use a lot at first, but Glen kept buying them bit by bit and eventually, well. Still, the more the better. For me, now, anyways. Not that any of you give a shit about me. All you want is the kid.'

'I do, Tina. I genuinely do. I want everyone to come safely out of this. Maisie's parents want their daughter back. You and Jennifer–'

'My little doll. She's my little doll.'

I focus now. Something in her voice alerts me.

'Dolls. You like dolls, don't you? I saw the ones you made. The ones you cut out and wrote messages on. Did you use a template?'

She's holding the phone close to her mouth and I can hear every breath. There's a long pause. Then she laughs again.

'No. It's in my head. The shape's in my head.'

Imprinted. I was right. I play it cool.

'Right. I'm a fan of birds myself. I always buy tea towels with birds on them, because my granddad had an aviary. I used to talk to the birds.'

I look down the road. Lauren's car is in the distance, speeding over the hill.

'And did they listen?'

'I don't know. Maybe they did?'

'My doll listened. Whenever I had a problem or Mum and Dad were fighting I'd go and talk to her. Tell her everything. Most of the time it was the only place in the world I wanted to be.'

'Is that why you're here, Tina? To find your doll?'

She laughs again. The sound smashes against a little girl shouting for her mummy and I'm finding it hard to keep my patience. But I must.

'I don't have to find her. She's right here. I'm here with her. Like I said, I always come here. But she's not much help now. No answers today.'

None of it makes any sense. I can't for the life of me think of any dolls in Saddleworth. Not even a toyshop. 'Where are you, Tina? I can come there if you want. To fetch Maisie. Then you can talk. I'll listen to you.'

She starts to cry. 'But it's too late, isn't it? Even if I get Jennifer back it'll be the same. I'll still feel numb and keep crying and she won't sleep. It's just not meant to be. So, what's the point of me? Eh? Jan? You're the one with all the answers. What's the point of me?'

Lauren arrives and gets out of the car. She slams the door loudly and Tina hears it. I back away from Lauren slowly.

'I thought you said you were there on your own. I just heard a car door slam. Away from you. You're not on your own, are you? You're a liar, just like everyone else.'

'Tina, please, just tell us where you are and I'll come and help you.'

She's hysterical. I can hear her heavy breath and the pounding of her feet. She's running again and the noise fades into the distance.

'It's too late now. Too late. I can't keep this up anymore. It's better like this.'

She ends the call. I lean against the dry-stone wall, suddenly exhausted. Lauren looks over into the ravine to the left of us, down to the craggy rocks at the bottom. Only two things in the conversation remain with me, the doll and the end. I close my eyes and breathe in the damp air. Right from the start of this I've known that doll shape. I wrack my brains to find it in my memories of the area, but it's just not there.

I know that Keith has scoured the internet and local officers have been asked about it, but not one person has any recollection of anything to do with dolls around here. But Tina had said that she's right here. Lauren interrupts my thoughts.

'Steve's organising a search of the area now. I think he's given up on this line. He's properly pissed off.'

'Me too. But I suppose it was a long shot.'

I get back into the car and Lauren drives up back along the road until we reach a turnoff.

'Just pull in here, Lauren.'

I need to think. She gets out of the car and lights a cigarette, which surprises me because I never imagined that she smoked. I can still hear *The Red Shoes*, over and over again, on repeat in my head with Tina's and Maisie's cries echoing through me. My head hurts and I touch the scar hidden deep in my hair. I need to think fast.

What would I do? If I was coming back here full of fear and I was cornered with no support, what would I do? This is where Tina and I are different. I have a support network, albeit a little shaky in the form of Kerry and some old acquaintances, and shakier still now with Kerry giving birth without me being there as I promised. But I had them and my job to haul me out of the mire. I'd do exactly what I did, come home. Back to the place I lived as a child. Tina's mother said she'd grown up in Uppermill. Behind Dovestones Reservoir. The area around the farmhouse has been searched extensively in the past couple of days but it might be worth another look.

I need to reach down into myself now, to put myself in Tina's shoes. God knows I've been angry like her, demented with desperation, and that's why I can do this now. That's why I can mould my thinking into hers, here, in the place she's come home to. Blind searching hasn't helped; we've had half the Greater Manchester Police force out looking and no one has stumbled across her. But she's somewhere around here, somewhere close.

We get in the car and I tell Lauren where to go. When we arrive, I see the farmhouse where Tina used to live, just as I had pictured it. Nothing changes much around here, particularly this far out. Lauren waits in the car as I walk around it and sit on the wall at the side of a huge pine forest. So, this is where she would hang out as a child. The other side of the narrow lane was a high dry-stone wall. Unlikely that she would go that way to roam on her own, as her mother put it.

There's no obvious pathway into the pine forest as far as I can see, but she could have easily climbed over the wall and, once over, she would have had run off into the huge forest and, in the centre, the reservoir. I'm split between exploring further or going into the village and asking everyone I see if they know anything about dolls or have seen the Range Rover. Or Tina. Although I'm fully aware that, at this exact moment, Steve and Keith will have arranged for resources to do just that. No. My job is to home in, to find out where Tina is. She's somewhere nearby and I need to find her quickly, quicker than a search team.

So, I focus. I summon up the blood. I blank out everything else and test my instincts. The doll. It's where she goes when she is alone. Dolls. I didn't need to phone Cat or ask Petra what dolls mean. A doll is a confidant. Keeps you safe from harm. You're never alone when you've got a doll. I imagine Tina rushing out of the turmoil-ridden farmhouse to escape her parents and running towards the only place she felt safe. Running through the pine forest – she would have known every step like I know all the moorland around my childhood home – and she would still know it now. Those things never fade.

Her own personal doll. A friend when she had no one. Something she could depend on, cling to when times were bad. Something good. By all accounts Tina was a handful her whole life. Maybe she's always thought that she was less than, a little bad, and the doll represents her good side. Tina hasn't had a good life. I was solitary by choice and I still am. Tina was forced away by her parents' domestic situation, and then pulled away from the place she loved, and her doll, to the other side of Manchester.

But her heart was here, and it's here she's returned. When people are stressed and isolated, they revert to coping strategies they have used before. At a previous desperate time in her life, Tina wore her red shoes and went to her doll and told her all her fears. Now she's back. She knows she's always there for her. They're with you always. This doll has certainly been with Tina all her life. Listening to her, at the forefront of her mind. She'd drawn it and made paper chains. Decorated her house with it. How would she have first found it? And why does no one else know about it? Is it hidden? Is it a doll at all? Or is it part of something else?

CHAPTER TWENTY-FOUR

I hurry back to the car, shouting to Lauren.

'We need to go into Uppermill. To the visitor centre.'

She puts a blue light on the top of her car and in minutes we're there. I push past a couple of hikers and Lauren shows her warrant card. I skip the exhibitions of local flora and fauna and go straight for the old photographs. I scan each one quickly and Lauren asks people if they know of any local toy shops. I'm about halfway round when Steve calls.

'Jan, any luck? Steve patched me in on the conversation between you and Tina. Do you think...?'

'Yes. I do think. My professional opinion is that she's highly volatile and capable of anything. I'm in Uppermill now trying to find out what that doll is. Or symbolises. But to be honest I'm hitting a wall. We're down to looking at photos in a museum now. No one's heard of it or seen it or anything remotely like it. But she grew up round here and I'm certain it's somewhere around where she used to hang out. It's somewhere around the Dovestone area.'

Steve's silent for a minute. 'Bloody hell. That's acres. We've been over it dozens of times with the helicopter. I've got people searching areas leading off the roads all around the reservoir. But the trees are dense in some areas. The thing is, Jan, if she's near water with that pure sodium...'

I remember Petra's films of the effects of the ammonium sulphate and the pure sodium. Her repeated warnings about the combination of the chemicals. Her sad eyes following me when I last saw her, her concern for me.

'I know. I know. Look. You carry on with the searches and me and Lauren will try to pinpoint her. Let me know if you find anything at all.'

I go back to the pictures. Lots of old artefacts from times gone by but no dolls. Eventually we go outside. I text Tina's phone telling her to call me. I picture her running through the forest with tears streaming down her face while Maisie is strapped into the car with the story on a deafening loop. I'm lost. Undecided what to do next. Then I remind myself that it's only because I come from the same area as Tina that I feel so guilty. Other people on the case come from Uppermill. Even Petra, who lives on the other side of the village, can't make sense of it.

Lauren looks pale and despondent. She's worked hard on this case and none of it is paying off.

'Come on, Lauren. We've done our best. We need to leave it to the search teams now. Problem is, that forest is so big. She could have done something dreadful before they find her, or got away.'

'So, do you think she'd really do something like that?'

I look closely at her. This case is really getting to her. It's getting to everyone. I know that grown men in the operations room would be fighting back tears at Maisie's cries when the last call was relayed into the SMIT suite. We all know the bottom line and the closer we get to Tina, the worse it will be if we don't find her and something terrible happens.

From the first moment in Maisie's bedroom to right now, I've known that this was not what any of us originally thought it was. I didn't buy the organised crime campaign Steve suspected because it was so messy. The problem with investigating serious crime is that when something comes along that doesn't fit the box, we try to force it in. We started with an abducted little girl being held for ransom by a gang of activists who were driving around a bomb.

Now the scenario is very different. A troubled young woman, on the edge of her sanity through her situation and mental state, tried to put things right and made a terrible misguided mistake in her desperation. Spiralling ever downwards, she's now in a car full of water-explosive chemicals on the edge of a reservoir with a child she abducted by mistake. But she's asking for help, so there's still a chance.

Lauren lights another cigarette and I go to take one, but don't. Stay strong, Jan. What would you do? Follow Tina through every step. You need help but you've got no one to talk to. You're blind with desperation and not of this world through fear. People have let you down and you can't trust anyone. All you have are the depths of your own self and you're not even sure if you can trust them. Where would you go? What deity would you consult and beg for advice?

I've been there, awakened from forced sleep and suddenly all alone in a world where you thought you were supported. It dawned on me, like it will have dawned on Tina, that there is no one to help. In her case, no one to take Jennifer for a night while Tina got some sleep. No one to talk to about the problems you face. No one to tell you that you are doing a good job, regardless of a nagging demon inside that screams, 'Bad Mother!' No one to tell you that you are acting strangely, to see you never smile and cry all the time. With no audience it's hard to see yourself.

In my case, there's no one to advise me what to do next, no

sanity check, no reassurance that everything would be all right, because it wouldn't be and it still isn't. So, when I found myself without a home for the first time, temporarily living in a hotel in London with two weeks to make plans to get the hell out and strict instructions not to discuss my predicament with a living soul, who did I turn to? I turned back time and had an imaginary conversation with my grandfather. He was never the most talkative man when he was alive, but in my visualisation of him he provided a perfect foil for the dilemma I found myself in.

I managed to convince myself that there was goodness in the world, and that I would be okay. That I could do anything because when you've faced what I had, then there's only up. I just hope that's what Tina is doing now with her dolls. Making a deal with life that she'll carry on and face everything that is a consequence of this. But until then, it's a battle of wits between Tina with this desolate moorland as the battleground. A war to survive.

But what is this doll that no one knows about? What the hell is it? Again, I wonder if it could be something else that she thinks of as a doll. Symbolised. How has she driven to it? She can't be deep in the pine forest. It's far too dense to have driven to it. Yet she must be near it, because I heard her running through the trees, branches snapping under her feet. She's beside the forest. The huge fir tree plantation lies on the far side of the reservoir and that's where I had assumed she was, because it's accessible from the road. That's where everyone's been looking for her. But what if she'd driven across the moor? After all, no one was looking for her when she first arrived. What if she was on the other side?

The far side of the reservoir is mainly craggy rocks and has no roadway leading to it. There's a stone pathway that was built for hikers to get from one reservoir to another, but it's not wide enough to drive up. She could have driven across the moorland from the end of the sailing club entrance and hidden the car in the ravine beside a wide storm drain. There are huge overhanging rocks to shield her and she couldn't be seen from the road. At the watery end of the ravine is a small plantation of trees, paid for by people whose relatives have been cremated and have no headstone or memorial, but who want something to remember them by.

The plantation was built on the grounds of a huge now demolished Gothic mansion called Ashway House. I'd walked there as a child and seen it, and my father had told me that it had been the location for a filming of *The Hound of the Baskervilles*. He'd taken me out on the moor many times, and each time he'd told me stories of a mist descending and, if I ever stayed out here, how I could die of exposure. He was diagnosed with early onset dementia and he would repeat the same stories over and over again until I was the only person who would listen to him. But I loved walking with him and seeing the huge house that looked like a castle nestling between the rocks.

I clearly remember him bringing a picnic each time and showing me the house as if it were the first time. Then, years later, I was taken there every year with my school to do a play. The house had a ballroom, big enough for all the kids in the remote school to fit in and watch, spellbound, as the older children acted out Shakespeare and Roald Dahl.

Five years later, it was demolished as unsafe and he was gone. Most of it, anyway. I remember picking through the ruins and seeing scary gargoyles and figurines lying amongst the rubble. They'd stare up at me, dead-eyed and crumbling in the often-extreme weather.

I dial Keith quickly.

'Which primary school did Tina go to?'

He checked quickly. 'Roundhouse Primary. Uppermill.'

The same one as me. But she would have been in the year below me. I focus on the last year, when we performed *Romeo and Juliet* at Ashway House. I breathe in slowly and try to capture the conversation, the scenes afterwards. The posters that appeared just before I left primary school. The little girl on the posters, wrapped in a brown shawl and wearing clogs. The teachers rewriting the play with a happy ending. *The Red Shoes.*

I turn to Lauren, wide-eyed and suddenly excited by my realisation.

'I know where she is. I know where Tina is.'

She jumps up. 'Where is she? Ring through and tell Steve.'

'No. I'll do that when I'm sure. I'll direct you.'

We're hurrying to her car and she's annoyed.

'You mean you think you know?'

'No. I'm almost sure. But I want to be absolutely certain before we call in the troops. I want to try to resolve this myself without anything happening to Maisie. Tina's in a fragile state, and hundreds of police stampeding across the moor isn't going to help.'

I give her directions and she drives at breakneck speed until we reach the sailing club. Once out of the car, I point up to the gap in the rocks.

'She's up there.'

Lauren's eyes follow my finger up to the high rocks, on an incline across the moorland.

'With a car? I doubt it.'

'She is. She's driven across the moorland and into the gap between the rocks. There's a massive storm drain up there, an overflow from the reservoir above. It's quite sheltered up there, but she'll be able to see across most of the open land in front of her. So, we'll have to take the long way round.'

I look at Lauren's feet. Trainers today under her smart black trouser suit. I'm wearing my standard flat shoes and black trouser combination.

'Which is the long way round then? Naturally, I'll follow you.'

I point up to the rocks again. 'We'll follow the outline of the rocks along the bottom. It looks like there's an overhang and some small rocks that will shield us if she looks out. But we need to stay very close to the rock face.'

I look out over the horizon. Right in front of me is a rock formation that resembles an Indian's headdress if you turn your head sideways. There are a few dog walkers over by the sailing club and, on the other side of the water, a small group of windsurfers. Over on the forest side there's a walking group but they won't make it this far for a while yet. I try to judge the distance from the ravine to the edge of the water. Probably only about fifty feet. So, if she saw us coming she could drive the car into the reservoir with Maisie in it.

It's a risk. But it's one I have to take. If I can just reach her without being seen I've got a chance of rescuing Maisie.

'When we reach the end of the rocks keep down and we'll see what the situation is. If she's there, we'll phone Steve for backup and then approach her. Until then we need to turn our phones off.'

Lauren looks doubtful. 'No. What about control? They'll see our phones are turned off and think something has happened.'

'Okay. I'll text Keith first.'

She's still not happy. 'The thing is, Jan, I'm trained for this and my risk assessment is that we should wait for backup. You're not even supposed to be doing this.'

'Look, Lauren, I know it's risky but what choice do we have? Every second counts. We've already lost time searching in the wrong place. If we wait for backup we'll be too late. I just want to talk to her. That's what I'm trained to do. Negotiate. And she knows me. She knows what I've done before and I think I've begun to gain her trust. If we leave it and wait and she does anything...'

She doesn't really have any choice, except to go back. But she stays.

'Okay. But if she's armed...'

'She's got a car full of chemicals. I doubt if she'll have any firearms. Why would she? But agreed. If she's armed, we'll wait.'

I see the fear in her face. She's right. I'm not supposed to do this without agreement from Steve. But I've found myself in desperate situations so many times with people that I know the script. I know when to act and when to wait and what's borderline. It occurs to me that I might be influenced by my lack of fear in general, and my seemingly eternal optimism, but I can't stand by and watch. Yes, it's got me into deep trouble and nearly cost me my life but in this situation, like the others, a life is at stake. In this case a tiny life. A small girl whose parents are relying on me to rescue her. I promised them that I would do everything in my power to get her back and a promise is a promise. Ten, fifteen minutes waiting for operations and another twenty waiting for them to strategise, all the time in full view of Tina, could have fatal consequences.

So, I have no choice. We have no choice. I could offer Lauren the chance to wait here while I go on my own, but despite her protests she wouldn't take it. The reason she is here is because SMIT doesn't give up. Our team on the Met used to say 'there's no I in a team. Or hero'. While it was a different set-up, less planning and more winging it, it's the same idea. We get these difficult cases because they're difficult. Difficult cases, difficult decisions.

We switch our phones off and walk to the rocks. I touch their coolness and lean against them.

'Keep out of the heather. There are birds in there, lots of them, and if you walk near them they'll scatter and she'll know we're here. Same with the pollen. If you disturb the plants the pollen will rise and she'll see it. Lauren, if you don't want to do this, stay here and I'll go to talk to her.'

She swallows hard and I know she's thinking about it. I know she's thinking about her twins, safe at home with her husband. What would happen to them if anything happened to her? She turns up for work every day with that on her mind, but now it's drilling into her, because this situation is critical.

'I still think we should call for backup. But I'm not letting you go on your own, Jan. I couldn't do that.'

I pause for a second and wonder if this is just desperation. I have no real proof that Tina is there between the rocks. None at all. Just instinct. But isn't that what Steve called for? Extra? Isn't that what everyone expects me to do, think outside the box? But what if she's not there? I look out across the heather. It's uneven and at this level it's impossible to see two rows of tyre tracks. If I were her, I would have driven close to the rocks, like we did, and not through the centre of the moor. I would have been aware, even at that point, that the baby I'd taken was being missed and that the police would be out in force looking for her.

But then again, I'm privileging Tina with a sense of reasoning. And isn't this what it all boils down to? Her bad decision-making due to her condition? The skewed thinking because of her being at the end of her tether? I signal for Lauren to stay where she is and I crouch low and inch my way through the heather. It's a risk as if she is there, she might see me. But I have to be sure. I bend low until I'm almost level with the tall heather and the gorse and move farther out. Eventually, I come to a gap. The heather is flattened to the ground in a line. I stand up just enough to be able to see a matching gap alongside it, leading in a curve to the rocks and then swerving to the right.

I make my way back to Lauren.

'She's here all right. You can call Steve now and then we'll set off.'

CHAPTER TWENTY-FIVE

W e scramble up the gap in the vegetation beside the rocks and reach the edge of the turning. I know Tina is around the corner, but unsure how far up the ravine she is. Lauren is tucked in close behind me and as we approach we can hear *The Red Shoes*. It sounds slightly muffled. It's audible from the car, so it can't be too far up the slope.

I turn to Lauren and whisper to her. 'This puts the odds further in our favour. She won't hear us above that noise. And she'll probably have her earphones in as well.'

Lauren grabs my arm and hisses at me, 'I thought you were just going to talk to her?'

I turn back and crouch down. There's less chance of her spotting me if I'm not at eye level when I peep around the corner. I summon up the blood and look. She's about halfway up the ravine. The car is parked underneath the overhanging rocks as I expected. The crags and boulders almost form a tunnel up the memorial forest in the distance. No wonder the helicopter couldn't find her. From this angle I can't see if Maisie is in the front of the car.

Tina is walking around with her headphones on. She's

talking to someone, gesticulating, and at first I think that she's talking to herself. But as the story changes to another repeat loop, I hear snippets of her conversation. She's talking to Glen. I turn back and phone Keith. He answers in one.

'Jan, where are you?'

I ignore his question. 'Can you patch me through to Glen Wright's answerphone? She's calling his answerphone.'

'Yeah. I know. We've been tracking her calls. This is the third time she's called it. First two were phone down, but up to now she's just sworn at him and told him that she took the car. I'll patch you in now. How did you know she was calling Glen?'

No time to explain. 'Just patch me through.'

I suddenly hear Tina's voice on the line, echoing in front of me, filling in gaps that are drowned out by rushing water in the storm drain.

'...and you didn't even care enough to look after your own child. If you don't fucking like me, fine. I'm not that keen on you either. But Jennifer? And now you're going to have to look after her. Or she won't have anyone. She needs you when I'm gone, Glen. You...'

The call cuts out and I see her look at her phone and redial.

'You were right. I'm a shit mum. I can't make her happy.' She starts to cry. 'She's so beautiful, Glen, so pretty and funny. But I can't make her stop crying. All night. I can't do it. I feel... I feel... useless. So...'

The answerphone cuts out again and she screams and throws the phone towards the water. Her back is turned now and I look farther up the ravine. And there it is. A stone panel leaning against a rock. It's broken at the top right-hand corner and, over the years, lichen has grown over the joins to make it look like part of the rock wall. I recognise the style. It's from the demolished house. Decades have stretched the rubble from

Ashway House away from its original site and down the ravine, making a stone pathway up to the forest.

A cherub. It's etched into the panel and stands out in relief, exactly the same shape as the paper doll left in Maisie's bedroom. And what we thought were baby doll sketches in Tina's flat. But bigger. It's about five feet tall and, from this angle, looks as if it is standing beside the rocks rather than part of them. Tina retrieves the phone and dials again.

'This is it, Glen. This is the last time you'll speak to me, so look after her. I've done something stupid and I can't get out of this one. Remember when we used to say we could endure anything? With Magellan? It's not true. I'm deep in the shit and I can't climb out this time. I don't even know how I got here and I can't face the consequences. I've really fucked up, Glen. And I...'

She's almost hysterical now, and she runs over to the storm drain and throws the phone in. The story has looped back to the beginning and I think I see a slight movement in the car, a tiny head above the dashboard. Then crying. Maisie.

Tina puts her hands over her ears.

'The fucking headphones...'

The headphones were still attached to the phone when she threw it. She runs over to the drain and leans over the rush of water, looking for the phone. The voice booms out *The Red Shoes* from the car CD player. Maisie cries and I sense Lauren starts to shake behind me. Tina is screaming now.

'Stop it. Stop it. Stop the fucking noise.'

I feel every muscle in my body tense as she moves toward the car. Lauren feels it, too. I duck back behind the wall.

'Ready?'

She looks afraid.

'What are you going to do? You said you were just going to talk.'

'I'm going to stop her. And get Maisie.'

Lauren peers around me at the car. Tina is gathering up everything and pushing it into the back of the car. She tries to wrench the heavy cherub away from the rock face but can't budge it, so she leaves it. I look at Lauren but she's shaking her head.

'I can't, Jan. My kids...'

So, it's down to me then. I watch as she walks around the car. The back doors are swinging open still and she quickly jumps into the driver's seat. Quicker than I thought she would. The engine is turning over by the time I reach the car door. I pull it open but she's released the handbrake. The car is rolling slowly down the ravine and towards the water. It's gathering speed as it slides down the incline beside the storm drain.

I jump on the step of the car door and pull at Tina. She holds on to the steering wheel, screaming loudly. Maisie looks petrified and begins to scream too. In a split second I prise Tina's hand away from the steering wheel and pull her past me. She's still hanging on to my jacket, but can't keep her grip and tumbles onto the hard ground beside the water.

I sit in the driver's seat and my foot hits the brake just as the front wheels of the car hit the water. Every nerve in my body shudders as I pull on the handbrake and pray the incline is shallow enough to stop the car sliding into the water. I turn off the story and Maisie immediately stops crying and looks at me. Her face is dirty and her eyes red-rimmed. She stares at me dolefully.

'Want Mummy. Want Mummy.'

I gently unstrap her and hold her close. I know that a tiny movement could inch the car farther down the incline and into the water. I know that as soon as the water touches the pure sodium there will be a huge explosion. So, I keep very, very still, except for taking my phone and calling Steve. The car creaks and makes a tiny movement as I dial. Maisie is very still against me as he answers. I speak very quietly.

'Steve, I'm in the car with Maisie. I'm assuming that Lauren has apprehended Tina. Looking from the sailing club up the right-hand side of the water we're on the edge of Dovestones.'

'Roger that. Lauren's called. I've deployed the emergency services and bomb disposal. Sit tight, Jan. We're coming.'

I sit there holding Maisie and waiting. The suppressed fear and having to drive again lets loose a demon and it invades my mind. *I'm back in London, in my open-top sports car. I'm driving up Upper Woburn Street towards Russell Square. I turn the radio up as Don Henley's 'Boys of Summer' comes on and I start to sing loudly. My shoulders are moving and my head bobbing as the song plays. It's six months since Lando finished and somehow I've lulled myself into some kind of false sense of security where everything is right in the world again. I'm driving to my beautiful apartment where I'll look out at my view across London. Sleep peacefully between freshly laundered sheets and feel safe behind my double-bolted security door.*

I'm singing and laughing and thinking about Chinese food, so I hardly see the blue car hurtling toward me. I don't see the face of the driver although later I think he was wearing sunglasses. But I do remember the force of the crash, the shock waves that jarred my head from side to side and my car moving sideways and hitting the railings at the junction outside Hotel Russell. The smell of whiskey, stronger as it seeps over my legs, the broken glass puncturing my skin slightly, just enough to sting. I do remember a searing pain in my head followed by numbness. I do remember the blue car backing away and driving off, and angry onlookers chasing it and shouting that the registration number was covered.

I remember everything blurred and a sense of ironic euphoria as I realised what had happened. That I would never be free again. That no matter what happens they'll come after me. I remember my left hand straying to the seat beside me and then everything fading to grey, then to black.

Maisie stirs and I have the urge to rock her gently, but I dare not move. I think she's gone to sleep and wonder if she's been awake all this time because of the constant noise. I can see the other side of the reservoir and operations are clearing the walkers and windsurfers. Tiny figures in the distance are putting yellow tape at the end of footpaths. I turn my head slightly to the left and Steve is standing behind a cordon at a safe distance. He gives me a thumbs-up. Steve. So quiet and calm and who gets things done. We make a good team. Lauren's beside him holding a cotton pad over her eyes. I guess Tina didn't go quietly.

The car creeps forward a little and Maisie stirs in her sleep. I hear the water lapping around the wheels and look out of the open door. The incline into the reservoir is greasy and even a slight movement will move the car forward. Sitting here, finally being able to think about what happened in London; all of this makes me feel a strange calmness. Of course I'm afraid, but I can't change anything now. This is where team effort really comes into play. Trust. Knowing that the people around you will do everything in their power to get me out of danger.

If I hadn't been on the brink of death before I'd be surprised at what you think about. I'd thought previously that it would be a panicky feeling, a kind of desperation. But it isn't. Not for me anyway. This could go either way, so obviously there's hope. But there's also a sense of the inevitable. And that train of thought leads me to sorrow for the others. Steve, Lauren, everyone who's worked so hard on this operation. There should be a training module that tells us not to blame ourselves when something bad happens to a colleague. But then I realise that maybe I want someone to feel guilty about the past and scratch that.

I feel sad for Maisie's parents, who probably think they are in the most pain they could be now. But they aren't. Even Kirby. And Jean and Graham, my adopted parents, I now realise. They'll all be left behind with the pain.

And sadness for my future self and all the things I could do. I'd felt it back then as I lay in my crushed car, and in the hospital afterwards as I was told that I might not recover from my head injury. How, after I was discharged, I realised that I wasn't the same person. I was a toned-down version of myself, with the old me somewhere inside, emerging only when summoned. A sense of waste for my future life that grew into a plan as I realised that I would recover. I feel it now. All the things left undone, things I couldn't face. Kerry's baby. I'll never see them again. My beloved Manchester and its nemesis, the moors. Best of both worlds. But if this doesn't go well, I'll never run free across the heather again.

I check the time on my phone. It's quarter past twelve on a Tuesday morning. I smile slightly. At least we've wrapped up the operation in the recommended time. That'll please Steve. I can hear a helicopter above me now, circling around, and it wakes Maisie. I hold her very tightly as she wriggles and the car moves slightly. I look out of the door again. The front wheels are almost submerged, and the water is lapping into the car on the steep incline, washing around my feet and the pedals. I learned enough in physics to know that the weight of the water will eventually drag the car farther into the reservoir. The slippery surface won't help.

Survival mode takes over and I consider jumping into the water with Maisie. I mentally calculate whether I could get far enough away carrying a child in my wet clothes before the explosion. I'm still thinking about it, looking at the water, when I see it dimple more and more. Large drops of rain splash into the dirty wetness and, I realise, into the exposed back of the car.

I relax a little and look at Maisie. She's sleepy and I cradle her now, breathing in the smell of her hair. She reaches up and touches my hair, winding it around her fingers. It's almost inevitable now. There will be a risk assessment. With full emergency services here there will be no team heroics. I look out at my team behind the cordon. They're completely still. Steve has his hands in his pockets and Lauren's poker face has slipped and the horror of the situation is reflected in her expression.

There's a tiny paper doll spinning on a cord in the windscreen. I watch it as the car slips a little farther, its spinning, spinning, an ever-present reminder to Tina that she's not alone. One mixed-up young woman has caused all this misery. I'm angry at her and sorry for her at the same time. She'll probably get the help she needs now, but I doubt that she'll get Jennifer back. I don't know what she and Glen will get. Conspiracy to cause an explosion, maybe. Or worse. It's certainly not going to be an easy ride for them. Particularly if, or more probably when, what is now almost seeming like a given, as the car rolls forward, happens.

I feel tears prick my eyes. It's the first time I've actually cried in three years. I've been close a few times but forced the feeling back down with my worst memories and blocked them out with loud rock music and work. It occurs to me that Tina and I are more alike than I'd like to admit. But before the first tear escapes, I feel a jolt backwards and the car begins to back up. The water quickly drains from around my feet and an operations guy appears at the window, takes Maisie from me and begins to run. My legs are so cold that I can hardly walk so I throw myself onto the gravel beside the car and get up slowly. Then I run and run, past Steve and Lauren, past the waiting medics and up to the sailing club. Past the stone building and past the police cars and cars parked up at the side of Bank Lane.

I finally come to a halt at the stone wall at the top of the reservoir and sink to the ground behind it.

I try to control my breathing and take off my sopping-wet shoes. I can't believe I got out alive. I can't believe Maisie is safe and will soon be back with Marc and Amy. I can't believe that I got behind the wheel of a vehicle again. After I was discharged from the hospital, I'd taken delivery of a shiny new car. I'd sat in the driver's seat and even managed to turn on the ignition, but my feet wouldn't extend to the pedals. Physically they would reach, but as soon as I tried to depress them, even just a little, my body froze with fear.

I tried it many times but each time the same thing happened. I couldn't drive. As usual, I analysed myself and came to the conclusion that if this was the container that my fear was held in, so be it. A small price to pay. Never to drive again. But I did. I drove the car. I made it stop, anyway. In my addled, freezing brain I wonder if a chink of darkness opened and a little bit of fear escaped and, in future, I wouldn't be as brave because of it. No. No more driving for me. I can't see it happening again soon.

The echo of facing the car crash is still ricocheting around my consciousness. I've blocked it out for so long, avoided the pain. But I knew as soon as the Met became involved, the tendrils of memories would creep back in until eventually I had no choice but to deal with it. And one day I'll explore the full horror of it. One day, when all this is over and I'm settled I'll dig deep and uncover it all. But for now I need to get back to work.

Steve and Lauren are hurrying towards me with a medic. Steve's worried expression fades a little as he approaches me and sees I'm rubbing my feet back to life.

'All right, Jan?'

I nod and smile as much as my frozen face will allow. 'Yeah. Just a bit cold. Did you get Tina?'

Lauren's face is swollen and her lip split. Her smart black suit trousers are soaked and she's covered in silt. Our eyes meet and she's silently pleading with me not to mention her not being able to step up. But I understand. Not everyone is a lost soul like me. Lauren has connections, responsibilities. Steve laughs. It's an unusual occurrence but he's got good reason.

'We did. Or Lauren did. There was a bit of a struggle. But you're okay aren't you, Lauren? Quite the hero.'

She smiles weakly. I don't say anything, because there's no I in hero.

I'm just about to ask that Tina's assessed, taken care of, because she's ill, when there's a loud bang and the ground shakes. I watch as the explosion nearly knocks them off their feet, the shock waves making them stumble. I don't stand up because I can see the shock on Steve's face. The car will have disappeared into a thousand pieces and I could have been in it. It's moments like this, when we see the consequences and potential consequences of criminal activities, our resolve strengthens and reminds us of why we are doing this.

Lauren starts to cry. It's a release I understand completely. I stand up and put my arms around her. Steve's not a hugger, but he puts an awkward hand on her shoulder. The medic pulls a foil sheet around me and we stand for a while.

CHAPTER TWENTY-SIX

I went to the hospital and had a check-up. They let me have a warm shower and then put me in a private side room with an armed guard outside. They kept me in overnight just to be on the safe side, which was a relief because despite this case being over, I still can't go home. So as soon as I'm discharged I go back to headquarters to get changed. Lauren's taken a couple of days' leave to be with her family and allow her wounds to heal.

As I hurry up to the SMIT suite there's a buzz through the operations room. I walk along the glass corridor and look up and down Northampton Road. The black BMW is still there, in exactly the same place. I don't know why I ever thought it wouldn't be. I'm still on high alert after yesterday and I wonder if I'll ever be able to relax. I've seen this before in this game. In my peers. So involved in their work that they forget to have any down time. In this line of work there's always the worry that some disgruntled criminal will be released from prison and come to find you. In my case it's more of a certainty than a worry.

I enter the SMIT suite just as the partitions are being taken down. The screen has gone and Keith's comms station has been removed. I expect he's asleep at home having been awake for three days solid. I look in the rubbish bag and see more than twenty cans of Coke Zero. All the paperwork has been transferred into a wheel-along plastic bin for storage until the court cases come up. Even the workstations have gone, unplugged and stored away until next time. A couple of cleaners are wheeling in their trolleys and setting up vacuum cleaners.

Just as I'm about to find Steve, Petra turns up.

'I saw you come in. I wanted to see how you are.'

She looks me over and I smile widely at her.

'No harm done.'

'Yes. So I heard. Good work, Jan. Thank goodness you got little Maisie back.'

We did get Maisie back. It hasn't really sunk in yet.

'Without your input it could have all been very different.'

She makes an explosion sound but she's very serious.

'So, last thing now, Jan. You know the third sheet of paper, the one underneath the paper dolls? Well, we found a phone number on it. Probably not any use now, but you might need it for evidence.'

I'd completely forgotten that Petra was still working on this.

'Oh. Right. Have you rung it?'

She laughs. I know she wouldn't have. Petra avoids phones if she can.

'No. I leave that sort of thing to you, Jan. I'm not a people person. That's your area.'

She hands me the piece of paper and I see it's a local number. Tina has scribbled dolls and shoes around it but it must be important to her as she's left it legible and circled it several times. I get my phone out and dial. It rings then clicks onto an answering service. The woman on the line explains that this is a service for women who are suffering from post-natal depression. I look at Petra.

'Post-natal depression support. So she tried to get help?'

'Clearly not enough. It needs following up but rest now. Find somewhere safe and rest.'

She hugs me and walks away. Until the next time. The investigation is over and until we get the next Code Red we'll be on standby and this place will be emptied. The police officers working on this case will return to normal duty and everyone else will return to their normal lives. Except me. Normal life would be going home and helping out with smaller cases when they come up. Helping to sort out the evidence from this case. Expert witness work. Catching up on current theories and going to see Cat. In between I'd do some gardening, eat some good food, see my friends and walk Kirby. Have lunch with Jean and Graham.

Steve's in the corner reading some notes. I watch him for a moment, his awkwardness suspended when he's alone. He starts slightly when I sidle up to him. We're all a bit jumpy still.

'Jan, how are you? Shouldn't you be resting?'

I laugh a little too loudly to confirm the remaining nerves. 'Yeah. I'm going to find somewhere to stay. Petra offered but you know.'

He knows. He knows that I don't want to put her in danger. That's why he doesn't offer to put me up. He's got a wife and kids and it wouldn't be right. Instead, he gets me up to speed on the case.

'So now we know the outcome, Glen Wright's been charged with conspiracy to cause an explosion in a public place. He won't get bail. I spoke to Sally. Tina's been charged with the same thing but I've arranged for her to receive a care worker who will arrange everything she needs.'

'Thanks, Steve. And Jennifer?'

'Tina's mother has her. She's applied for temporary custody of her until we find out what'll happen to Tina. I know what you think, Jan, but she still committed a crime. She knew what was in that car and she took Maisie Lewis. The least she'll get is diminished responsibility.'

He's right. But I can't help but think if she had got help earlier this could have been avoided. I can't help myself. I have to ask.

'And the Met? Are they happy to wrap their end up?'

He doesn't detect my real reason for asking this, the meaning behind the questions.

'Yep. Sally said that they're more than happy with all the intelligence they got from the Magellan crew. Everything from counterfeit goods to protection. But you know how it is. Someone else will step into their shoes.'

'Sally? Sally did the wrap up? What about Pat? Was he happy?'

'Gone AWOL. Not turned in so Sally dealt with it. To be fair, their part was over. Probably taken some leave.'

Probably taken too much whiskey. Or spent too much in the casino. Pat's old school. No ringing in sick for him. He'll just ride the crap he gets and carry on.

'And Maisie?'

Steve walks me towards the door.

'Come with me. We're going to see Marc and Amy Lewis.'

He drives me up to the Lewis's house and they greet us at the door. Amy's holding Maisie and she walks out to greet us. It's miraculous. The grubby child I held so tightly yesterday is now a rosy-cheeked, healthy-looking little girl. I notice Amy's white-knuckle hold on her and know that they have more work to do before their lives return to normal. If they ever do. Marc shakes Steve's hand and bear hugs him.

'I can't thank you enough. For getting Maisie back. Thank you.'

Steve looks at me. 'It's Jan here that you should thank. There's something you should know about your daughter's rescue.'

We go inside. The house is warm and inviting and I feel a pang of fear about my own future. We sit in the lounge which has a very different atmosphere to the last time we were here. Steve's eager to tell them what happened so that we can put the final seal on the case.

'What we didn't tell you yesterday was that Jan only got to the car and your daughter in the nick of time. Tina was driving the car into the water. Jan dragged her out and halted the car and waited with Maisie until our guys came and pulled it back. Only seconds later the car exploded. If it wasn't for Jan, it would have been a different story. She hasn't been home since this case started.'

They stare at me without speaking. I'd rather Steve hadn't done this, put me on the spot. He could easily have come here alone to do this.

'Just doing my job. My intention was to negotiate but when I saw Tina... the perpetrator was about to act I had no choice. Right place, right time.'

Amy speaks now. Her arms encircle Maisie who is gurgling happily. I watch as she takes a strand of Amy's hair and winds it around her fingers.

'How can we ever thank you, Jan? We'll tell Maisie about this when she's older.'

I force a smile. 'All's well that ends well.'

They walk us to the door and wave as Steve drives us up to the junction with the A635. But instead of turning left towards Greenfield he turns up the road. In minutes we're parking near the sailing club. He gets out of the car but I sit here. I sit and look at the familiar landscape, the horizon that's even more deeply etched onto my memory now. He waits a few seconds then walks round and opens the door.

'Come on.'

I reluctantly get out and walk alongside him. The water is lapping at the edge of the reservoir and in the distance I hear the overflow drain's rushing water. It's a beautiful place, but I feel the fear that still hangs over it.

'I always do this. Come back to the scene afterwards. It closes a door for me.'

He's right. It does close a door. But it's not that simple.

'Did you go back to Manchester then?'

His head dips. Maybe I said the wrong thing. But eventually he answers.

'Not at first. It was too painful at first. I nearly didn't come back to the force. But eventually I did. When it was all rebuilt. But in that space between the doubts and fears, roots had time to grow. Weeds. Pull them up they bloody grow again. That's why I always come back.'

We're walking towards the cordon. Scene of crime are here going through the tiny remains of the car. I expect most of them would have showered into the water, lost forever. Apart from the yellow tape and the scene-of-crime officers in their white cover suits you'd never know what happened here yesterday, or nearly happened. I think about sand on the road after an accident. My accident. The only trace of the day that changed my life and changed me.

But here there's no sand. Ramblers clamber high on Indian's Head and the windsurfers are back. A group of cyclers arrive at the far end of the yellow tape and grump as they have to turn back. No doubt the press will report that Maisie Lewis was found safe and well with the ex-girlfriend of Glen Wright, a known activist. There are only so many words you can use to explain a crime. They won't want to know about Tina's story or Glen's story. They'd love to report on Magellan but if I know the Met, they'll never find out about it. They'll focus on Amy and Marc for a few days until they realise that they aren't going to sell their story and then they'll retreat.

No trace of this will be left, save for a few police records and images etched deeply on the memories of those involved, but rarely spoken about. They'll turn to the next big story and this case will be forgotten.

Steve's walking across the edge of the water and turns up into the ravine. I follow him until he comes to a halt in front of the cherub.

'Bloody dolls.'

She hasn't suffered much in the blast. The very tip off her nose is missing, but that may have happened before. I look more closely and there's a contented smile on the cherub's face. She's quite endearing. No wonder Tina loved her so much. Steve looks at me very seriously.

'I'm taking her in for evidence.'

I almost laugh. 'I'm not sure you'll get anything out of her.'

'No. I won't. Not my bag, dolls. I'm more of a less-complicated evidence kind of guy. But thanks, Jan. Thanks for tempering that. Never more than on this case. At one point I would have probably had the National Guard out. Not that we would have found her under here.'

I look above us. Solid stone. Not a splinter dislodged by the explosion.

'Combination of psychology and luck. If I hadn't been brought up around here, I might not have put it together.'

He nods and dusts off the cherub. She's well-made and obviously carved and not cast.

'True. But you were. I think that's why you came back.

That's all part of it. Why we're all in SMIT, because you have valuable local knowledge. How did that work in London then?'

I return quickly, eager to get him off that subject. 'Easy to get to know London quickly. Not so much round here. This terrain isn't that welcoming to those who don't know it.'

Then he asks the million-dollar question.

'So, what now?'

He doesn't look at me. I know his tactics. He's brought me here to face up to things. To make a decision. Psych 101.

'I'll stay around here for a bit.' I think about Salvador and my house and wonder if I can salvage something out of this mess. 'After that, I don't know.'

'You can't keep running forever.'

'I know.'

I know but I might have to.

'You know you'll always have support, Jan. We could bring them in.'

'On what charge? Sitting in a car watching someone?'

He's silent for a moment. Like me, he's struggling with the notion that although someone is committing a crime, we can't arrest them and charge them. We know they're doing it, but we have to wait for them to slip up so we can move in. It's almost unthinkable for us. I can see the pulse in his forehead quicken and his skin flush slightly.

'Threatening behaviour. The text messages. It might send a message to them. That they can't do it on our patch without consequences.'

He means well, and it matters to him. Not just me, but the fact that they're contaminating his beloved city.

'It's not the kind of message they understand. They'll just send someone else. And it won't stand up, anyway. The guys in the car didn't send the texts. They came from central London. So they'd walk.'

He's beginning to see my dilemma. Feel my resignation. Understand why I can't go home.

'What did you do to piss them off so badly?'

I almost say that I don't know but I owe Steve more than that.

'I broke their code. I pushed one of their crew to the very edge. Until he tried to kill me. Out in the open. Until then no one had been able to pin anything on them. Everything that happened to anyone who crossed them seemed like one big coincidence. But I knew how to press their buttons. I chose the most psychologically vulnerable of them and showed his family who he really was. Nothing illegal. Just constant arrests and questioning, always in the daytime. It broke him and he pointed a gun at me. We did a deal, and he grassed them up.'

He looks incredulous, eyebrows raised and mouth slightly open. 'But why you? Why not someone else in your team?'

'It was me who did the goading. It was my plan. His wife testified that I had it in for them, always turning up with the arresting officer, always being in on the questioning. And she was right. That's what I'm here for. To ask the difficult questions.'

He's shocked. I can see it cross his face.

'But at what cost, Jan? We all deserve a life and a family.'

I shake my head and walk back up the ravine. He catches up with me and I answer his question with a lie.

'I was just unlucky that they picked on me. Went after me. You know about the crash. It was played down as an accident because no one was sure it was them. Just a few words in the local paper. The Met were playing the long game with them. Still are. Police DC badly injured in hit and run in central London.'

Until they claimed responsibility when they thought I was dead. That's how I got away. I'd considered witness protection but I decided to take my chances. My death was all part of the plan. Win–win for the Met. They got Lando to formally own up, and I got to leave safely. Steve looks alarmed.

'You're kidding?'

'Nope. Even had a funeral. But it didn't work, did it?'

'Bloody hell. I didn't know all that. I didn't think they could do that.'

'You've no idea how big the Lando thing is. Massive. Involved in most of the crime and protection in London, and here by the looks of it. They're not into operations. They leave that to the minions. They're their own law enforcement. They protect the criminals and dole out punishment to anyone who crosses their projects. Their operatives just disappear or suffer a mysterious accident. No attribution of blame possible. We needed to get them and I suppose I was just collateral damage.'

'Jesus. I didn't realise.'

We're back at the car now. He drives me back to the station and drops me off.

'I'm going now, Jan. The operation's over but I'll write it up and send it to you. Where will you be?'

I look at the police station. There's the black BMW parked further up Northampton Road. Steve sees it too and I feel the concern he has for me. But he can't do anything. No matter how much he wants to, he can't do anything.

'Just send them to my email address. I'll pick them up.'

I watch as he drives away, then consider walking up to the BMW and fronting them. But what good would that do? They'd just deny all knowledge and I'd be back to square one. I linger outside for a while, silently goading them. They'd be able to see me, but couldn't take action as I was standing outside police headquarters. Maybe they are trying to frighten me into submission. I almost laugh at the thought of it, then a huge wave of relief washes over me as I suddenly realise that we did it. We got Maisie back.

It always takes a while to sink in. It always takes at least a day for the pressure to withdraw and a feeling of triumph to sink in. At one time I would have rushed into town and treated myself for seeing it through. But these days it hardly dents the surface. Even so, I lean against the doors and try to prolong the good feeling.

But as I stand outside reception, a stream of operations personnel rush out and towards the car. I move forward to warn them, to tell them to leave it alone – don't they know who they are dealing with? But I don't. I stand and watch as they surround it and open the driver's door surprisingly easily. One of them leans inside and then walks around the car, opening the boot. I watch carefully as he closes it again. He shouts to his colleague.

'No one in there. Get this sealed off and get SOCOs here.'

They walk back towards me and I ask him what's happened.

'Some joker phoned in just now and said there was a drunken guy outside HQ in a black beamer. No one in there. Empty.'

As he walks away the comms phone beeps. I'd automatically pushed it under my bra strap with my own phone when I left the hospital. My heartbeat speeds up as I see the familiar number from Lando and a text message appears.

> You can go home now, Rhiannon. Hollywood.

Pat Knowles. I text back.

> Confirm ID.

In a microsecond he's fired back a text.

Silver Bullet Band.

Definitely him. I text one word.

How?

He returns.

Need to know only. Let's just say I've learned my lesson. I think that just about makes us even. But here's some extra. Look out for a character called Connelly. He's behind all this at your end. In Manchester.

CHAPTER TWENTY-SEVEN

I don't know if it does make us even. I don't return his text. I don't know if I can ever forgive him. He could have left London and come with me. He could have come up north and lived with me. But in the final analysis he chose not to. He chose spite and mistrust. He chose not to read my heart and not to understand. He chose to think about himself. He threw me away and chose the next DC, someone to sit up the long nights with him and analyse his deepest whiskey-fuelled thoughts.

The day I left he was nowhere to be seen. I'd got a message to him that I was moving out and that he should come and collect his things. There wasn't much really. A couple of suits, a few CDs. His running gear. Most of the stuff to be moved was mine. I watched as the removal men cleared what was left in the flat. My beautiful furniture, all going into storage. Later to be sold as a job lot at auction in my absence. My clothes. Expertly packed by moving professionals and couriered up north to my new home. I'd been careful not to be recognised. Wig. Glasses. After all, I was supposed to be dead.

But he wasn't there. Neither was his stuff. He'd clearly already been here and taken it. I'd waited for him at the allotted time but he didn't show. I'd stood outside the flat, looking up and down the road. I walked up to the coffee shop on the corner where we would have our breakfast sometimes to see if he was there. Involved in one of the novels he loved so much, or scanning the papers carefully. My memory of that day was of my being self-conscious. Afraid. Constantly afraid of being recognised, and worried that the people who'd come to know us would see me searching for Pat. But everyone was too wrapped up in their everyday life to see a woman who was displaced from hers. I'd called his mobile five times but he didn't pick up. Inside the flat I found a letter from him.

Dear Jan

   It was good while it lasted but I can't come with you. You agreed to everything without considering me and I deserve more than that. You think you're the only one hurting but I've got feelings too. You chose to disappear just at the time when we needed each other most. I love you, Jan, but it's too much. If you stay in London, there's a chance for us but if you go it's over.

   I hope you make the right decision.

   Pat xx

Very formal. Very unlike our relationship had been. There were two kisses on the bottom of the letter. I read it once and turned it over. I sat and thought for a few moments. About his hand over mine as we waited for the Tube in the mornings. The warm skin of his back pressed against mine when we wake. Tired eyes and tears at old black-and-white movies. Our own playlist of early 80s rock, a decade before our time but something we had in common. An old eyeliner lay on the floor of the nearly empty apartment and I picked it up and wrote on the back of the letter.

Pat

You don't know everything. When you do, you'll understand. I didn't choose this.

Jan

No kisses. Did I love him? By the strength of the pain of his betrayal, his refusal to understand, maybe I did. Love's a funny thing. At first, in the heat of steamy passion and lingering kisses you think you are in love. I'd never thought I was in love until I first kissed him. It was as if he'd breathed it into me, that feeling of excitement, and missing him when he wasn't there. But it's a learning curve. Eventually I came to care for him. I worried when I knew he was on a difficult case. I checked on him when he didn't phone me. Not because I was jealous or paranoid, but because I was scared that something had happened to him.

That romance turned to care and to love between us. He was exactly the same about me. I knew he was naturally a hard man. He would have made a good criminal if he hadn't chosen the right side of the law. But he melted when I was around. His expression changed and although we never announced that we were together, everyone knew. It was obvious. But you don't know if it's real love until you hit a brick wall. And we'd certainly hit one.

I left the flat with a small brown suitcase crammed with mementoes of the only thing that had really mattered to me.

Six months later I received a message from Peter Simpson, the one person in the Met who knew where I was. It was in a brown envelope and it simply said 'Sorry'. I knew it was from Pat. He would have been fully briefed on the case when he tried to look for me and realised the situation I was in. They would have shown him the tiny paragraph in the newspaper and explained how I had got away.

Only Pat could ever have understood how painful it was for me. I knew exactly what he would do. He'd sink onto his haunches and pinch the top of his crooked nose to stop himself crying. His nicotine-stained fingers would pinch and pinch until the tears retreated. I'd seen him do this a thousand times. Then he'd fully understand that I wasn't leaving him. I was staying alive when my life was threatened. And saving his.

But now he understands. He redressed that awful balance because it turned out in the end that he'd abandoned me. I was never named in the press. I heard that my funeral was low-key with just a few professional mourners to make it look real. I was free to reappear whenever I liked, but it wasn't recommended, because they would be waiting for me. And it would start again.

I thought Pat would have been there. I hoped he would. But it turns out he wasn't, and that hurt more than anything. He knew. He knew it was happening. But Pat would have eventually found all this out anyway, whether he was at the funeral or not. He would have realised that by moving north I was asking him to share my new life, protect me, be with me. He would have known how much it cost me personally to ask him to do that.

He never officially lived with me in London. We had our own apartments, but he stayed most nights with me. Even now, the searing pain in my soul when I think about how happy we were makes me feel faint. It went on for a while, our affair. And then suddenly it was over. I wasn't allowed to tell him what had happened at first, but I thought that he knew me so well that he would know I hadn't left him.

But the circumstances were not normal. We were both devastated. It turned out that we didn't have our own unspoken language when I'd thought we had. He didn't understand my heart and everything I had ever told him about home. Where I was born. Where I grew up. For a detective he was acutely blind to the clues as to where I had gone. All he could see was his own abandoned soul, and the pain surrounding it.

When I realised that he would be the investigating officer in London on this case I kept up the pretence, just in case I had read the situation wrongly and he didn't know the full story. Most of the people I worked with in the Met simply thought I had dumped him and left. My secret funeral was for the benefit of Lando and outside a select group of officers no one knew about it. And Pat, obviously, because of what had happened. So, it would be no surprise to Sally that I'd reappeared. Everyone else simply thought that I'd run away.

It had worked for a while. On the basis that everyone who needed to know thought I was dead and those who wouldn't notice I was gone wouldn't care anyway when they caught a fleeting glimpse of me. There had always been the chance that I would turn up and that was the flaw my superiors refused to recognise. Then it all fucked up. It was a delicate balance of trust and time and all it needed was someone to leak information to Lando about what the police had done. Where I had gone. How I had done it. That, in actual fact, I wasn't dead. Someone did. Someone from deep in the heart of the enquiry. It would have been impossible to stay in London after that.

As soon as the information got out, we all saw what a stupid plan it had been, but there had been a small chance we could pull it off. But we hadn't, and I ran.

Of course Pat knew. Of course he knew the risks. He'd been so professional that I had actually doubted that he sent the note at the apartment or knew about what happened. But he came through in the end. I've no doubt that this man who I was so close to will haunt my dreams and that I'll be tempted to ring him, just to see how he is. Just to see if I can recapture the passion we had. I know that I'll imagine that I can have that part of me that's buried so deep, the part that was Pat's partner in crime. It's in my blood. The extra. The drive that makes it possible to summon up my fight and with Pat it was right there, crackling between us. I know that I'll keen for it, want to go back to the woman I once was. But I won't, because this isn't the end of Lando, it's just a pause in the proceedings. And maybe I do love him too much to get him involved. Even though he is.

I dread to think what he's done. How he's dealt with the two guys in the car. How he knows about this Connelly guy. I know Pat. He's got an evil side that he doesn't keep too well hidden. It's a bad combination in a copper, evil and professionalism, but he pulls it off. I collect my things from the empty SMIT suite and call a cab. I go home and push the queasy feeling of fear down as I push the door open. It's just the same as I left it, save for a few instances of over neatness that I spot immediately. It's hard to believe that it's been turned over. Pat must have been here, too. Seeing how I live. Putting it all right for me.

I open the back door and whistle for Kirby. I feel a normality settle over me again as Jean comes to the fence with her.

'Back sooner than I thought. I thought you'd gone, love.'

Kirby nuzzles my hand and fetches her ball.

'Well, I wasn't sure how long I would be, Jean. Have you and Graham been all right?'

She looks flustered. 'It was funny, you know. There were a lot of comings and goings at your house and this nice young man came and had some dinner with us. Said he knew you and you'd asked him to come. I made him a chicken dinner.'

I feel a smile coming. Jean always does that to me. She looks put out but I know that secretly she would have enjoyed sitting the officer down and feeding him.

'Well, I'm back now. How's Kirby been?'

'Great. Missed you, of course. But she's only a baby, isn't she?'

We chat for a while and then Graham joins us.

'We're having a bit of a barbecue tonight. We didn't know if any of your police pals would be popping by, so we got enough for quite a few people. Glad to see you back, love.' He leans over the fence and hugs me awkwardly.

'Sorry, Graham. I'll have to give that a miss. I have to go out again.'

'Oh, all right, love. It'll save until tomorrow.'

I go into the kitchen and pour out Kirby's meal into her bowl. I run the tap and wipe the side over. All these things are the basics of life that you don't miss until they're gone. That, and the everyday routine that people get so used to that they take it for granted. I probably won't stay here now. Pat's message will only last so long and they'll come looking for me. But I've got time to think and time to make decisions.

I take a shower and dry my hair. I leave it curly as I'm off duty. I lie on my bed for a while then pluck up the courage to call Pete.

'Hi, Pete. Sorry I couldn't be there–'

He interrupts me. 'Ah, Jan. There's someone here wants to say hello to Aunty Janet.'

There's silence then a little grunt. Then Kerry comes on the line.

'Jan! I've had a little girl. Seven pounds two. Perfect weight even though she's a bit early. We've called her Karen Janet.'

For once I'm lost for words. I quickly recover and congratulate them.

'Oh my God! Congratulations to the both of you. All three of you. I'm so sorry I wasn't there, Kerry. How did it go?'

She laughs loudly. 'Well, it hurt a bit. Not recommended. Probably won't have any more. You're not missing anything. And it's all right. It's perfectly fine, Jan. Pete made it back in time for the birth. I had her at lunchtime yesterday. I didn't ring because I knew you were tied up with that child abduction. Saw your picture in the paper. Don't beat yourself up, love; you've got plenty of babysitting to do.'

She was born at lunchtime. Around the same time that I nearly lost my life. Pete comes on the phone now.

'Are you coming up tonight? I'll pick you up if you like?'

'Yes. I'd love to meet Karen. I can't wait. But I'll make my own way there. I need to do something first.'

'See you later, then. I'll pick up some champagne and we can wet the baby's head.'

I end the call. I can't believe that Kerry's not mad at me. Maybe they expect me to be a little bit unreliable. I'd forgotten all about the silver Range Rover and my picture in the paper.

I go out into the garden and cut some flowers. A beautiful bunch of daisies and yellow roses. I tie them with a white ribbon and wrap them in a piece of old wrapping paper I kept from one birthday or another. I work carefully and with focus because this is very important. I call a cab and it takes about twenty minutes to arrive. That's fine as I'm in no rush.

As the cab reaches its destination, I feel the butterflies in my tummy. This is a first for me. The first time I've ever been here. But the time is now right. And who knows what might happen tomorrow? I get out at the gates and walk through the grounds. The last time I was here was at my grandfather's funeral. He was well loved throughout Saddleworth and his coffin had been carried in a horse-drawn hearse. Not a flashy glass carriage, but a simple wooden affair. My grandmother was already dead, and my parents had died two years before, within six months of each other. My grandfather had been ninety-eight when he died, but still fit and active.

People at the funeral told me that he'd walk miles every day. He never caught a bus or taxi unless he absolutely had to. He cycled any distances too far to walk. They'd lived in a tiny cottage on the outskirts of Uppermill and since he'd retired, he'd grown flowers which he sold at the side of the road. Prize-winning chrysanthemums. He'd go around cutting men's hair for a small charge and spent most of it in the bookies. He had his faults. He drank far too much and would get up on tables singing old anthems. And he'd fall off. His body was covered in battle scars from drinking too much whiskey. But between the gambling and the drinking he was a caring man.

He spent a lot of time showing me right from wrong and telling me that in the end we're all alone with our conscience. I suppose I'd been looking for someone like him in my own partner and Pat had fitted the bill. If only our misunderstanding hadn't been so monumental things could be so different. There I go with my 'if onlys' already. I reach my grandfather's grave and take a yellow rose from the bunch I'm carrying. I place it carefully on his grave. I still remember not understanding when they lowered him in, wanting to jump in and tell them they'd made a mistake.

But we have to be dignified in this life and, sometimes, take what we're dealt and run with it. I carry on through the graveyard, getting my bearings and reading the gravestones. They vary from traditional stones to Celtic crosses. There are even a few cherubs. I stop at my parents' grave. They're buried together. My father died of lung cancer in the end and my mother had a heart attack. Or died of a broken heart, as my grandfather put it. He told me that the best thing you could hope for was to die before your children but that hadn't happened for him. He outlived my mother. I take two more yellow roses and place them at the head of the grave. So sad.

Then I turn the next corner and I see it. My own grave. I stand still at a distance at first. I wonder if I should have taken their advice and changed my identity. Gone for witness protection. But I guess something inside me was waiting for Pat to come and find me. Funny. Now he has, it's too late. The old Jan, the one he knew, is deep inside. I'm not that woman anymore. Not most of the time, anyway. My phone beeps a text. I glance at it. Salvador. Sal. The Italian chef who I know is my future calling me.

I approach the grave and bend down to pick out a few weeds that have grown on it. There's a vase at the foot of it and I arrange the flowers neatly in it. The inscription on the headstone says, 'Janet Elizabeth Pearce. Taken from the world too soon at the age of twenty-two.' The date underneath will forever remain a terrible anniversary for me. The date of my supposed car crash. The one that made me collateral damage. That caused the injury that changed me. The date I entered the terrible world that my grandfather had warned me about. I go around the side and run my fingers over the golden letters underneath my own inscription. I haven't been here before, because I couldn't bear to. Something that's trapped inside of me, the one thing that drives me on and summons up the blood, disguises fair nature with hard-favoured rage, shifts a little. But I had to come. Because it's always personal.

Amelia May Pearce-Knowles
Lies here with her mother who passed the same day.
Taken too soon at the age of nine months.

THE END

A NOTE FROM THE PUBLISHER

Thank you for reading this book. If you enjoyed it please do consider leaving a review on Amazon to help others find it too.

We hate typos. All of our books have been rigorously edited and proofread, but sometimes mistakes do slip through. If you have spotted a typo, please do let us know and we can get it amended within hours.

info@bloodhoundbooks.com

Printed in Great Britain
by Amazon